W0013335

9788870595726

The Raven Spell

Within the ancient woods, where druids find their
dwelling,
An oath is sworn with stone and spell, forever com-
pelling.
To guard the Earth, its truth untold,
And shield its secrets from the bold.
The raven takes flight, its wings a shadow in the sky,
Casting a spell with watchful eye,
A keeper of the world beneath,
Where nature's mysteries lie, concealed from our reach.
It witnesses the rise and fall of men,
Their scars etched upon the glen,
The pain they bring with their own hand,
Yet, wisdom it bears, as only ravens understand.
For the raven carries a profound hope,
Unfolding nature's beauty, boundless in scope,
Though draped in somber hues, it spies,
Both wistful and wise, through ancient eyes.

Prologue

IN AN ANCIENT TIME known as the age of the druid, our world thrived with untamed vitality. Dense forests held secrets of old, and nature's spirits commanded respect from all who dwelled in their realm. Among this wild landscape, druids emerged as protectors of sacred groves, stewards of the natural world, and defenders of the delicate balance between life and death.

Seven sacred groves spread across the land, each possessing a unique essence and purpose, yet all connected to the Elder Tree. These hallowed grounds served as refuge, where druids gathered for timeless rituals, offerings to ethereal spirits, and shared wisdom. They were not only places of spirituality but also sources of knowledge, where new druids learned the ancient ways of nature and the primal magic coursing through it.

The druids lived in harmony with the land and its creatures. They healed with nature's magic and defended against those who threatened their way of life. But an earth-shattering event, the sundering of the rift, disrupted the balance. Nature's spirits descended into chaos, once-thriving woods became shrouded in darkness, and creatures twisted into grotesque forms. The brave druids fought to preserve their way, but the odds were against them, and their decline seemed inevitable.

Today, druids are few, scattered like forgotten embers. The sacred groves have faded from memory, and the ancient magic of the natural world has dimmed. Still, a glimmer of hope remains in those who hold fast to ancient wisdom. Committed to their oath to protect and restore the delicate balance of nature, they are poised to rise when destiny calls, ready to face looming challenges and rekindle the splendor of the natural world.

1

An Ill Omen

MY EYELIDS THREATEN TO flutter open, but I resist the urge, knowing that yielding would shatter the spell enveloping me. The melody of the ancient forest grows more intense, its haunting tune filling my ears. Only those attuned to the natural magic of the Ageless Isles can hear this symphony, a connection to the essence of this veiled, wild land.

Then, a soft creak of a branch reaches my senses, followed by a sense of movement above me. A bird lands on the branch, its beady eyes fixed on me. Though I can't see the bird, I sense its trepidation, feel its heart racing. It wants to convey something, I'm certain. I wait, holding my breath, wondering why the forest has sent this messenger.

I refuse to open my eyes, not now when the forest's melody is at its zenith. Ancient trees seem to chant an enchantment, and I can't afford to break the spell. But then, a raven's ominous caw pierces the harmony, stealing my breath. I try to calm my racing thoughts, focusing on anchoring myself. Something is amiss, or perhaps it's another test?

Ravens are harbingers of death, messengers of conflict. My heart stills, threatening to cease altogether, before thundering with the impending news carried by this unwelcome messenger. I pant, my pores threatening to flood me with salty sweat. What does it mean? Why today of all days? Then, as suddenly as my breath quickened, it slows, just before I lose my meditative state. I can't afford to lose focus, not when I stand at the brink of a crucial shift. I've waited and prepared for this moment my entire life. Doubts and hesitations swirl in my mind, but I grit my teeth and try to push the bird's warning to the back of my thoughts. I have to concentrate; nothing can disrupt the shift.

With all my might, I silence my doubts and surrender to the forest's rhythm. The ancient music returns, and the breeze strengthens. Brittle leaves descend gracefully, heralding the imminent shift. I take a deep breath, allowing the magic to consume me. Only through steadfast meditation, years of study, and arduous preparation can one attain the shift, as ancient as the Isles themselves.

Finally, I open my eyes, and the blurry surroundings gradually come into focus. I can sense that the shift has occurred. The forest's magic teases my senses to life. I've been in deep meditation for four days, preparing for the pilgrimage—an ancient rite of passage for Wood Elves like me on the Ageless Isles, my home.

"My name is Faelyn Nightsky," I whisper to the wind. I'm a druid in training, and after this pilgrimage, I will unlock the ancient wisdom of my forebears—if I can navigate the treacherous path that lies ahead.

As I open my eyes, I'm instantly awestruck by the beauty of the forest. When I closed my eyes four days ago, the forest had been the same familiar one I had grown up in—full of beauty and wonder, but nothing compared to what I'm seeing now. A soft glow emanates from every leaf, branch, and blade of grass in sight. A gentle rhythm flows through the forest like never before, a rhythm that has been unseen until this very moment.

The ancient forest guardians dance merrily, still unaware that I can now see them. The forest is alive. It's a living entity with a wondrous voice that hums playfully in octaves my keen Elvish ears overhear for the first time. It's something I've been told about and have studied all my life, but until this very moment, no scroll or lecture has done it justice. Particles of glowing dust and leaves waft in the gentle breeze, and everything in this enchanted realm pulses with a rhythmic energy.

As I breathe deeply, I revel in the forest's flavor, losing myself in the moment, and even the scent is intensified. A disturbance interrupts me, and I shake my head awake because I'm forgetting something extremely important—I have limited time.

Even with my acute perception and quick reflexes, I take too long to respond to the thunderous thrashing of leaves behind me. It all happens in the blink of an eye. Before I can turn, a blur of furs and leathered boots races past. I won't let anyone catch a spirit guardian before me. I leap to my feet—and in one fluid motion I snatch my blackthorn staff and race after the owner of the leather boots, Neason Dreamleaper—one of the fastest elves I've ever known, second only to me.

Swiftly catching up to him, I shove him aside as I rush by. He falters momentarily but steadies himself before leaping over a rotting log and cursing me.

"I won't be last, Neason," I declare, rushing forward and reaching for a fleeting sprite who now knows we can see it. There are five of us neophytes, all competing to catch a sprite and race to the Lunar Grove to unlock the secrets of our ancestors. Only one of us will receive the druidic Oath, and I'm determined it will be me.

"Always cheating, Nightsky," Neason huffs behind me. I can hear him swipe at several glowing sprites in vain as they blink in and out of existence at will.

"You're just too slow, Dreamleaper." Getting a sprite is no simple task. They are tiny balls of light that defy the physical restrictions of our world. Even with our Elvish speed and agility, the sprites seem to be one step ahead of us, and time is running out. The spirit sight will last only a few more minutes, and whoever doesn't catch a sprite can't continue the pilgrimage, facing exile from our village—the same fate that befell Malvolia Willowbane.

Not being able to catch a sprite is an ill omen, casting a dark shadow on one's fate. According to my father, eighteen years ago, in a ritual similar to this, Malvolia had been a neophyte just like me. The forest had been cast with magic as jet black as her hair, and despite her being the favored one to get the Oath, she hadn't been able to capture a sprite. She had returned empty-handed, and they say she had been possessed with rot and decay. The villagers had banished her immediately, and she had fled to the Feral Expanse, a punishment as harsh as death, and some say, even worse.

Barlan Willowlock, an excessively bothersome elf, bounded ahead of us, chasing a sprite with the agility of a demon. Neason and I struggled to keep up as we pushed through the dense foliage of the forest floor. Suddenly, Barlan's outstretched hands grasped the sprite as he leaped off a long, creaking branch, avoiding a fatal fall with a swift roll.

"I'm favored by the forest guardians!" he boasted.

I rolled my eyes at his foolishness, hoping he would fail the pilgrimage and leave us in peace. I adjusted the strap on my leather pauldron, feeling the weight of my hide armor against my skin. As a Wood Elf, I valued agility and mobility over heavy equipment.

"I will catch a sprite or die trying," I vowed to myself, determined to prove my worth and avoid the fate of an outcast like Willowbane.

My heart raced as Maeddes and Cokko Barkblossom, two arrogant High Elves dispatched from the Capital, barged into our race, catching me off guard and shoving me to the ground. Despite the chaos, Neason stood firm and sprinted to their side. I loathed High Elves with their self-righteous demeanor, sickly pallor, and garish hair. They fancied themselves as the ones closest to the ancient spirits, but no one was more attuned to the forest's magic than us Wood Elves.

I scrambled to my feet and charged ahead, focusing all my energy on catching up before all the good sprites were gone. As I crashed through a thorn bush, my heart sank as

I saw both Maeddes and Cokko laughing and saunter-
ing back to me, taunting me with their freshly caught
sprites. I took a deep breath, feeling the cool air fill my
lungs, and raced deeper into the heart of the forest.

Dammit.

I see Neason leaping and bounding within a glade,
still unable to catch a sprite. I still have time. Maybe I
won't be the last. I reach for a sprite right in front of
Neason, but he elbows me out of the way and launches
himself halfway up a wide oak, then scrambles onto
a thick limb after the sprite. I lose sight of him, but
within moments I hear him boast, "Beat you, Nightsky!
Looks like you're the last neophyte to catch a sprite. If
you can catch one at all."

All I can do is curse at him, then feverishly search
the thicket for my sprite. I have to get one. I just have
to. I won't be like Willowbane. I can't be like Willowbane. I throw the thought from my mind and scramble
across a capsized log fallen across a bubbling brook.
The slippery green moss squishing under my leathers
do nothing to deter my speed.

I see a cluster of sprites and make my move. Leaping
into the air, I outstretch my hand and grasp at one, but
it vanishes before I could snatch it. Another pops into
sight as I land gracefully on the ground, and I cup it in

both hands but am dismayed when I open them and see nothing.

Frantically searching now, I see a stray sprite floating back across the mossy log, and I race toward it, gripping it in my hand. I am ecstatic and electrified simultaneously. I am euphoric with glee until I'm not.

Darkness washes over me, and I lose control of my body. My elven eyes watch as the sprite in my hands blinks from white light to darkness and back again. I am rigid and paralyzed with fear, unable to move, breathe, or think. My eyes snap shut, now awash with a murder of ravens, befouling my sight and addling my senses, delivering a vile message of nausea and dread. I can't tell if they are actually surrounding me or if it's a dream, but it seems so real, so nauseating.

A putrid acid rumbles in my belly as the dizzying horde of demons now sully and defile my mind. They are made of smoke and ash, blurred and featureless. A face appears in my mind and starts hissing and screeching at me.

I am powerless to stop it as it overtakes my mind's eye. I feel myself falling into darkness, and for a moment, I am certain that my destiny has taken a perilous turn.

2

Alban Hefin

MY HEAD THROBS AND my stomach sours as my eyes flutter open once more. This time, the forest is blanketed in silent darkness, and the once playful tune of the ancient woods has vanished. The spirit sight of deep meditation has worn off, and all that's left is my keen darkvision. I'm dazed and confused as I regain my roots. Time has passed since I fell, and the creatures of the night stalk the shadows. Although the raven has gone, so has the vision of the ashen demons. I sit up and reach for my head because it feels as though a troll tried to wrench it from my shoulders. At this point, I wish there had been a troll that yanked my head off because I wouldn't be suffering. It'll take more than my father's willow bark potion to soothe this headache.

I run my fingers over my arms, feeling the goosebumps rise on my skin as I peer into the inky darkness of the glade. I sigh heavily as the weight of my failure settles on me like a thick cloak, suffocating me with its despair. Malvolia Willowbane's fate flashes through my mind, a warning of the consequences of dabbling with dark magic. And whatever happened to me with the vision, was dark magic. I just don't know how it was able to breach the enchantments of the Isles. Thoughts race through my mind, trying to piece together the utter failure of the day. I groan as I push myself to my feet not wanting to make the trek home empty-handed, meaning I'll be banished for sure.

Despite my usual light step gait, my footsteps drag along the ground, each one heavier than the last as I make my way back to the village. The wind whispers around me, mocking my failure, while the trees creak and groan, as if disapproving of my inability to capture a spirit guardian. I can already see the disappointment etched onto my father's face, his usually warm eyes now cold and unfeeling. My mother's absence looms like a specter, reminding me of the grief that consumed my father after her death. Exile would be too much for him to bear.

I was barely a teenager when I lost my mother to a malevolent evil witch, and her name was Malvolia Willowbane. The memory of that fateful day still haunts me, and today's ominous events only serve to exacerbate the raw emotions that time has failed to heal. It feels as though I'm reliving the worst day of my life all over again, the pain as fresh and relentless as ever. The mere thought of Malvolia Willowbane still lurking in the shadows, possibly plotting her wicked revenge on my people, sends an icy shiver down my spine. My mother had been a beacon of hope, a guardian who sacrificed everything to protect our peaceful village from her dark sorcery. And now, as I stand accused of being akin to Willowbane, I can't help but feel that her sacrifices were in vain, that her legacy, and everything she fought to preserve, is now tainted by my perceived connection to the very evil she gave her life to oppose. The weight of that guilt and despair is a suffocating burden I'm not fit to carry, knowing that my actions may have unwittingly undone all that she had strived to protect.

I can hear my mother's voice in my head, urging me to focus on my purpose. She was always pushing me to be my best, to become a druid and serve our people. But now, my purpose has shifted. As an outcast I have several options, and none of them are pleasant. As I trail my fingers through the damp, dew-drenched grass, I can't help but imagine the intricate dance of destiny hidden within every seed pod clinging to the slender stalks. With each pod I carefully extract and set free on the capricious winds, I feel an unsettling sense of connection to the world around me, stirring not only the mournful chorus of crickets concealed in the swaying verdant sea but also a creeping unease that whispers of hidden secrets and the relentless march of fate.

The journey home is a tumultuous river of emotion, every step bringing me closer to the looming disappointment of my father, my heart an anchor dragging me down into a sea of despair. As the village edges into view, I stand paralyzed on the precipice, unable to breach the protective thicket that guards my home. It's only the persistent hooting of an owl, mocking my hesitation, that goads me forward, through the forest's reluctant embrace and down the moonlit hills where my childhood laughter once echoed. Even the scent of home, once a comforting embrace, now crumbles like seedcake under the weight of my dread. The haunting visage of the Elven face, an echo of that evil vision, superimposes itself over my thoughts, and I can't help but feel it bears a striking resemblance to the malevolence of Malvolia Willowbane. The irony is suffocating.

My heart drums in my chest like a captive bird, each beat a painful reminder of the night she stole my mother from me. The mere thought of Malvolia's dark magic and the anguish it inflicted upon my family and village engulfs me in a relentless tempest of anger and grief. I'm acutely aware that I should be preparing what I'll say to my father, but the paralyzing fear that history may cruelly repeat itself threatens to swallow me whole. My mother's voice, a spectral whisper in my mind, pleads for strength and unwavering focus, urging me to master the chaos of my emotions. How can I not harbor a burning, insatiable rage for the creature that took her away? I grit my teeth and inhale deeply, attempting to quell the storm of emotions raging within.

The willow tree stands before me, the very heart of our village, a sacred symbol of unity and life. But now, it signifies the impending doom that awaits me. The whispering leaves, rustling in the breeze, sound like mocking laughter, a cruel reminder of the fate that looms. I stumble forward, my legs weakening, catching myself on a nearby tree, and the thought of facing my father, the Sage and Chancellor, is a leaden weight in my chest. He is the embodiment of strength and wisdom, a pillar of our village. How can he remain blind to the truth of my delinquency? How can he bear to cast his own daughter out into the abyss? A lump lodges in my throat, and a sob I dare not release, until I can't hold it any longer, and I croak. I grit my teeth and clench my jaw and lurch forward, step by awkward step.

The distant sound of merriment, the music and laughter of the Waking of the Forest celebration, accentuates my profound solitude. How can they revel while my world crumbles around me? A silent scream of despair wells within me, but I swallow it back, understanding the futility of conveying my pain to those who cannot comprehend it. I inhale deeply, wiping away my tears, determined that though I may be exiled from this village, Malvolia Willowbane shall not claim victory. With my back to the only home I've ever known, I cling to the resolution that once I'm banished to the Feral Expanse, I'll find Willowbane and kill her.

The weight of betraying my druidic heritage gnaws at my conscience like a ravenous wolf seeking entry into my soul. The memory of my mother's tragic end urges me forward, my determination steeled by the acrid taste of vengeance. I clench my fists, an internal storm raging, ready to forge a path to hunt down Malvolia without the sanctity of the Druidic Oath. My destination: Hellfast, a corrupted city within the Expanse, where I may find mentors in the shadowed art of daggercraft. Maybe I'll turn into a shadowblade, relying on my natural speed and agility to slip through the shadows like a stealthy assassin. I choke back an anguished sob at the thought. I already miss the mossy smell of the forest, and I haven't even left it yet.

I gaze up at the imposing ladder hanging from the colossal willow tree and begin to ascend. With every step, a profound sense of heaviness envelops my chest as I climb higher and higher, fully aware that this journey could signify the end of my days as a free elf. The surrounding woods, with their majestic willow trees and their roots intertwined with the earth, seem to morph into a gallery of torment. Every step is filled with fear and anxiety, as the vivid image of my upcoming exile is etched deep in my mind. The looming prospect of the village's rejection, and the label of being an outcast destined to wander the realms endlessly, hangs over me like an ominous specter with each rung I ascend.

At last, I ascend to the treetop, greeted by the breath-taking sight of our village. The wooden huts, their designs melding seamlessly with the trees, interconnected by bridges adorned with intricate guide rails and ethereal leaf-shaped lamplights, take on an otherworldly charm. Vines, woven intricately into the railings and footbridges, present the illusion of an enduring alliance between nature and our people. Even the High Elf King, Eldrin, might reluctantly acknowledge our humble village's splendor, notwithstanding the prideful posture of the Eagle Clan of Faelyndelle.

Rounding the corner, I'm met with the lively sounds of the Waking of the Forest celebration. The village square dances with the mirth of elves lost in the bliss of music, their laughter and glee a stark contrast to the weight of my fate. They twist and twirl in rhythmic unison, under the moonlight's embrace, while the soothing music of the flute fills the air. The elfin lights cast an enchanting glow, illuminating the scene. The quartet of bards harmonizes seamlessly, playing a melody of enchantment as they stand beside the tables laden with elvish delicacies and barrels of Alfenwine. Yet, as I stand on the fringe of the jubilation, the knowledge of what tomorrow promises overshadows the revelry. The neophytes are on the brink of their pilgrimage to the Lunar Grove, while my own path is banishment into the unforgiving Expanse. I question whether I possess the strength to endure such a desolate place or if I'll merely languish in my despair.

As I skulk along the outskirts of the euphoric celebration, my heart echoes the somber melody of my plight, the cheerful atmosphere a painful contrast. A burning resentment toward my predicament wells within me, threatening to engulf my every thought. My father's advisors, Guro and Madief, revel in the festivities, blissfully unaware of my looming calamity. The fragrant aroma of elvish delicacies wafts through the air, but my father's untouched plate speaks volumes about his distress. He is a study in worry, his face etched with lines of apprehension, the hope that I might prove my worth slowly waning. I break free from the crowd, realizing that I can no longer bear the weight of their celebration, their obliviousness to my suffering.

In the center of the dancefloor, I standalone, extending my empty hands in a gesture of shame. The dancers, their revelry disrupted, retreat from me as if my very presence is a contagion of black knot. My father's gaze, once filled with worry, now bears the mark of incomprehension, a silent plea etched upon his face as he sees my empty hands. His gaze implores me for an explanation I can't provide.

A crowd of drunken dancers raises their cups and exclaims, "Alban Hefin!" The traditional greeting for this day, a fortnight before the summer solstice, now morphs into an unexpected salute, and I shudder with the weight of their misplaced enthusiasm. I extend my empty hands in a desperate display of my inner turmoil, the lump in my throat growing heavier by the moment. The square falls into an awkward silence until it's broken by heated whispers filled with judgment and speculation.

My father's anguished voice rends the silence, "My daughter. My dear Faelyn, what has happened?" I flounder for the right words, but nothing emerges, nothing that can make sense of the chaos that has unfurled. How do I explain the vision, the raven, or the specter of Malvolia Willowbane? The words evade me like a shadow slipping through my grasp, leaving me with nothing but a lingering sense of frustration and longing.

"I fell," I stammer, "and wasn't able to catch a sprite."

A collective gasp shivers through the crowd, a buzzing swarm of whispers and pointed looks. My father's voice slices through the clamor, commanding silence, "Quiet!"

The hush descends like a heavy shroud, leaving only the lapping of waves against the distant piers and the serenade of crickets to accompany the midsummer night. The moon's judgmental glow pierces through the clouds, illuminating my shame. All eyes are on me, their scrutiny an unbearable weight. I pull my hood tighter, as if it could shield me from the searing spotlight of their attention.

"What do you mean you fell? Where is your guardian?" my father questions with a furrowed brow, the accusation in his tone a dagger aimed at my heart.

"I wasn't able to catch one," I reply, the words bitter on my tongue. I close my eyes briefly, wishing for an escape. "It happened so quickly. Something...affected me on the moss log, and I slipped."

"Slipped on a log?" my father interjects, skepticism etched across his face. I hear muffled laughter from the neophyte table and cringe. He shoots them a nasty stare and they become silent. "My daughter slipped on a log? The fastest and most sure-footed elf I've ever seen slipped on a log?"

"There was a raven," I utter, hoping it will bridge the gap between my father's expectations and my failure.

My father shakes his head in disbelief, a storm of emotions etched across his face. "I..I don't believe it."

"Father," I plead, but my words are swept aside.

"Impossible," my father interrupts. He gestures angrily, as if pointing to an invisible phantom, while the cloud of questions and doubts continues to hang heavy over the gathering.

With a deep breath, I continue, unable to conceal the fear and confusion that gnaw at my heart, "There was a raven before I opened my eyes from meditation. It landed on the oak branch above me."

My father's eyes narrow, dissecting my words, searching for meaning and finding only bewilderment. "And then?" he prompts.

"Then, I felt...unsettled for a moment. I stilled my mind and opened my eyes, only to find myself with the spirit vision, so I began the hunt," I recount, hoping to convey the surreal nature of the ordeal.

My father turns to my words with a desperate plea in his gaze, as if he could find the answer in my explanation. "What happened to the raven afterward?" he inquires.

My memory falters, a glaring omission. "I don't know," I confess, a lump forming in my throat, "It wasn't there when I opened my eyes."

My father paces over to Guro, the Oathkeeper, and questions him. "Guro. You must have answers."

Guro pushes himself from the table, scrutinizing me with his enigmatic eyes, a piercing focus that forces me to confront my uncertainty. "You never actually saw the raven?" he questions, his voice like a sentinel guarding the truth, neither sceptical nor comforting.

I stumble over my words, hesitating, and then finally admit, "No, I never saw the raven, but I felt its presence."

Guro's scrutiny intensifies, and his hooded features become more inscrutable as he searches for answers I cannot provide. "Ravens bear messages," he declares with a weighty finality, his words directed at me alone. "Did you receive a message?"

I flinch, my eyes betraying me as they dart around, grasping for an answer that doesn't implicate the specter of Malvolia Willowbane. "I... I saw darkness." I falter, the admission heavy with unspoken truth.

A collective gasp ripples through the crowd, and my father's anguished voice breaks the silence, "My daughter... what have you seen?"

I'm ensnared in a trap of secrecy, my words a double-edged sword, and I cannot reveal the name that lingers unspoken. Instead, I reply, "Darkness... that's all."

Guro continues to scrutinize me, his silence laden with implications, until he finally speaks, his voice a harbinger of doom, "The laws are clear, Chancellor. Even for kin. A neophyte unable to attain a spirit guardian is not fit for the druidic Order."

My father's desperation surges, and he beseeches Guro, "There must be a way, Guro. You can guide her, teach her to shield herself from the darkness, to block the Rift."

I silently plead for Guro to offer salvation, to find a path that leads to redemption rather than exile. But Guro's solemn words shatter those hopes, as if he were the bearer of irrevocable fate. "I'm afraid I can't, Chancellor. After the summoning, these are dangerous times, and the Rift itself senses our vulnerability. With Faelyn here, without a guardian, she could become..."

My father, unable to bear the unspoken ending, intervenes with anguish in his voice. "Don't say it."

The unspoken threat looms, casting its malevolent shadow over the square, and the gravity of my impending fate drags me deeper into despair. My father, once a pillar of strength, is now broken, his voice barely a whisper, "My Faelyn... My only daughter. I can't bear to lose you." He buries his face in his hands and weeps.

Tears streak down my face, but I wipe them away quickly, trying to remain steadfast for my father. I square my shoulders and stand tall, though my heart is sinking into despair at my impending exile.

Guro, his demeanor unyielding, scratches his chin in contemplation, his gaze an unsettling force that probes the depths of my soul. He walks around me as if looking for something, anything. "There's something on you," He declares, diverting the impending tragedy for a moment, and my heart races, my palms slick with dread, but I maintain my composure, hoping that Guro's discovery will bring this painful ordeal to its conclusion.

I reach behind me and pull out an object that was concealed within my cloak. In a swift motion, I toss it at Guro's feet, disgust etched on my face. "There's something wrong with it!" I exclaim, my voice trembling with a mixture of revulsion at the sickly looking thing.

Guro gazes at the object, a shattered sprite, and then turns his penetrating stare back to me, suspicion clear in his eyes. The gasps of the onlookers and the collapse of my father plunge the gathering into a morose silence, the heavy curtain of fate descending upon us all.

3

The Revival

GURO STEPS FORWARD, PLACING a reassuring hand on my shoulder. "We must act quickly if we want to save the sprite," he says, his voice steady, though the urgency in his eyes is unmistakable.

I nod, knowing that time is of the essence. The sprite is a vital part of the forest, and its loss would have catastrophic consequences.

"We must save it," Guro continues, his tone unwavering. "But not here, not within the confines of the village. We must seek the essence of nature."

My father sits up stark straight, his eyes widen with fear as he realizes the implications of what we need to do. Stumbling up, he says, "But interfering with the passage is forbidden," he says, his voice barely above a whisper.

"We have no choice," Guro whispers. "The sprite's life is in our hands. Faelyn, we need you to act as if nothing is wrong. Can you do that?"

I take a deep breath, anchoring my roots for what's to come. "Yes," I say, my voice firm. "I'll lead the way."

We make our way down to the sea, the sound of the waves providing a calming backdrop to our hurried foot-steps. The full moon casts a silver glow over the water, and I can feel its power pulsing through me.

As we near the water, my mind races. I know the risks of breaking the druidic laws, but I also know that this is the only way to save the sprite.

I lead the way, my feet tracing the familiar path through the sandy hills to the beach. My senses are heightened, and I can feel the sea's rhythmic energy pulsing through me.

Suddenly, I hear a rustling in the coastal sage, and I freeze. My father and Guro come up behind me, their faces tense with anticipation.

But it's only a deer, its eyes wide with fear when it notices us, then it darts across our path and disappears into the darkness.

We continue on, and finally, we reach the beach, and Guro leads us into waist deep water and says that we're far enough from the village and out of sight. Guro and my father begin the complex series of chants and gestures, their hands glowing with a soft lunar light.

I cradle the sprite, a glowing orb of flickering light against my chest, its weak breaths barely noticeable against my skin. My father, Kaelen, and Guro stand before me, their faces etched with concern.

"What have you done, Faelyn?" My father's voice is stern.

"I found it like this, Father," I reply, trying to keep my voice steady. "You saw as I did. It was stuck to me."

Guro steps forward, his hands glowing with the soft lunar light. "We'll do what we can, but reviving a sprite is no simple task. It requires ancient rituals and a sacrifice to the Lunar Grove."

"A Sacrifice." I gasp. My mind reels. A sacrifice means taking and upsets the balance, but I'm only a neophyte, so maybe I just don't understand. Sprites are the protectors of the forest, and their loss can have dire consequences, so Guro must be right. We must do everything in our power to save it.

"We'll do whatever it takes," I say, determination in my voice.

Guro looks sternly at me, "You need to collect Lunar Seaweed for the ritual to work."

"Okay, where do I collect it?" I look at the surrounding shores for any sign of the Lunar Seaweed.

Guro shakes his head and points to the black horizon of the sea. "It's out there. At the bottom of the sea floor and only grows where the depth of the sea is over forty feet deep."

With determination in my heart, I wade out into the unforgiving sea, where the icy waters clutch at my skin and pierce through my bones. In preparation for the perilous dive, I use my earth magic to conjure a small air bubble that swirls before me. Gasping, I suck it into my lungs, extending the breath that must sustain me in the treacherous depths.

As I descend into the frigid abyss, my mother's tales of the Kraken, a monstrous sea-dwelling entity said to stalk the ocean's hidden depths, flood my mind. The horrifying stories she shared with me echo, and the realization of the sea's mysteries wraps around my thoughts. Fear tightens its grip as I remember her vivid descriptions of its colossal tentacles snaking through the waters, ready to seize any unsuspecting victim.

As I dive further down, the pressure mounts and my insides feel like their being crushed, but I am relentless in my pursuit. Several times I catch sight of some sea creature and startle, but nothing bothers me so far. My head spins as the weight of the sea swirls overhead.

In the dim, shadowy depths, I finally lay eyes on the Lunar Seaweed. Its ethereal, otherworldly beauty dances amidst the unforgiving currents, its soft, radiant glow captivating. Yet, my awe is short-lived, for a colossal, amorphous form emerges from the murky depths. Panic surges through me, and the tales of the Kraken race to the forefront of my thoughts.

Before I can react, a massive, inky tentacle shoots out from the creature, darting towards me like a sinister serpent of the deep. My heart races, and I dodge to the side just in the nick of time, the tentacle barely grazing my side.

Desperation and terror fill me as I snatch the Lunar Seaweed and yank it from the sand. I hold it tightly and kick with all my force unfurling a torrent of sand. The monstrous entity is not satisfied with its initial attack, and it pursues me relentlessly towards the surface. My lungs burn, my vision blurs, and every fiber of my being aches for precious air.

The race to escape the relentless Kraken's grasp intensifies as I kick upwards with all the strength I can muster. Several times it wraps a tentacle around my ankle and I'm barely able to kick free, but it slows my ascent enough that I fear my breath will run out. The surface seems impossibly distant, and my survival hinges on reaching it before the monstrous creature can claim me in its watery embrace.

Suddenly the light of moon shines brighter, illuminating every ripple of water and somehow, the creature stalking me loses interest and sinks into the darkness of the sea just as I breach the surface and gasp for air. Holding the Lunar Seaweed possessively as I swim to shore, I gasp and struggle until I reach a depth where I can walk. Then on wobbly legs, I make my way to Guro and my father.

I hand the seaweed to Guro and buckle at the knees gasping for breath. Guro snatches the seaweed and my father rushes to my side. "Are you okay?"

Not wanting to startle him further, I just nod. "It was deep is all." I lie.

Guro looks to my father and says. "Time is running out. We must act now." My father leaves my side and stands beside Guro whose looking up to the moon and they start chanting. The druids' voices rise and fall in an otherworldly language, and their hands move in intricate patterns.

As the rituals continue, mist from the sea forms around their hands, then around the dying sprite, and its breathing becomes stronger, and its tiny glow begins to flicker with a soft light. Tears prick at the corners of my eyes, relieved that our efforts have paid off.

Finally, the rituals are complete, and the dim flicker of the sprite becomes a little brighter and doesn't sputter out as much. But suddenly, I see the belly of a fish breach the surface of the sea, then another, and another. Until the surface is covered with dead fish. I squeal with fright.

Kaelen turns to Guro, his face stricken. "I'm not sure this was a good thing."

Guro steps forward, his eyes darting around the beach. "We must go back, quickly," he says urgently. "The sea is angry."

I nod, sensing the danger. The balance of nature is delicate, and we may have upset it by reviving the sprite. As we make our way back to the village, I can feel the power of the sea growing stronger with each step, the wind picking up and the waves crashing against the shore with ferocity.

As we reach the village, panic sets in. The normally peaceful village is in chaos, with a violent wind howling, the trees bent and threatening to snap, and villagers screaming in terror. My heart sinks as I realize the consequences of our actions. We've brought a curse upon our home.

Something catches my eye atop one of the tallest trees, the moonlight above casting it into silhouette, but I know what it is instantly: the white feathered raven. The branch it sits on, the only still branch in the village as it gazes down on me, and only me, its eyes unwavering. It caws at me, then flies off into the night.

Then, suddenly, the wind stops, and just like that, stillness engulfs the village. And I know it's not a curse but an ill-omen. One that is following me like the plague.

I turn to Guro, confusion, then relief, and now foreboding washing over me. "What just happened?" I ask, still trying to process the sudden calm.

Guro's face is grave as he responds, "The sprite. It has angered the sea with its revival. We had to do it, but at a cost."

"Did you see the raven?" I ask.

Guro's face hardens, but he shakes his head no.

4

A Mother's Gift

SUNBEAMS BREAK THROUGH THE dense Willowbrook forest canopy, casting dappled shadows on the forest floor. The birds' melodious chorus is a symphony that fills me with encouragement. After last night's events, encouragement is what I desperately need. I inhale the crisp forest air, a mix of earthy moss, dew-kissed leaves, and the faintest hint of blooming wildflowers. This forest has always been my home, but today, its familiar sights and sounds feel tinged with uncertainty.

As I complete my preparations, the gentle breeze that rustles the leaves dances through the open window, carrying with it the forest's secrets. I meticulously inspect my blackthorn staff, its polished wood cool to the touch. My fingers trace each knot and rut, searching for any imperfections that might hinder me in the upcoming trials. When my gaze reaches the staff's intricate, twisted knot at the top, I find solace in the knowledge that its grains run true.

Satisfied that my staff is flawlessly honed, I place it beside the arched doorway, a sentinel of strength.

Our home, crafted from the living trees, exemplifies Wood Elf craftsmanship. Each piece of carved wood, every inch of our arboreal haven, serves as a testament to the magical harmony we share with the forest. It's a delicate balance, ensuring that our presence doesn't harm the ancient trees, and the forest repays us with its abundant blessings. To coexist with the woods is not only an integral part of being a Wood Elf but also a fundamental aspect of the Druidic Order to which I belong, well, almost. As long as my sprite isn't dead, and I don't get banished for that, and I can make my way to the Lunar Grove successfully. No pressure.

In the kitchen, my hand glides along the curved wooden walls, an intimate farewell to the house where I've grown up. A place that, despite my doubts and banishment fears, I hope to return to. From a clay pot in the pantry, I gather a handful of seedcakes, a perfect travel ration. Each one represents a piece of home, portable nourishment on this uncertain journey.

My gaze is drawn to the almost imperceptible sprite inside the clear vial, its light barely flickering. I wonder if I inadvertently crushed the life from it during my fall. My father's abrupt entrance interrupts my thoughts.

"Faelyn, my dear," his emerald green robes shimmering like the forest canopy, he exclaims as he leans over to kiss my brow. His worried lines from the previous night have now faded, but his eyes still reveal lingering concerns. His gaze drifts toward the distant sea, hardening with determination.

"I'm not a child, father," I remind him while stuffing the last of the seedcakes into my travel sack and adjusting it to hang low on my back. While Elvish time stretches like a taut hide, my age in Elvish years may still classify me as a teenager, but my nearly thirty years of life belie that. It's a paradox I'm used to—my High Elf heritage clashing with my Wood Elf upbringing.

He closes the gap between us, his bronzed skin radiant in the sunlight. "I know that, my Faelyn. It's just that I was so worried last night at the Waking the Forest celebration. You gave everyone quite a scare. And the sea..." His eyes seek answers in my gaze, his grip firm on my shoulders.

"Like I said, it was a mistake. The white-headed raven threw me off my game." My voice carries a hint of excuse.

"The white-headed raven," he murmurs, concern wrinkling his features. "There are no white-headed ravens. Are you sure you saw it?"

My nod confirms my certainty. Confusion washes over me when he walks past and disappears into his room without further comment. "Alright. I guess I'll see you later?" I call after him, puzzled.

After some rummaging, he reemerges, holding a small box. "This is for you. It was your mother's."

As I hold it, an arcane energy seems to surge through my veins, prompting me to ask, "What is it?"

"It's yours now. Open it," he insists.

Lifting the lid reveals a deep blue silken cloth cradling a pair of bracers—my mother's bracers. Heirlooms I thought were lost when she passed away. "I thought these were gone."

"Garm's bracers," my father explains. "They were a gift from her father, and it's said they're imbued with the Wolf Guardian's magic."

The revelation stuns me. "I can't accept this, father. They're yours. Mother would have wanted you to have them." I push the box toward him, but he pushes it back gently.

"No, she wouldn't have," he insists. "She loved you so much."

I slam the box onto the table and cross my arms, bitterness welling up at the memory of her relentless training and harsh discipline. "But she was so hard on me."

My father's hand brushes a strand of hair from my eyes, his expression softening as he speaks. "You look so much like her. You have her eyes, you know." His gaze wanders, lost in a memory.

"Don't remind me." I cringe at the thought of my heterochromatic eyes. Instead of the expected blue or green of High Elves or Wood Elves, I have one of each. An enduring reminder of my mixed heritage and a constant source of feeling out of place.

"There's nothing wrong with that. High Elf blood is nothing to be ashamed of." He speaks sternly, his emerald eyes warm and reassuring. "Besides, she was hard on you because she was preparing you for the Oath."

I can't help but respond with a sarcastic tone. "If calling it 'preparation' when she antagonized me with brutal training, then yes, she really prepared me."

"You joke," my father says, "but it's true. I believe her Oath was connected to you in some way. She was sure you were someone special, and her training was her way of preparing you for that destiny."

"I know, father, but it doesn't make it any easier." I shake my head, still haunted by memories of my mother's relentless training.

"Your mother felt the same way you do now," my father continues. "After receiving her Oath, she became wise and patient. I believe the same will happen to you."

I scoff, unable to contain my skepticism.

"It's true," he insists. "Her Oath gave her purpose, and that purpose was you."

My curiosity is piqued, and I ask, "What do you mean?"

My father seems hesitant, searching for the right words. "A druid's Oath is a sacred pact with the Lunar Tree, and your mother never shared the details of her Oath. But when you were born, she became convinced that you were someone truly special. She doted on you tirelessly, more than any mother tends to her child—it was something deeper."

"Right, if you call antagonizing me with brutal training 'doting,' then sure, she really doted on me." I respond with a heavy dose of sarcasm.

"You may not understand it now, but her dedication was driven by love," my father says, his emerald eyes kind and warm. "You have your mother's eyes, and that's something to be proud of."

I cringe at the mention of my unusual eyes, yet another factor that sets me apart from my kin. "But her harshness..."

My father's voice holds a sense of nostalgia as he counters, "Your mother was different. She knew the path she walked was unique, and she didn't want you to face any less of a challenge."

I yell in frustration, swatting his hand away. I turn to face the window, which now seems cast in shadow. "She left us alone for... what? To make some pilgrimage for a meaningless Oath?" A surge of anger and sorrow threatens to overwhelm me, but I bury it deep.

He folds his arms, his gaze unwavering. "So quick to pass judgment, my daughter. The Oath is an integral part of our heritage, and your mother's choice was hers alone. It was her way of protecting Willowbrook."

"She didn't do enough," I growl, bitterness creeping into my voice. I turn away and walk over to my blackthorn staff, picking it up to drum my fingers on impatiently, eager to end this conversation.

Before the accident, she had been Oathkeeper for a hundred years."

"It was no accident, father; she was murdered." I correct him firmly.

"Yes, murdered." He cringes at my correction. "And now, every seven years, neophytes travel to Willowbrook to learn the ways of the Druidic Order and make their pilgrimage. Seven years ago, twenty Elves became neophytes, but the numbers have dwindled since. This time, there are only five. I fear the next generation may bring none at all."

I think back to previous pilgrimages and realize he might be right. "So what? Maybe more will come next time," I say, though deep down, I'm not so sure.

He shakes his head. "Your mother believed differently, and so do Guro and I." He steps forward, resting his hand on my shoulder. "To wield the power of nature, you must not only understand it but also be in harmony with it. Only then can you learn the ways of the Oathkeeper. Daughter, I believe you will be our next Oathkeeper."

The notion leaves me dazed, and I stand there gaping at him as he retrieves the box from the table. "Oathkeeper?"

His smile, one of understanding and conviction, remains unwavering. "Garm's bracers are extraordinary. They will grant you abilities beyond your understanding."

"Like animal friendship and intuition," I recall from my mother's lessons.

"Indeed," he agrees, "but these are one-of-a-kind. They will also allow you to harness the elemental powers of nature through your staff." He gestures toward my blackthorn staff. "Use their magic wisely. All magic has a price, and while blackthorn is durable, excessive magic will eventually crack it."

He kisses my forehead and states, "Now go and prepare for the summoning tonight. I need to meditate to recharge my magic."

Still stunned by the weight of his revelations, I croak, "Oathkeeper?"

He gives me a knowing look, hands me the box, and says, "You must find your own path, Faelyn. Do not let anyone else dictate your destiny."

I take the box, a heavy token of my mother's legacy, and ask one more time, "Oathkeeper?"

My father looks back at me, a hint of pride in his eyes. "Your mother's path was different, but I believe yours will be even greater."

Leaving my home, I step outside. The village in the treetops is bathed in warm sunlight, the wooden platforms alive with activity as Wood Elves go about their day. The sounds of life are all around—the rhythm of hammers crafting, the aroma of fresh bread, and the fragrance of blooming wildflowers. As I traverse the village, the lush foliage envelops me, and I'm once again in sync with the forest that's always been my home.

The Elven homes, nestled within the trees, blend seamlessly with nature. Each home bears unique designs, yet all echo the forest's enchanting allure. Some homes have balconies that offer glimpses of the forest below, and I catch sight of other Elves going about their daily activities.

I make my way to the training grounds, carrying the weight of my father's expectations and my own doubts. I set my staff down and take a deep breath, seeking to clear my thoughts as I focus on the summoning tonight.

Suddenly, I feel a presence behind me and turn to find Riven, a childhood friend. Her long, dark curls cascade over her bronzed skin, the epitome of a true Wood Elf. "Hey, Faelyn!" she exclaims, hugging me. "What's the matter? You seem off."

"Were you at the solstice celebration last night?" I ask, wondering how much she knows.

She shakes her head, her dark eyes curious. "I couldn't make it. We just returned from the Capital. My father needed help with the supplies."

I sigh, not wanting to reveal too much, but I offer this: "You missed quite a show last night."

"Oh?" Riven's curiosity is piqued.

Though I can't confide all my thoughts in her as I used to, I can't keep her entirely in the dark. "My father wants me to become the Oathkeeper," I tell her, gesturing to my staff, "but I'm not sure it's what I want."

Riven regards me with understanding. "Faelyn, you must follow your own path. Don't let anyone else dictate your destiny."

Her words resonate with me, and clarity washes over me. Maybe I don't have to become the Oathkeeper. Perhaps there's another way to make my mark. "And I won't let those snooty High Elves win this year," I add with determination.

A smile graces Riven's lips, and she nods in agreement. "That's the spirit."

I pick up my staff, filled with renewed purpose. "Thanks, Riven. I needed to hear that."

She slips her arm around my shoulder. "I'll walk you out of the village. I'm already headed that way."

As we walk together, the forest canopy overhead and the whispers of the treetop village behind, I can't help but feel a newfound determination. The summoning tonight may be significant, but it's just the beginning of my journey.

5

The Raven's Curse

THE AFTERNOON'S LULL HAS taken hold, where the sun's rays have turned a deep golden hue, casting elongated shadows over the undulating hills. The world seems to be holding its breath, waiting for something unknown. I pause and take a deep breath as I approach the training grounds, the salty scent of the nearby sea filling my nostrils and the distant sound of waves crashing onto the shore. It's a reminder that we're surrounded by nature's unpredictable beauty.

The towering sycamore trees encircle the area, their branches reaching high into the sky, like ancient guardians watching over us. The training grounds themselves are a wide expanse of rolling meadow grasses, bathed in the soft, golden light of the late afternoon. The beauty of this place remains undisturbed, an oasis of serenity amidst our training's demanding nature.

As I step onto the training grounds, the sound of clashing weapons fills my ears. Neophytes are sparring with each other, their wooden quarterstaffs clattering together as they practice their combat skills. The rhythm of their training, the swift moves, and the focused expressions on their faces create a mesmerizing spectacle.

The first station I see is dedicated to survival skills. Here, druids are practicing their tracking and hunting abilities. Some have their animal companions by their side, moving in perfect harmony. Others work alone, their connection with nature evident in their every move. I watch as a druid tracks a deer, their keen senses in perfect sync with the forest's heartbeat, and they take down the prey with a single, masterful arrow, displaying their skill and precision.

I move on to a station where druids are practicing with slingshots, throwing knives, and staffs. Some of them harness their elemental powers, their weapons coming alive with sparks or the added force of nature's elements. It's a vivid reminder of the profound connection between the druids and the world around them, their powers an extension of their very beings.

But as I delve deeper into the training grounds, my attention is once again drawn to the mysterious white-headed raven. It's perched on a nearby branch, its dark eyes watching my every move with an intensity that's anything but coincidental. The legends speak of ravens as messengers between worlds, and the weight of its gaze fills me with an inexplicable dread. My heartbeat quickens as I wrestle with the sense that it heralds something ominous, something beyond the realm of ordinary occurrences.

My thoughts deepen, a storm of doubt and fear brewing within me. Can I truly become the Oathkeeper, the protector of this village, with such an omen hanging over me?

As I press forward, I encounter a group of young elves in the fledgling area, their faces determined and focused as they practice combat skills. Their sparring is intense, their movements swift and fluid. I can't help but feel a pang of envy, yearning for the simplicity of their training, before my life became embroiled in mystery and dark omens.

Suddenly, a twig snaps behind me, a sharp, jarring sound that rips through the tranquility of the moment. My hand instinctively goes to the hilt of my hunting knife, heart pounding with anticipation. But the shadowy figure that emerges from the trees is one of the druids, returning from a solitary meditation. As my tense muscles relax, the unsettling feeling of being watched remains, an itch in the back of my mind.

The sense of unease threatens to engulf me, but I muster my resolve, attributing it to mere superstition. A deep breath steadies my nerves as I prepare to face the training that lies ahead, knowing that my journey will be fraught with obstacles, both internal and external.

As I near the Novice's Retreat, I spot my fellow neophytes - Barlan, Neason, Maeddess, and Cokko - all engaged in preparations for their forthcoming pilgrimage to the Lunar Grove. My heart carries a heavy weight. Although I haven't been banished, a sense of foreboding looms over the Summoning Circle. Doubt gnaws at my core, like a relentless beast.

Barlan and Neason stand locked in a heated argument, their voices rising in a tempest of emotions. Frustration rushes through me. Why are they arguing when they should be celebrating? I'm compelled to step forward. But as I approach, I sense their mistrust and the tension in the air. Barlan insists on a longer, safer route to avoid a dangerous wolf pack, while Neason champions a shorter but riskier path to save time. It's a pivotal decision that could determine the fate of our journey. With determination, I suggest a compromise. Their eyes turn to me, seeking answers.

Barlan shakes his head, "The best way is over the pass in the hills. It's longer but at least we'll avoid the wolfpack. And Faelyn, tell Neason that the village is NOT cursed."

I groan, not wanting to discuss the raven further, but I lament, ready to defend myself.

"Bout time you showed up Nightsky," Neason sneers. "Thought maybe you and your broken sprite got banished like Willowbane." Neason's sneer and mocking tone pierce through the air as he greets me, an unwelcome presence. However, my attention is diverted by a sudden explosion from behind a sycamore tree. Both Maeddess and Cokko emerge from the soot-covered cloud, choking and stumbling.

Silence descends upon us, laden with anxiety, and we exchange anxious glances. My heart skips a beat as I see the ground beneath the sycamore tree, charred and blackened, smelling strongly of sulfur and ash. I voice my concern, "What kind of magic are they teaching you in the Capital?" I exclaim, frustration creeping into my voice. I see something from the corner of my eye and everyone's gaze shifts upward, the raven circles overhead, plunging us into deeper unease.

"Nightsky brought that ill omen." Maedess says, her accusation lands like a blow as she points to the circling raven, implying that I brought ill-omen upon us. The eyes of the others turn to Neason, expecting his support.

I retort with a mix of frustration and defiance, "It has nothing to do with me."

Barlan attempts to diffuse the situation, "let's not to point fingers," yet the accusations linger, refusing to dissipate.

The air is thick with tension, then Neason says, "You probably pissed off the spirit guardians when you sat on yours."

Neason's nasty words echo through my thoughts. The soot-covered Maeddess and Cokko share knowing smirks, fanning the flames of suspicion.

As the accusations escalate, the raven continues to circle above us. An internal tempest brews as I grapple with their judgment. I reiterate my innocence, my voice firm, leaving no room for doubt. My mind races to unravel the mystery of the explosion, seeking answers beyond the surface.

I turn to Barlan, searching for guidance. "Do you have any idea what could have caused the explosion?" I ask, my voice trembling with doubt.

Barlan's solemn gaze meets mine, and he shakes his head, leaving us with more questions than answers. "Our Pilgrimage is at dawn. We have no time for this."

The raven lets out a haunting caw, its cry echoing through the still air. It takes flight, vanishing into the sycamore forest. Dread courses through me as the truth dawns - the village is cursed, and it may be my fault. Maybe the Krakken... or the sacrifice. No. I had seen the raven before all that.

I stress the importance of unity and vigilance, convinced that we face an unknown threat. "I think this is all connected." I point to a trail of soot leading into the sycamore forest, a silent invitation to investigate.

He looks at me and says, "I don't think we should go."

I head into the trees, and everyone follows, albeit reluctantly. The darkness in the air wraps around us like a shroud as we follow the trail.

I bend and touch the ashy ground, I recoil from the pungent scent of sulfur and ash, realizing that it's no ordinary burn. Dark magic is afoot.

Maeddess remains critical, "This is stupid and we should go back to the village."

But I hold my ground, "Whatever this is, it's dark magic and has no business in the Isles." Each step forward feels like we're walking into an ominous trap, the heavy silence amplifying our shared unease.

A sudden snap of a twig behind us forces us to whirl around, weapons drawn. But it's only a group of feral boars, foraging in the underbrush. They barely notice us as we stalk by, hidden in the shadows. The forest's shadows come to life, and I can't shake the feeling that we're being watched. Neason brushes by me, taking the lead, but I maintain focus on the trail of soot, my instincts telling me something isn't right.

As we cautiously trek deeper into the darkened forest, where the trees seem to close in on us, Neason wonders about the trail's destination. "I don't like this." He stares up to the treetops then back down again. "It's suddenly cold. Very cold."

I see my misty breath and agree, then I take the lead again. Maeddess's fear becomes more palpable, and Cokko unsheathes his dagger in readiness. The trees guard their secrets, and the air is charged with dark energy. Even though the raven has disappeared, hidden by the thick canopy, its presence is undeniable, watching and waiting.

My heart races as I come to a grim realization, acknowledging the accusations that now weigh upon me. I must protect not only myself but also my fellow neophytes from the malevolent magic that seems to have been awakened.

The group moves stealthily, vigilant for danger, our surroundings growing more ominous. Neason's whispered question lingers in the tense air, and the darkness closes in around us.

"I don't think we should go any further," Maeddess's voice is a tremor of unease, her eyes darting for threats. Cokko stands prepared to defend but they keep sharing furtive glances.

Barlan suggests we retreat, but I'm not convinced. A nagging feeling insists there's something hidden, something we're meant to uncover. "Wait," I murmur, scanning the clearing with determined eyes. "There must be something we're not seeing."

As we search, I notice a faint rustling from a thicket of bushes. Cautiously, I approach and peer inside, spotting a small, hidden tunnel leading deeper into the forest floor. Jagged cut stones sculp the opening while moss covered steps lead into darkness. Our shared glances confirm that this might be our only chance to unveil the truth hidden within the shadows.

With a deep breath and a surge of determination, I step into the tunnel, aware that we may be stepping into the unknown, our destiny uncertain.

As we move deeper, the air grows icy and the light dim, a chill sweeping through us all. Maeddess and Cokko exchange fearful glances, lingering behind, as though hesitating to proceed.

Abruptly, the tunnel opens into a small, circular chamber. In its center stands a pulsating, green-glowing portal, its unnatural light casting eerie shadows. My skin prickles as the fine hairs on my neck stand on end. It's clear that this portal is what the trail of soot led us to.

But before we can investigate further, Maeddess and Cokko, gripped by sudden fear, seize each other's arms and begin retreating, their faces etched with terror. "We have to leave!" Maeddess's cry reverberates through the chamber.

Barlan and Neason edge closer to the portal, their curiosity piqued. I hesitate for a moment, torn between caution and my insatiable desire to uncover the truth. Then I see it. A flash of jet black hair and a cackle erupts from the portal, snapping us all out of our stupor.

I step forward but the portal slams shut with a deafening roar, plunging us into darkness. The weight of what we might have just missed crushes down upon me.

As we turn to leave, suspicion creeps into my thoughts regarding Maeddess and Cokko. Their fear and haste strike me as unnatural. Something isn't right, and I'm determined to uncover the secrets hidden within the heart of the forest.

6

The Summoning Circle

WEST OF THE VILLAGE is the summoning circle, nestled amidst the towering oak trees. It emanates magic that soaks deep into my bones. The other neophytes, Barlan included, and my father stand with me, all of us eagerly awaiting the passage of our spirit guardians to this realm. This sacred ritual will bind us to our spirit guides before embarking on our pilgrimage.

The wind howls around us, whipping through our hair and sending shivers down our spines. But despite the chill in the air, my heart beats with excitement, and my mind races with thoughts of the journey ahead.

As the Evening's Serenade turns to the Moon's Blessing, the glow of the moon flickers through the leaves above us. My father begins the summoning ritual, his voice low and steady, resonating with the power of the Elder Grove. The magic in the air hums with anticipation, and the hairs on the back of my neck stand on end.

"I've dreamt of this moment for as long as I can remember," Barlan, the do-gooder among us, whispers. "To have a spirit guide by my side, to embark on the pilgrimage – it's all I've ever wanted."

His words touch my heart, reminding me of the dreams and hopes we all carry. I steal a glance at Guro, our Oathkeeper and steadfast sentinel. He wears a look of quiet determination, his eyes fixed on the summoning circle.

Barlan smiles, "We're in this together, Faelyn. Our spirit guides will guide us through the unknown. I can't wait to see what mine will be like."

"Have you ever wondered about those strange occurrences lately?" Neason, known for his curiosity, asks. "The raven, the explosion in the training grounds, and that mysterious soot trail?"

As Neason's question hangs in the air, we exchange knowing glances, I can't help but feel responsible. If they only knew the full truth. "Maybe these events are intertwined with our upcoming pilgrimage?" Barlan suggests.

The summoning ritual continues, and the anticipation rises. The atmosphere crackles with power and mystery. I can't help but wonder what challenges lie ahead in the Ageless Isles and the other realms. Are our spirit guides truly our allies, or do they have their secrets? Is the white headed raven watching me now? And what if my spirit guardian is actually dead?

As my father, the Sage, begins the summoning ritual, I take a deep breath and focus all my attention on the bond I am about to form with my spirit guide. As I'm almost in tune with the chanting, a violent growl breaks through and startles me. Guro hushes us although the worry in his eyes implicates his hidden fears.

It's nearing midnight, and Guro walks the perimeter of the circle, casting protective enchantments to ensure no unwanted spirits from the Rift breach our circle. The growling that was once so loud fades as if running from the light.

My father is standing in the centre of the circle behind a large stone altar, and he raises his hands to the heavens and begins chanting. We can sense the charge in the air, and even the High Elves seem giddy.

But then, a flash of lightning descends from the clouds, electrifying my father's hands. The bolts crackle and separate into chain lightning, encircling us with an electric storm of protective magic.

As my father summons the ancient lightning deity, the bolts of lightning skip from tree to tree, leaving no harm, and I can feel the protective barrier taking hold.

The rest of the neophytes inch towards the summoning table, where our spirit guardians rest inside glass vials. My sprite flickers slightly on the stone summoning table, mostly laying dormant. But my father says that once he summons them, the glowing orbs of energy will be no more, and each one will take a terrestrial form.

I peek at the others' sprites, and they are all more animated than mine. But then I remember how it got there and wonder if there is something special about it. Nevertheless, I focus on the ritual, and my heart beats with anticipation as my father begins to chant again, and the spirits of our guardians are summoned to be bound with us.

How it got there and why it didn't disappear after my spirit sight faded, I can only guess. But what I know is that something isn't right with it, and despite my relief at not being banished, I wonder if the thing is even alive.

Chain lightning dances from the protective circle of the trees to my father's hands, then streaks towards the table, engulfing the vials, including my limp spirit. Infusing them with energy.

This goes on for much too long, and I'm getting nervous. The other sprites take form, while mine is stagnant. I search my father for answers, but he has become a conduit, channeling the light of the moon, and is incapable of anything while the magic streaks through him.

Finally, after several minutes, thunder erupts, and my father cries out; a cloud of smoke billows on the stone table, obscuring my sprite.

When the cloud settles, Barlan's sprite comes into view, a tiny translucent cherub hovering just above the stone table. It notices Barlan and zips up to his shoulder, chattering to him eagerly, as if it's known him forever. He seems to communicate with it, but I don't see Barlan's lips moving or hear anything.

Suddenly, two apparitions emerge from the cloud, and I startle, thinking they're spectres. But when they don't attack, I inspect them closer. The two High Elf-looking apparitions don't notice me, as they sashay towards Maeddess and Cokko, apparently able to communicate with the pair. How is that fair? Already, the High Elves have an advantage. A silken elemental fog blinks into, then out of existence, only to reappear again. Tiny lightning strikes within the velvet mist as it weaves its way towards Neason's shoulder.

Three unique spirit guides—the question is, what will mine be? Each one of their spirit guides seems to resemble their neophytes in one way or another. Do-gooder Barlan gets a Cherub, The High Elves get the snooty looking High Elf apparitions, and Dreamleaper gets some odd dream weaver cloud. I think to my High Elf heritage and wince—I better not get stuck with some kind pretentious doppelgänger.

Before I catch sight of my sprite, my father drops to his knees. I race to him. He's weary and drained. "You're not well."

"I'm fine, Faelyn," He whispers. "Just a little tired. Your sprite is stubborn." He gives me a weak smile.

I groan at my father's attempt at humor, knowing full well that he means my sprite is stubborn like me. And as I pull him up, I hear a hiccup followed by slurred muttering. What in the grove?

The rest of the billowing cloud clears, and my guardian sits up, looks at me, closes one eye, seemingly unable to focus, then passes out again. A tiny flask tumbles from its grasp, and golden liquid puddles on the stone table. "Mines not like the other sprites." I blurt out, and my father and I exchange weary glances.

I glance over at my father, hoping he has a solution to this mess, but he just looks confused. "Just give it some time," My father reassures me as he leans on me for support. "Sometimes the passage between realms is difficult."

Suddenly, I think it's dead, but then I hear a loud snore, a choke, and a cough all within moments. Its wiry white mustache and beard cover most of its tiny face and body, and a patchwork of stitched cloth covers the rest. His wide-brimmed, battered brown hobo hat has three mushrooms growing on the top of it. I turn to my father and say, "I think mine's broken."

Maeddess snickers. "It looks like a hobo. It fits this place."

I'm too busy fretting about my sprite to reply. Suddenly he sits up stark straight, lets out a crusty cough and a thunderous fart, and scratches his ass, flashing us all in the process. He grabs his tiny leather flask and tries to suck it dry. "Blasted Alfenwine is drained." He bumbles around, searching for more.

I bend down so I'm eye-to-eye with my sprite and say, "I'm Faelyn; what's your name?"

My sprite finally notices me and startles. He throws his tiny flask at me, and it bounces off my nose and rattles on the stone table. "What in Elder Grove is going on here?" He belts out a series of hiccups and falls on his ass.

"Are you drunk?"

"Are yooouu drunk?" He slurs nastily, crawling towards his flask.

The other neophytes burst out laughing, and that sinking feeling I had earlier rears its ugly head, and now I'm convinced banishment to the Feral Expanse may be the better option.

"What is it saying?" My father questions.

Before I can answer, the sprite goes on a rampage. "My name is Moonbean Flatterwort and I've-" He stumbles around, trying to catch his balance, then starts wagging his finger wildly at my father and continues. "never been caught in a thousand years by some schtuupid Elf before." He leans menacingly towards my father, still wagging his finger dramatically. "So there's been some kinda mishtake."

"I'm over here." I correct him.

Moonbean gives me a quick glance, then repositions himself and continues wagging his finger at me. I have no words as I watch Moonbean stumble around drunkenly, trying to catch his balance and figure out who to talk to, until his eyes roll into his head and he crashes face first into the stone table and starts snoring.

"Yup, he's definitely broken."

My father worries, "Looks like you have your work cut out for you, Faelyn."

I can't help but feel a twinge of worry, "But what if I can't fix him?"

My father places a reassuring hand on my shoulder, "You'll figure it out. Remember, your spirit guide chose you for a reason."

7

The Pilgrimage Begins

As the Moon's Blessing's sets and Dawn's Blossom is about to bloom over the village, I feel a mix of excitement and nervousness churn in my stomach. Today, my fellow neophytes and I will set out on our pilgrimage to find our path and begin our journey as druids.

I stand in the center of the village square, surrounded by my companions and my father. Guro stands beside him, a solemn expression on his face. My father clears his throat and addresses us, "Neophytes, today marks the beginning of a journey that will shape your lives forever. You will face many challenges and dangers on your pilgrimage, but I have faith that you will overcome them. Remember to always listen to your spirit guide and trust in your own abilities."

Guro steps forward, holding out a small pouch to each of us. "These pouches contain one magical refill of essential supplies for your journey, including rations, healing herbs, and wild root. Use them wisely."

I take the pouch and feel a surge of gratitude towards Guro. He has been our mentor and guide throughout our training, and I will miss his wisdom and guidance on our journey.

Guro looks at each of us in turn, his eyes shining with pride. "You have all grown so much since the day you arrived in this village as raw recruits. Some of you were born here, and some have travelled from great distances but I am honored to have been a part of your journey, and I know that you will make us all proud."

My fellow neophytes and I exchange glances, feeling a sense of camaraderie and solidarity. We have been through so much together, and now we are ready to face whatever lies ahead.

Guro walks to the table set with an intricately carved wooden box then takes it and stands infront of us expectantly. My heart beats faster as he steps forward and opens the box, revealing a swarm of glowing fireflies fluttering inside. Their glowing lights, illuminating the square.

"These fireflies represent the spirits of the forest," Guro announces to the crowd. "As the neophytes set out on their pilgrimage, they will release these fireflies into the air to symbolize their connection to the spirits and their commitment to their training as druids."

I watch in wonder as Guro hands each of us a handful of fireflies. The tiny insects crawl over my fingers, their soft glow illuminating my face. I feel a sense of connection to the forest and the spirits that inhabit it, a connection that I know will guide me on my journey.

With a deep breath, I raise my hand and release the fireflies into the air. They swirl around me, creating a breathtaking display of light and movement. My fellow neophytes do the same, their fireflies joining mine in a dance of flickering light.

The villagers cheer and applaud, sending us off with their blessings and well wishes. I feel a sense of pride and gratitude for the community that has supported us throughout our training.

My father steps forward and places a hand on my shoulder, "Faelyn, I am so proud of you. You have shown great determination and bravery in your training, and I know that you will make a great druid."

I smile up at him, feeling a sense of warmth and love. "Thank you, Father. I will make you proud."

We stand in a moment of silence, each of us lost in our own thoughts and emotions. Then Guro steps forward and raises his hands in a farewell gesture. "Go forth, neophytes, and may the spirits guide you on your journey." With that, we turn and begin to make our way out of the village, our hearts beating with excitement and anticipation. The road ahead is long and uncertain, but we are ready to face it together.

As we make our way down the winding path leading out of the village, I can't help but feel a sense of foreboding. This is it, the moment we have been training for, the moment we pilgrimage for the Oath. But with that comes the realization that there is no turning back, no safety net to catch us if we fall.

I look around at my companions, noticing the same mix of determination and fear in their eyes. We have all come so far, but we have so much further to go.

The road stretches out before us, winding through dense forests and rolling hills. We walk in silence for a while, each lost in our own thoughts and emotions.

Then, suddenly, we hear a rustling in the bushes. We stop in our tracks, our hearts racing with fear. Guro had warned us about the dangers that lurk in the wilderness, and we know that we must be on high alert at all times. But we're so close to the village, I've played here many times before, why am I suddenly so full of fear?

My hand instinctively reaches for my staff, the source of my power. I can feel its warmth and energy pulsing through my fingers, reminding me that I am not alone.

We stand frozen, waiting for whatever is lurking in the bushes to reveal itself. Seconds tick by like hours, and I can feel the tension in the air mounting.

And then, with a sudden burst of movement, a rabbit darts out of the bushes and scurries across the path.

We all let out a collective sigh of relief, our nerves frayed and frizzled. It's a reminder that we must stay alert at all times, that danger could be lurking around any corner.

As we continue on our journey, I can't help but wonder what other challenges and dangers await us. But I also feel a sense of determination and excitement, knowing that we are embarking on a journey that will change our lives forever.

Neason nudges me with his elbow and grins, "Hey, Faelyn, is Moonbean still passed out from all the Alfenwine?"

I roll my eyes, feeling slightly irritated at his teasing. "Yes, he is. And my father says the transition from Realms can be hard."

Neason chuckles, "I don't know how you'll manage the pilgrimage with a sprite as lazy as Moonbean. My sprite, Blaze, is always raring to go." His silky cloud crackles with lightening ontop his shoulder, and I have no idea if it's communicating with Neason right now or not.

I bristle at his comment, feeling defensive of Moonbean. "Moonbean is not lazy, he's just more laid-back. And he's always..." I can't finish the sentence so I march ahead, leaving Neason in my dust.

Neason raises his hands in mock surrender, "Okay, okay, I was just teasing. Don't get your wild root pouch in a twist."

I groan, knowing that Neason means no real harm, but loathe being made fun of.

Barlan calls from behind as he streaks up beside Neason, and says, "It's okay Faelyn, maybe some sleep will do Moonbean some good." All of the other neophytes burst out laughing at Barlan's comment.

I groan again, knowing that Barlan means well, but is as naive as the rabbit we crossed paths with. He can be a bit gullable at times, but he's also one of my closest friends and a reliable ally.

As we continue walking, I take a deep breath and try to focus on the task at hand. We have a long way to go and many challenges to face, but I am determined to see it through. And with my determination and the guidance of my spirit guide, if he ever wakes up, I know that I can overcome anything that comes my way.

I steal a glance at Neason and notice his mischievous grin. "You're enjoying this, aren't you?" I ask, trying to keep the annoyance out of my voice.

Neason shrugs, "Can't help it if you're an easy target, Faelyn. Besides, it's all in good fun."

I scoff, "Yeah, well, I don't find it very fun." We walk in silence for a few moments before I decide to break the tension. "So, Neason, what does your spirit guide tell you anyway?"

Neason's expression turns serious as he considers my question. "That's for me to know and you to find out whenever yours wakes up." He bursts out laughing and darts ahead, telling Maeddess and Cokko what he said. I hear them cackle and grit my teeth.

Barlan catches up to me, a concerned look on his face. "Hey, are you okay? Neason can be a bit of a jerk sometimes."

I shake my head, "It's not just Neason. I'm just feeling a bit overwhelmed with everything that's happening."

Barlan nods in understanding, "I get it. It's a lot to take in. But we're here for you, Faelyn. We'll get through this together."

I smile gratefully at him, feeling a surge of warmth in my chest. "Thanks, Barlan. Hey, I was thinking about that strange portal?"

Barlan's expression turns serious. "Yeah, what about it?"

I shrug, "Were Maedess and Cokko acting weird to you that day?"

Barlan's brow furrows, "Maybe. I didn't really have time to scrutinize them. I was too excited for the pilgrimage." He smiles as he spins around, looking to the sky. "And now we're on our way to the Lunar Grove."

I laugh at his simplicity, feeling a sense of relief at having someone to set my roots.

As we tread along the wide ridge, an expansive oak forest flanks both sides of our path, the tree tops just below our feet. The sun casts dappled shadows, and a soft breeze rustles the leaves, carrying the earthy scent of moss and mossberries. A unique feature on this ridge is a series of large, flat stones scattered intermittently, which provide excellent spots to rest, talk, or even enjoy a midday meal. In the distance, beyond the forest's lush canopy, we spot towering, jagged peaks shrouded in mist. They stand as silent guardians of the wilderness.

Turning my attention back to my companion, I continue my conversation with Barlan as we pause for a moment on one of the flat stones, gazing at the distant mountains and enjoying the serenity of the forest. "So, Barlan, what does your spirit guide tell you anyway?"

Barlan, walking beside me, smiles warmly. "Ariel is a bit mischievous," he begins, "and he loves playing games, which is how he usually gets his point across. Whenever he wants to convey something, he'll make peculiar patterns in the wind, like swirling eddies or gusts of air that tickle my face. It's like he's laughing or nudging me in a playful way."

I listen with fascination, thinking of the unique relationship between Barlan and Ariel. "That sounds delightful, Barlan, a bit different from the straightforward nature of Moonbean."

Barlan chuckles, nodding in agreement. "Indeed, it is. Ariel's riddles sometimes drive me a little crazy, but they're always in good fun."

But as we continue on our journey, the weight of uncertainty begins to press on me. I can't help but feel a pang of worry as I glance down at Moonbean, who is snoring on my shoulder, his translucent-like form lazily drifting. He's hardly moving, giving the impression that he's either half-asleep or floating in a trance. "Barlan," I murmur, "I sometimes wonder if Moonbean is prepared for this journey. He's always so... disconnected."

Barlan turns to look at Moonbean and then back to me, his expression full of understanding. "I've noticed that, Faelyn. It's true that Ariel is different, but that doesn't mean Moonbean isn't prepared. Each spirit guide has its own way of guiding us, and perhaps Moonbean's approach is simply more..." he pauses then smirks. "Relaxed."

I sigh, my doubts not entirely dispelled. "I guess you're right, but it's just that... he's not helpful. I see you guys with your guides and I'm jealous. I worry that maybe I'm not ready for this journey."

Barlan smiles warmly at me, his cherubic guide Ariel swirling playfully around him. "Faelyn, you are more than prepared. You've always been the top of our class, and full of courage, determination, and kindness throughout our training. Moonbean might have his moments of... relaxation, but I believe that when the time comes, he'll guide you with wisdom and care."

Moonbean shuffles over and lets out a fart and I wince. Barlan looks at me with questioning eyes. "Is something wrong?"

"No." I lie. "It's just that Moonbean has impecible timing."

Barlan scratches his head as he looks from me to the sleeping spirit guide on my shoulder and says. "Did he just communicate with you?"

I laugh. "Something like that."

8

The Pillar of Truth

As we walk through the dense forest, I can feel the weight of my destiny on my shoulders, and I can't help but think that running away to the Expanse would be the easier option. My spirit guide, a drunken fool who's been snoring on my shoulder since he hit me in the face with his flask, is no help at all. I'm not even sure if he's still alive, but the occasional snore and fart tell me he's at least breathing. I stop to adjust my staff, which is strapped to my back, and my spirit guide falls off my shoulder yet again. I pick him up and continue on my way, knowing that he'll just appear on the other side if I leave him behind.

This is how my journey begins, and it wasn't the sendoff I'd been hoping for. Sure, the fireflies were beautiful, and my father's and Guro's words were uplifting, but my spirit guide has done nothing yet.

Suddenly, Barlan blurts out. "I'm sorry about the other day," he pants, "Maeddess and Cokko had no right to blame the raven on you. I don't think it's your fault."

I give a small smile but say nothing, feeling the sting of their accusations still fresh in my mind.

"Really though," Barlan continues, "I know you were asking about them being wierd and all, but I think they're just different. You know, from the Capital."

I nod in agreement. "I've never been there, but I've heard stories." The mention of the High Elf Capital of Faelyndelle triggers a vivid, foreboding memory of my mother's stern training. She had been a strict but loving mentor, preparing me for the challenges that lay ahead in our pilgrimage. Her lessons had been a stark contrast to the warm tales she told, a necessary push to mold me into a druid.

My mother's voice echoes in my mind as I recall her words. "Faelyndelle," she would say, her tone serious, "it's a place of tradition and politics, where no one is to be trusted, especially those from the Capital. The grand spires and magnificent bridges are more than just beauty; they symbolize the eternal connection between our people and the spirit of the land."

She would continue, "In Faelyndelle, every action has a hidden motive, and every word is a potential trap. You will be expected to uphold the ancient customs and demonstrate your dedication to the balance between the natural world and our kind."

Her training had been relentless, pushing me to the limits of my abilities. She had taught me to harness the raw power of nature, weaving spells with precision and discipline. My mother's expectations had been high, and she demanded perfection.

"But, my child," she would say, her eyes softening just a bit, "never forget that in Faelyndelle, as in life, your roots are your foundation. Stay true to who you are, for it's your uniqueness that will set you apart and define your path. Trust no one, but trust in yourself."

I would look up to her, determined to live up to her standards and make her proud. Her memory fills me with both anxiety and resolve. She knew the challenges that awaited me, and her teachings continue to guide me, even on this perilous pilgrimage.

I turn to Barlan, a determined gleam in my eyes, as I share the memory with him. "My mother was strict in her training, but she was preparing me for the Oath and the daunting path ahead. Faelyndelle is a place of tradition, politics, and deceit, and my mother's lessons remind me of the strength within me. I just hope I'm ready for what's to come."

"My mother tells me that things used to be different."

Curiosity piques within me. "How so?" I ask.

Barlan clears his throat. "She says that the Druidic Order used to be more accepting of outsiders, that they were more open-minded and welcoming. But now, it feels like we're closing ourselves off from the rest of the world."

I nod thoughtfully, mulling over Barlan's words. The dense forest surrounding us is alive with the rustle of leaves and the chirping of birds, creating a symphony of sound that echoes through the trees. The path beneath our feet is uneven, with roots and rocks jutting out at every turn. The shadows cast by the towering trees make it difficult to see far ahead, adding to the sense of mystery and danger that permeates the air.

As I continue walking, I can't shake the feeling that we're being watched. I turn my head this way and that, scanning the trees for any sign of danger. My spirit guide, Moonbean, stirs on my shoulder, sensing my unease. He opens his eyes and stares off into the woods, his ears perked up, and his nose twitching as he sniffs the air. Then suddenly, he lays his down, rolls over, and snores.

"I wish Moonbean was more like Ariel." I grumble.

Barlan chuckles. "What, you want endless riddles and obsessive cheerfulness?" I smirk at the irony and Barlan shoots me a knowing glare then adds. "I'm not obsessively cheerful. Just optimistic."

As we walk, the path grows steeper, and the trees close in around us, creating a sense of claustrophobia. Dread creeps into the pit of my stomach, a feeling that only intensifies as we come to a fork in the road. Two paths lay before us, one leading left and the other right.

Barlan looks at me, his eyes filled with uncertainty. "Which way, Faelyn?"

"I don't know." I say then I close my eyes and take a deep breath, hoping to connect with my spirit guide and find the answer. But Moonbean remains silent, and the forest seems to offer no clues.

With a deep sense of unease, I point to the left path. "This way," I say, hoping that I'm making the right decision.

As we continue on the left path, the trees thin out, and we come upon a small clearing. In the center of the clearing stands a massive stone pillar half-covered in moss.

A shiver runs down my spine as I approach the pillar, my heart racing with anticipation and I have no idea why. It towers over us, reaching towards the sky like a giant sentinel guarding the secrets of the forest. There are faint symbols and markings etched into its surface are like nothing I have ever seen before. They are faint yet complex. Some of the markings are familiar, resembling the symbols

I have seen in ancient texts and druidic lore, but most are alien and unknown.

As I draw closer, I can feel the hum of energy emanating from the pillar. It's like a pulsing heartbeat, a rhythm that echoes through the clearing and reverberates in my bones. I reach out to touch the surface of the stone, and a jolt of electricity surges through my hand, making me recoil in shock.

Despite the initial shock, I am fascinated by the pillar. It's as if it's calling out to me, inviting me to decipher its secrets and unravel the mysteries that it holds. But there is also a sense of danger lurking beneath its surface, a warning that I should tread lightly and approach with caution.

As I stand there, gazing up at the towering pillar, the mysterious markings scratch deeper into the surface, glowing and writhing, like a puzzle waiting to be solved. My fingers dance along the grooves of the stone as the markings appear, as if searching for some hidden message or secret code. They become highlighted and pulsing in vivid detail. I start to see the groves, spirit guides, water, trees, druids and then a raven and darkness. I leap back in fear and stumble into Barlan.

"What in the Groves Faelyn?" He grumbles looking at me with quizical eyes.

I ignore him and gaze at the pillar again as if mezmer-ized. And then, a spark of recognition ignites with-in me, like a forgotten memory resurfacing from the depths of my mind. I realize with a start that I am look-ing at ancient druidic symbols, long lost to the current generation of Druids. Filled with curiosity and a sense of reverence, I find myself compelled to speak to the pillar. "What secrets do these symbols hold?" I ask, my voice hushed with awe.

Barlan leans into the stone pillar, studying it, then questions me, "I don't see any symbols, Faelyn. And who are you talking to?"

Somehow I glean meaning from touching them, and they tell me a story of a veiled past, of an ancient druidic civilization that existed long before our time, a civiliza-tion that possessed knowledge and power far beyond what we could imagine. But the civilization fell, and its knowledge was lost to time. Could these symbols hold the key to that lost knowledge?

I turn to Barlan, my eyes alight with excitement and my heart racing. "Barlan, I think I've uncovered some-thing incredible."

Barlan looks at me with equal measures of surprise and anticipation. "I don't understand Faelyn? What are you talking about?" He places his hand on the stone, studying it with renewed interest, but he clearly doesn't see the symbols.

"These symbols," I say, pointing to the ancient markings etched into the stone, "are from a time long forgotten by our Order. They tell a story of a civilization that possessed knowledge and abilities beyond our wildest dreams."

Barlan's expression darkens, and he steps closer to me. "This is just a stone pillar."

Suddenly, a loud rumbling sound fills the air, and the ground beneath us judders. Barlan and I stumble, struggling to maintain our balance as the earth shifts beneath our feet. I feel a sense of panic rising within me as I realize we may be in grave danger.

Just as suddenly as it began, the shaking stops, and a voice echoes through the clearing. "Who dares disturb the sacred ground?"

Barlan and I look at each other in shock, both of us unsure of what to do or say. "Did you hear that?" I ask.

Barlan nods with wide eyes as he steps back. As the rumbling ground settles, my mind races to a memory of my mother's voice, recounting a tale about a similar ancient pillar. She had spoken of a time when she ventured into the heart of the forest, her eyes gleaming with the thrill of discovery.

I remember her words vividly: "A pillar of truth, my dear, is a sentinel of ancient wisdom. It guards the forest's deepest secrets and channels the energy of the earth. It's a place where the spirits of the wood intertwine with our world, and its secrets are both a gift and a curse."

Her voice had been filled with a mixture of reverence and caution as she continued, "The pillar may offer guidance to those who seek it, but it also tests the intentions of those who approach. It demands truth, for it cannot be deceived. To approach the pillar with falsehood in your heart is to invite misfortune."

With her words echoing in my mind, I look at Barlan, and we share a brief, knowing glance. My mother's tale becomes a guiding light in this strange encounter. We are not to take this encounter lightly, and the pillar's guardian won't be fooled by empty words.

I take a deep breath, steeling my resolve, and address the unseen presence in the clearing. "We are Faelyn and Barlan, and we are here on the Pilgrimage, seeking guidance from the forest. We mean no harm, and our intentions are pure. We ask for the wisdom and guidance of the pillar of truth."

There is a long pause, and I hold my breath, waiting for a response. Finally, the voice emanating from the ancient stone pillar replies, "You have been chosen, Faelyn, and the forest has guided you here. But it is you who must choose truth over shame."

I shiver, feeling the weight of the pillar's words and its subtle allusion to the white-headed raven that had appeared in my visions. The raven, with its cryptic messages, is a mystery even to me, and I can't deny that it's a source of unease and shame.

As I falter for a moment, unsure of what to reveal about the raven, the forest seems to sense my hesitation. The earth beneath our feet trembles, and a deafening crack splits through the air. The tree near the pillar, once strong and proud, now splinters and crashes to the forest floor with a thunderous boom. The sound of the cracking tree echoes through the forest, and for a moment, the world seems to hold its breath. Barlan and I stand frozen in place, watching as the massive tree splits down the middle, its once-sturdy trunk now a splintered mess.

The voice from the pillar is now even more enigmatic. "You carry a secret within you, Faelyn. A secret that may yet define your journey. The forest senses your hesitations and uncertainties, and it will not be fooled. Seek the truth within yourself, for that is where the answers lie."

I look to Barlan, my eyes wide with both awe and dread, and he returns the sentiment. We have unwittingly awakened a powerful guardian, and it was clear that our journey has taken an unexpected turn. With the realization that the forest holds secrets even older than our Order, I swallow hard as I confess my unease, "Barlan, there's something not right about this place."

"I agree. Something isn't right. Is it talking about the raven?" He takes another step back and unsheaths his staff and steps behind me so we are back to back. Another loud rumble reverberates through the forest as another massive tree collapses nearby. A chasm opens before us, splitting the clearing in half, and is a neverending abyss of blackness, seemingly drilling down to the Rift itself.

As we turn to run, a low rumbling growl surrounds us, and I feel the hair on the back of my neck stand on end. The sound seems to come from all around us, and the pillar speaks again over the chaos, "Lift the veil Faelyn, that is the only way." Then suddenly, the voice fades away and the growling intensifies.

I grab Barlan's arm, and yank him. "We need to go, now!" I shout, pulling him along with me as we race through the forest. But we're too late. The earth quakes violently as the chasm splits apart further, leaving only tiny islands of land to traverse.

Barlan and I cling to each other for dear life, our eyes wide with terror as we scramble along the edge of the chasm, leaping over debris and ducking under low-hanging branches, desperate to escape the violent shaking of the earth. It feels like hours before we finally collapse, gasping for breath and trying to calm our nerves. Barlan's voice shakes as he speaks. "What was that? I've never seen anything like it."

"I don't know," I reply, my voice trembling with emotion. "But we have to tell someone about this. The village needs to know."

Barlan shakes his head. "We can't risk letting Maeddess and Cokko getting to the grove without us. We can't let another High Elf get the Oath."

I tremble as I stand. "We have to keep moving." With that, I pull Barlan to his feet and we make our way back to the Pilgrim's Path, our minds reeling with questions and fear. As we walk, I can't help but wonder what kind of ancient power we've awoken, and what kind of danger we've put ourselves in. And how did it know about the raven? And what veil was it talking about? Does it have to do with the raven? I'm so confused.

As we walk deeper into the forest, Barlan is looking at me funny, but won't say anyting, so I ask. "What's up Barlan?"

He mutters several times without saying much, until he finally spits out. "You lied to the pillar."

"I didn't lie Barlan. I hesitated." I say kicking a stray stone that had found a home on the Pilgrims Path, harder than necessary.

Barlan grunts but doesn't say anything further so I clarify. "You didn't see the symbols, but it meant something, but I didn't have time to decifer them all. It showed me things, and-"

"That was a pillar of truth Faelyn. I've heard about them before. They are rare. Very rare and to cross one is monumental. And anyone stupid enough to lie to one-"

I stop mid stride and twist to face him and he staggers to a stop as I poke my finger in his chest. "First off, I'm not stupid. Take it back." I poke him again for good measure and he winces.

"There were no symbols Faelyn. And stop poking me." He rubs his chest and steps back.

I step forward again with tenacity. "There were symbols and it showed me what was in my visions." I growl. "And, I was confused and hesitated because I was scared."

Barlan narrows his eyes and stalks past me without another word. We keep walking for hours without saying anything until Barlan blurts out. "We need to make camp." So we search for a suitable spot and find a small clearing next to a babbling brook. I gather dry twigs and branches to start a fire while Barlan sets up our makeshift shelter.

As we sit around the fire, I can still feel the fear and adrenaline from our earlier encounter coursing through my veins. I try to shake it off and focus on the present moment. Barlan breaks the silence. "We should have never come this way," he says. "Going left was the wrong decision."

"I didn't see you making a decision." I say. "And we can't turn back now. We're on pilgrimage, and we have to see it through." I tear a piece of seedcake off, chewing agressively while Barlan barely nibbles on his ration of hard cheese.

Barlan looks weary, until he tucks into his shelter and pulls his cloak tight. "I think I'll head out early tomorrow and travel alone for a while."

I nod in agreement and pull my cloak over my head and turn my back on him without another word. As the night grows darker, the forest seems to come alive with strange noises and eerie whispers. As I close my eyes, I can still hear the cracking tree and the rumbling growl. But I try to push those thoughts aside and focus on the warmth of the fire and the sound of the babbling brook. As I drift off to sleep, I realize this journey will be like nothing I've ever experienced before.

9

The Wailwraith's Curse

SITTING BY THE MORNING fire, savoring the freshly brewed mugwort tea and nibbling on the seedcake, I let my mind race with thoughts of the pillar we found yesterday. I wonder if it was just a trial of the pilgrimage, or is the hidden truth defying my mind. The chirping birds and rustling leaves of the forest surround me, and the dewy grass and nearby trees shimmer in the pink glow cast by the rising sun. The rainbow hues refract through the dew droplets, creating a magical display that fills me with wonder. And after yesterday, wonder is exactly what I need. There is no sign of Barlan, or his stuff, so he was true to his word and left me alone. Good riddance.

However, my peaceful moment is rudely interrupted by Maeddess' sashaying out of the bushes. My heart sinks, and I brace myself for her taunts. "What's that on your shoulder, halfbreed?" she sneers, kicking debris onto my fire, causing a wave of ash and soot to splash on me.

I leap to my feet, preparing to strike with a flying elbow, but she ducks and avoids it. "Won't the King be disappointed when his two stuck-up cronies lose to a Wood Elf?" I retort.

Maeddess lets out a harsh laugh and backs away, keeping a safe distance. "Half-breed, the Wood Elves haven't claimed an Oath in over thirty years," she mocks.

Frustration builds up inside me. "Stop calling me that!" I grip the handle of my Shillelagh, ready to strike, but I hesitate, knowing that my father would not approve of such behavior. "I'd thrash you with Shillelagh if my father didn't care so much about protocol," I say through gritted teeth.

Maeddess appears unimpressed with my threat. "Shillelagh?" she says dismissively.

Grabbing my blackthorn staff, I twirl it menacingly in my hands, feeling the power of Garms' bracers racing through my veins. It invigorates me, and if my mother's lectures are accurate, I can call on any elemental source in eyeshot and imbue it with my staff.

Maeddess scoffs, "You named your staff? How pathetic."

"Not when it can do this." I close my eyes and call on the ancient magic of the hills to power my staff. I hear a swish, and when I open my eyes, the moisture from the grass surrounding me leeches into the staff, empowering it with waves of sticky dew that splash around the butt ends of Shillelagh.

Maeddess eyes Shillelagh warily but chastises. "Wow, you can suck the dew from the grass. Impressive." Her eyes flash white, devouring her pupils, she flicks her hand as if lifting something from the ground, and suddenly a mass of thorny vines erupts from the grass beneath my feet. Dammit—she's trying to entangle me. I won't let her.

I spring up and over the horde of vines with ease, then swing Shillelagh in her direction, intending to send a storm of water at her, hopefully drenching her and teaching her not to mess with me. Instead, one vine wraps around my ankle and trips me, and Shillelagh's butt-end violently stabs the ground, sending me face first into the dewy grass. A thunderous wave of water drenches me, soaking me to the bone.

Maeddess chokes out a laugh just as Cokko, Neason, and Barlan breach the crest of the hill behind us. I can hear them all laugh in unison. Even do-gooder Barlan laughs. Ugh.

"What a loser." Maeddess runs away, more than likely to brag to Cokko about what just happened.

As I lay in the grass contemplating my future as the laughingstock of the Ageless Isles, I hear a cough, and

Moonbean sputters awake, "What in the Groves? Why am I tied up and soaking wet?"

Ugh. Great. Just what I need. "Now you're awake?"

"Untie me, you fiend."

I push myself up from the grass and sulk. "Untie yourself, you drunk."

"Who're you calling drunk?" Moonbean croaks. "And why do I have such a splitting headache?"

I eye my shoulder and scoff. "Because you haven't had a drink since yesterday. You're sober."

"I don't like it. Where's my flask?"

"No clue."

"I remember it bouncing off your nose."

Wanting this conversation to end, I leap to my feet and yank Shillelagh from the grass, wring out my hide shirt, and unstrap my leather pauldron, releasing Moonbean, who then tumbles to the ground with a thud.

He staggers up and stretches. "Thanks, lass. Now where's my drink?"

"You're not getting any until we get to the Lunar Grove." I say firmly.

"Ah, right. The pilgrimage." Moonbean says, suddenly remembering.

"Moonbean, you need to stop drinking," I scold.

"What? You're taking away my only source of happiness?" Moonbean replies with a pout.

"You're my spirit guide, and you can't even stay awake. You need to be focused, and I need you to help get me to the Lunar Grove," I say, trying to sound firm.

"Fine, fine. I'll lay off the drink," Moonbean shrugs. "But you should know, I'm an ancient sprite, and I've never been captured before. I've a lot of information to share with you."

"Really? What kind of information?"

"Well, I know a lot about the ancient spirit guardians that protect this forest," says Moonbean with a twinkle in his eye. "Back in the day, we were powerful beings who protected the forest from any harm. We were like, the guardians of the guardians, if you will."

"Interesting," I say, looking around the forest in awe. "What happened to them?"

"Ah, well, over time, our powers faded, and we became more like..." a disapproving look washes over Moonbean, and he falters. "Guardians of the elves who snatch us up and use us for pilgrimage." Moonbean gestures around them.

I shake my head, hoping I was finally getting through to him, and yet he still gives me no guidance. I shrug and walk away. "Try to keep up."

After several paces, he abruptly appears on my shoulder with his arms crossed, facing the wrong way. "So I can't even sulk in peace. I've got to be tethered on your shoulder the whole time?"

"I guess so." I mutter.

As I venture further into the ancient Hinterlands, towering trees surround me. They're not like the one's back home on the coast. These ones seem older and wiser, reaching for the sky with their branches like they have a secret to share. The sunlight peeks through the leaves, playing a game of light and shadow. The thick undergrowth of ferns and brambles adds an extra layer of excitement as I try to catch glimpses of deer and rabbits darting through the foliage. We hike up hills and down into valleys, our journey mostly uneventful, but I remain alert nonetheless.

"Wow, this forest is amazing," I say, taking it all in. I've never been this far north before and am startled by how abrupt the change came when we entered the Hinterlands. The quick drop in temperature, the surrounding forest becoming more wild, and a sense of danger around every tree.

"Yes, it is," agreed Moonbean, taking a swig from his flask.

"Hey, I thought you weren't drinking anymore," I scold. "How'd you even fill that, anyway?"

"Oh, right. Sorry," Moonbean apologizes before stealing another swig, then corking it with something resembling an acorn. "I'll try to be more helpful. Although, to be fair, I'm not much of a fighter. I'm more of a thinker." He taps his patchwork hat and winks at me.

"Right," I say, patting Moonbean on the head. "Just get me to the Lunar Grove. I have a feeling we're going to need you awake more than anything."

I turn away from Moonbean and start walking; the Midday's Bloom on my back as I head north towards another sunken valley. The ancient forest that surrounds me is rocky and imposing, with trees that grow larger and more gnarled with each passing mile. I can feel the chill in my bones as the temperature drops rapidly.

Moonbean shivers atop my shoulder. "Wretched beasts ahead."

"What?" I say, trying to focus on the treacherous tangles of deadwood at my feet.

"The Hinterlands." Moonbean starts. "Are full o' treacherous and gnarly beasts long forgotten by your kind."

"I'm not afraid." I lie as I hear a shriek in the distance. "What was that?"

"Can't be certain." Moonbean grimaces. "Could be a harpy, a chimera, or a unicorn for all I know."

"Unicorns don't exist."

"They used to."

I scoff, but the shrieking continues in waves. I pinpoint where it's coming from and shudder. A sunken cave entrance comes into view after I breach the crest of a weedy knoll. Hidden between two gnarled trees with a mass of long forgotten bramble is the entrance to a hidden cave. I think of Barlan and then of Maeddess and Cokko. What if they've shut him in the cave and somehow, he's crying out in pain?

"That's not a good idea." Moonbean warns, taking a long pull from his flask.

"Put that away." I scorn. "I need you to help me. Isn't that your job?"

"My job," Moonbean slurs as he dances a wobbly jig on my shoulder. When he's spun round twice, he says. "Is to flutter in the forest as a glowing orb of nothingness, minding my own business, and dancing the days away. Living merrily, and mostly unseen, to the shriekers and other nasties that call this ancient forest home."

"Shriekers? What's that? Is that what's making that awful sound?" I ask, but Moonbean doesn't hear me or is ignoring me, so I wrap my cloak tighter around me and march forward to the sound of the wailing coming from a cave in the distance.

Reaching the entrance, I pause, listening closely to the eerie sound, and decide to investigate. With my staff at the ready, and the hairs on the back of my neck standing on end, I feel a chill in the air worse than that of the coming dusk's bloom. "You feel that?"

"I do." Moonbean hiccups. "An' I don't like it. Let's skip it. No point in bein' a hero."

"What if someone's in there? What if Barlan needs my help. Maybe Maeddess locked him in there?"

"What if it's just an echo?" Moonbean suggests. "I won't tell if you don't."

"It could be a trial. A test of the pilgrimage."

I step into the cave and the wailing grows louder, echoing off the cavern walls. As I delve deeper into the cave, the shadows closing in around me, my heart pounds in my chest, and I'm almost on the verge of turning back, but I step lightly, keen to my surroundings. The wailing stops momentarily and the echo of drips and something fluttering stops me. I hold my breath, readying for a fight, but nothing comes at me. My breath icy now, I can sense something just around the corner.

"It's not too late to turn back." Moonbean whispers. "Think of my mortality. If I die in this form, I'm not sure I'll survive." He gulps.

"You are supposed to be my spirit guardian. Do something 'guardian like'."

I can feel Moonbean's knees shake as we turn the corner and I gasp. "Cursed Wildwoods! A wraith." I yell.

"That's not just a wraith." Moonbean screeches. "That's a Wailwraith!"

"What's a Wailwraith?"

"Its just one of the deadliest kinds of wraiths. It's a harbinger of death with a ghostly form, and a voice that wails or shrieks to foretell a death."

"What's it doing in the Ageless Isles?"

"No clue, kid, they usually can't manifest here. But stop yakkin' and get out of here. You're not ready for this fight."

Too late.

The Wailwraith shudders as it notices us and sets its ghastly eyes on me. Its unkempt hair defies gravity and writhes around its cadaverous leathered face. A look of torment and pain wrenches its very movement as it glides towards me, and strands of its torn, translucent gown threaten to entangle me.

"What do I do?"

"Don't let it hit you with its wail. One blast from its earsplitting holler and you're as good as dead."

"Okay, so I dodge it. I'm light on my feet."

It shrieks at me, and I dive out of the way, just as the waves of its shriek crash into the cave wall behind me, then absorb unnaturally into the stone. "Moon's mercy, girl. Get out of here, not deeper into the cave."

Too late. Now that I dove out of the way of the Wailwraith's blast, it's blocking the entrance, and I have to race deeper into the cave.

I hear it screech again, but I'm already turning a corner, and I can feel the blast of shrapnel as it misses again; my luck will only last so long and I know this. I stumble into a dead-end, and now I'm in trouble. Frantically scanning the room for a way out, I find none. I'm as good as tree rot if I don't find a way out or I need to find a weakness. "Does it have a weakness? An elemental affinity?"

"There's nothing you'd be able to harness. Nature's fury or a moon blessing might give you a fighting chance, but you're nowhere near ready for that!"

The Wailwraith glides into the room, and fury overtakes her already exaggerated features. She's in pain, which I can sense, but there's something more. Her eyes shoot daggers through me and settle on something behind me. I extend my staff, keeping the wraith as far from me as I can while I circle the room. My mother's voice rings in my ears, and recites almost all the knowledge of lessons past, until something finally sticks with me, "What about 'echoes of the ancestors'." I blurt out.

"You're not powerful enough!" Moonbean yells as I dive out of the way of another shrieking wail. The blast hits the cavern wall and chunks of rock explode around me. Shrapnel pummels my back as I roll away. Tumbling to the far corner, the Wailwraith tries to claw me but misses as she glides to where I just stood, as if guarding something. Then I see it—something glimmers in a wood-rotted, half-opened chest buried within the dirt. A guarded treasure. That's why she's so possessive of this cave.

"That's what binds her here." I point to the rot-ridden box.

"You're bright kid, but stupid. Stop worrying about it and get out of here. The path is free now."

"I can't leave. Something pulled me here." Memories of the hand gestures required to call on the forest's ancestors race through my mind. "I think I can do it."

"Not like this. Not in a cursed cave with a Wailwraith about to kill us with a death-shriek!"

I practice the hand gesture, and something doesn't feel right. Moonbean curses and shows me the gesture several times, each one different from the last.

"Which one is it?"

He curses again. "It's like this." He gestures differently from the previous three.

The Wailwraith shrieks and rushes us.

I steady myself and call to my ancestors, pleading with them to help me. Instantly I'm focused and in tune with my surroundings, even though the wraith screeches towards me, its claws extended and intent on ripping me to shreds. My hand extends, with the middle and forefinger bent and my thumb closing the imaginary circle, and with a flick of my wrist, I chant the incantation,

"Ancient spirits, guardians of the forest, hear my call, heed my plea. With your power and your wisdom, protect me from the Wailwraith's misery. Echoes of the ancestors, arise and surround me, envelop me with your gentle embrace. Let the Wailwraith's voice be silenced and banished

to its rightful place.
With your guidance
and your strength,
may the forest's bal-
ance be restored.
And may the Wail-
wraith know its de-
feat, as its form fades
into the shadows."

Suddenly, the wraith is encapsulated in a protective barrier, unable to move. I open my eyes, hand still extended as the energy from the cave absorbs into and through me, holding this thing in place. It scratches and wails, shrieks and bellows, but none of its deathly magic escapes. I'm impressed, and so is Moonbean. "By the roots of Yggdrasil, kid."

"What do I do now?"

"You send it back to the Defiled Rift where it came."

"How did it get here?"

Moonbean shrugs. "Something's wrong. It shouldn't be here."

"How do I send it to the Defiled Rift?" I ask, focusing on holding it in place.

"With a flick of the wrist to complete the incantation. But be careful, it's a slight movement, and if done wrong, it will have dire consequences."

Reading and hearing about the incantation many times and then successfully performing it with the immediate danger of a powerful wraith inches from me is nerve-wracking. "What if I do it wrong?"

"You shouldn't think like that kid." Moonbean scolds. "Just do it like this." He flicks his wrist several times, each one different from the last.

"Which one is right?" I yell.

"This one." He slurs and tries again, but fumbles it and somehow topples over.

The aid of my companion proving futile. I take matters into my own hands. With a swift and elegant gesture, I flick my wrist, and a powerful surge of arcane energy envelops the wraith, causing it to writhe in agony and unleash a cacophony of anguished screams. Just as a mystical portal materializes below the spectral being, attempting to draw it back into the realm of the dead, it lashes out in desperation and scrapes my flesh with its numinous claws. However, the wraith's strength is no match for the gateway's pull, and it's eventually dragged through the portal and vanishes into the ether.

Instantly, I'm overcome with dizziness and collapse to my knees.

"This isn't good." Moonbean tumbles off my shoulder, hitting the dirt face first. He runs up my arm to where the wraith cut me above my bracer. Blood gushes from my forearm onto the dusty stone floor. "You need medicine I don't have."

Reaching into my pouch, I fumble around and pull out the night flower ointment my father gave me. I know this isn't powerful enough, but it's all I have. Dipping my finger into the pouch, I smear a glob of the strong scented ointment onto the cut and snatch the small glimmering object from the half-opened chest without inspecting it, and stuff it into my travel sack. I need to get out of this cave.

Moonbean races back up to my shoulder as I stand on wobbly legs, and after several turns, I stumble out of the cave and collapse into the night.

10

The Healing Circle

THE CAMPFIRE CRACKLES, CASTING eerie shadows
that dance in the dark woods. My eyes remain stub-
bornly shut, my attempts to open them futile. While my
sight is trapped in darkness, my other senses remain vigilant. Crickets hum in the trees, and the low murmurs
of my fellow neophytes by the fire reveal their worry.
They've discovered me here, in Evening's Serenade, and
the mere sound of their voices confirms it. It's a strange
kind of homecoming, given the vivid encounter with
the Wailwraith in the cave. It seems my condition is
worse than I thought.

I struggle to sit up, but the searing pain that shoots
from my arm to my forehead stops me dead in my tracks.
Paralyzed or not, I can't move. The neophytes' mur-
mured voices continue, speculating on my state. They
mention Willowbane, and my blood runs cold. Willowbane, the embodiment of all we fear. I strain to listen,
but my efforts to join their conversation are fruitless.

"She collapsed again. I'm worried she's like Willow-bane." Neason whispers, as if just by saying the name will summon her. "Did you just hear a raven?" He questions and I can hear him swivel his head from side to side as if searching the trees for a raven. What a fool.

Barlan scoffs. "Not likely. I've seen no ravens and Malvolia is long dead. Banished to the Feral Expanse to never be seen again."

"That's not what I heard." Neason whispers. "I heard she's back and-"

"Shut up." Barlan scolds. "Can you just help me with the tea. Faelyn isn't okay and we can't lose her." He shifts the clay pot at the corner of the fire over the piping hot embers. A hot ember has a certain sizzle to it, and my keen ears intuitively know that his 'mugwort' and 'elderflower' tea is about to boil. If it boils, the bitterness will spoil the brew and the healing potential will be diminished. But I'm sure he knows that.

When he doesn't pull it off on time, a whisper of irritation slips through my lips, and I croak, "Your tea's about to boil. Pull it off before you spoil it."

Barlan rushes to save the tea from over-boiling, cursing and burning his fingers in the process. My frustration simmers beneath the surface. Neason kneels beside me, his worry etched on his face. "You alright, Nightsky? What happened?"

Blinking, I try to focus on his blurry form. "Water."

Neason acts swiftly, pouring cool water down my throat. I sputter and cough, but the liquid soothes the fiery discomfort in my throat. "Wailwraith," I manage to gasp.

The camp falls silent again, and Barlan questions my experience, "Wraiths don't manifest on the Ageless Isles, Faelyn."

I retort, my body throbbing with pain, "Then how do you explain my arm?"

He sets the clay pot with the almost boiled elderflower tea beside me. The sweet scent of the elderflower and the earthy flavor of the mugwort overpower the other ingredients, but it has a calming effect on me. The soothing liquid dulls the pain, though it lingers like an unwelcome guest. He places a hand on my forhead and says, "I don't even know what a Wailwraith is Faelyn. I can't trust you after what happened at the pillar. Too many secrets Faelyn."

"I didn't lie about the pillar or the raven. I hesitated."

Neason chews loudly on some seedcake, dropping crumbs all over his leathers. "What pillar? And I thought you said you haven't seen a raven?"

Barlan waves him off.

I hear Moonbean chime in, "Your arm looks infected, despite the pine resin and bandages."

Well, I'm glad Moonbean didn't run away like I thought he would. "How do I heal it?"

"With a hell of a lot more than pine resin and elderflower tea!" He squeals I can't see the little bugger, but I know he's hopping mad.

"What's your hobo going on about?" Neason asks. My vision clears somewhat, but I'm still as good as blind.

"He's asking why you haven't done more to quell the infection raging in my arm."

Neason scoffs and wipes his hands of the remaining seedcake crumbs. "Not everyday a neophyte has so many issues with fainting."

Barlan tips the clay pot of elderflower tea to my lips and I slurp it down. Instantly, the pain numbs, but the throbbing in my arm haunts me like a phantom. "I was waiting for you to wake up before attempting *healing touch*."

I spit out the remaining tea. Most of it sprays on Neason and he curses and shuffles away from me and sits by the fire. "That's not possible. Neophytes can't do that level of magic. It's too complicated." He looks around the camp in dismay, "and especially not out in the field."

"I spoke to my spirit guide Ariel, who is a powerful healer, and he thinks I can do it." The Cherub, Ariel, flutters on Barlan's shoulder. His round face and chubby cheeks are childlike, but his eyes pierce through me with ancient knowledge that encases the small being with golden light.

I agree to the procedure because Ariel seems competent, and I know Barlan means well, but I'm unsure because healing touch is one of the most complex spells a druid can cast, let alone an unexperienced neophyte trying to heal an complicated wraith's scratch. But something tells me the Cherub knows his stuff.

"I know that Cherub." Moonbean slurs. "He's a snob like the rest o' them." He gurgles down a swig of his flask. "These new guardians are all alike. Think they're special. Better than us, old guard."

"He's trying to help me, Moonbean. What are you trying to do other than drink? And how do you always have a full flask?"

"Ha! When you're as old as I am deary, you learn some trichhs." He hiccups.

Barlan listens to Ariel for a long while, as if the golden being is describing how to perform surgery. Barlan's brow knots as the conversation goes along. Then he looks at me and asks, "In your travel sack, do you have agate quartz?"

"Agate quartz?" I mutter as another shooting pain grips me. "No, I don't have agate quartz in my bag. I have some-"

I clench through the violent throbbing in my arm and gasp. "Wildroot and ointment."

Barlan talks to his Cherub again and Ariel points to my bag and nods. Barlan points to my bag, "Ariel says you do."

I'll prove the Cherub wrong and maybe wipe the smug look off its round face, so with my good hand, I reach into my bag and fumble around until I feel something unfamiliar. It's smooth and cold and I remember the shining object I found in the cave.

I pull out the object and bring it to my face. I can only make out the blurred details, so I ask. "What's this?"

"An agate quartz ring. Like Ariel said. Just sit still."

"And what is agate quartz supposed to do?"

Barlan hesitates, then says, "It catches and amplifies the moonlight. Then I can direct the moon's energy into the wound and heal it."

Neason shakes his head. "It's not that easy, Barlan. Healing a wound from a wraith with Healing Touch could go wrong. Very wrong. And where did she get agate quartz, anyway?"

"He's right." I say, even though every bone in my body aches at the thought of agreeing with Neason. As the tea wears off, the throbbing pain increases. "I'm not sure what kind of-" I strain as the pain overtakes me, then when the throbbing eases, I say, "I found it in the cave. The wraith was guarding it."

Moonbean stumbles down my arm and bends at the hip, staring at the wound then sniffs. I'm half worried he'll spill some of his hooch on the wound. Then again, it may not be the worse idea ever, only if Barlan hadn't already set the pine resin over it. "Infection has set in. This isn't a good idea." He looks at the agate quartz in my hand and shakes his head. "There's something about that ring I can't quite put my finger on."

"What else can we do?" I question the sprite.

Moonbean squints at the moon, its white glare bouncing off his frumpy brown hat highlighting the makeshift stitching, then he croaks, "If we amplify it and it turns sour, it could spread and contaminate the rest o' us." He fumbles his way back up my arm and plops down on the round of my shoulder crossing his arms for a long while, then he turns and hiccups, "I don't trust that Cherub." He shoots a menacing look at the golden Cherub, whose whispering something in Barlan's ear. "He's creepy."

I look down at the drunken hobo sprite sitting on my shoulder nursing a half empty flask of hooch and mutter, "He's the creepy one?"

"Um hmm." Moonbean nods and takes another swig.

"Right." I turn to Barlan. "Are we ready? Because I-" I tense as the shooting pain tears through my arm to my head and back again, and thunder erupts and echoes off the walls of my skull. "Ugh." Is all I can muster. I'm getting worse by the minute and if we don't do something now, I'm not sure I'll make it past my next breath.

"It's getting worse." Barlan places the back of his hand on my forehead. "You're burning up."

"Do it Barlan."

He kneels beside me and places both hands over the ring and chants. I try to watch, but the pain is too great and I'm in and out of consciousness. Suddenly the bugs and wind silence, or I just don't hear it anymore, I can't be sure. Even the glow of the fire dims, and suddenly, a light flashes and Barlan glows as if the moonlight is within him. He's gently rocking now and the glow from his hands cascades down to the ring which cools in my hands. I can feel the light drift from my hands and up my arm as it circles the wound. I can hear something sizzle and am uncertain if it's the fire or my arm, or both.

I hear Moonbean mutter something, then he falls off my shoulder and shuffles around, trying to climb back up, but I can't concentrate on him. Neason paces behind Barlan, scanning the surrounding forest as if something is just going to jump out from the thicket.

Barlan hums and the Cherub that was contently sitting upon his shoulder slides down his arm and places his tiny hands over Barlan's, further amplifying the light. And now a golden light mixes with the moonlight and makes its way to my arm. Once there, something happens.

A thunderous clap erupts, reverberating through the trees and there's a streak of light, but it's not moonlight. My vision blurs momentarily, and I wonder if the clap is in my head again, but it's not. Neason is on his knees, covering his ears, and Barlan stumbles over, breaking the Healing Touch. That can't be good. I don't think he was done.

The moonlight and golden Cherub magic suddenly vanish, and all that's left is pain. But something happens, and I'm suddenly able to move. I crawl to my knees and set eyes on Barlan whose convulsing on the ground, writhing in pain.

I look at Neason, who leaps to his feet and reaches for his dagger. With it in hand, he's stumbling around the fire, yelling at someone or something. I can't tell because I can't see anything but shadows. Somehow my vision, even though much clearer than when I first woke, is still not the same. "Neason!" I croak, but he doesn't hear me and wildly stabs at something.

I crawl to Barlan and shake him awake, but he only writhes as if something is strangling him. I search around me looking for the rose quartz, and when I find it, I place it in his hands and when our hands lock, I'm inundated with a vision. And not only that, Barlan is there, and I'm convinced he's not a figment of my imagination.

I hear Neason screaming and fighting but can't see him. Shuffling and clanking, biting and gnawing, and the crackle of fire, but none of that is in my vision. I'm floating over a blackened river that drains into the sea, sullying it with death and decay. The darkness eats away at the light and pollutes all that it touches. Barlan and I stare at each other and without words, we communicate with one another and we agree that what we're seeing is real and we try to discern it all.

My eyes follow the slow-moving river until a black tower distinguishes itself from the horizon. Small at first, but somehow we're floating towards it just above the trickling stream and through a desolate forest of deadwood and fallen trees. Beings morph in and out of existence, most in some form of torment and pain; I can only assume are the Foresaken. They claw and crawl their way out of the dusty, ashen ground, only to be sucked back into it, and then it repeats. It's as if they're made of ash, the same stuff that covers the bare earth. It's dry and hot and full of despair.

As if paralyzed, I can't feel my body as I float towards the ever-growing tower, but when I look down, I see my fingers tearing at my chest as if trying to claw their way to my heart; I focus and try to stop them but realize I can't. I'm not in pain, and my fingers can't seem to tear through my hide shirt and leather pauldron. A deathly screech echoes and surrounds me. It's everywhere and nowhere at once. Both Barlan and I see a portal open up above us and from the blackened sky falls Neason and ash demon with glowing red eyes. It claws at Neason as they plummet to the ground. When they crash to the ground, they immediately sink into the dusty ashen earth.

Neason sees us and reaches out in desperation as the blackened soil covers his body until only his eyes and a bit of his forehead are visible. With his outstretched arm clawing for us, he takes one last breath then is dragged under, vanishing into the earth.

I gasp and cry out, but I can't even move to him and am bound by some unseen force.

Suddenly, I sit up and screech. My call echoing off the surrounding trees. The cool night air threatens to choke me as I gasp for breath and am now fully aware that I'm no longer in the Defiled Rift. I desperately scramble to my feet and search for Neason, hoping it was just a dream but can't find him.

I trip over Barlan, who is just coming to, and he mumbles something under his breath as he rubs his head. Worried something will appear and drag me to my death, I stumble back over him and scoop my staff and get into a defensive formation, swiveling at every sound.

"What was that?" Barlan croaks stumbling to his feet.

"The Defiled Rift." I say, remembering my mother's lessons. Who could forget her descriptive tales of the forsaken realm? Unseen by the common folk, and only accessible to the dead or demon kind, the Defiled Rift somehow summoned us to it and I'm now convinced it snatched Neason Dreamleaper from our realm and dragged him to his death.

11

The Unsettled Ring

"WHERE ARE MAEDDES AND Cokko?" I ask Barlan, sweat trickling down my brow despite the frosty air, as we slog through the brambles up a hill, deep into the heart of the Hinterland forest. Each step is like a heavy burden, but I'm on my feet, at least. He doesn't meet my eyes, just stares into the distance, his usual cheerfulness overshadowed by the looming darkness.

"They're scouting the path ahead," he mumbles, "didn't want to wait around when Neason and I found you nearly dead in that damn cave."

I can sense his unease, the weight of Neason's death heavy upon him. It all feels connected: the raven, the pillar, the wraith, and that infernal ring. "You and Neason were close," I prod.

He gives a half-hearted shrug, still avoiding my gaze. "I can't make sense of any of this. Wraiths can't manifest on the Ageless Isles. Yet, here we are. There's something you're not telling me."

I remember the cave, and I drop my travel sack and rummage through the contents, searching for the ring. I pull out the strange object, its agate quartz gemstone glinting under the dappled sunlight. Barlan leans in to examine it. "It's changed since yesterday."

The ring gleams, its intricate patterns dancing beneath the surface. The agate quartz seems alive, swirling with red and green hues, both enchanting and ominous. It draws me in like a moth to a flame. I feel its power, a deep well of energy, yet a lurking darkness that sends shivers down my spine.

"When I last saw it, it was a solid red," I whisper. "Now, it's restless, in constant metamorphosis."

Barlan's eyes bore into mine, his unease clear. "There's a dark energy to it. Maybe that's what attracted the Foresaken?"

I nod, transfixed by the ring. "The wraith was tormented. To manifest in the Isles, it must have an attachment to something enchanted or cursed."

Neason circles around me, his mutterings almost lost in the wind. He's fixated on the ring, and his Cherub whispers to Barlan, their exchange a cryptic puzzle. I turn to Moonbean for his insight, but he's snoring away on my shoulder, blissfully ignoring our troubles.

Neason stops suddenly, his voice sharp. "I'm sure that's why the Foresaken broke through. It's this damned ring. Get rid of it."

I clench my hand around the ring, and shoot him a defiant glare. "No."

"It's the reason your arm is infected," he insists, his eyes filled with a mix of concern and frustration, "and you might not make it to the Lunar Tree."

Barlan mutters something about the significance of the number seven. I'm no longer surprised; his knowledge always seems to stretch into the oddest corners. "We both held the ring when we glimpsed the Defiled Rift. It's some sort of key."

I nod, a hazy memory surfacing. I'm not sure how I know, but I do. My mind's still foggy, and the pain in my arm throbs relentlessly. My vision blurs, and I struggle to maintain consciousness.

Barlan's patience snaps. He swipes the ring from my hand, and I'm jolted back to reality. "Get rid of it!" he yells.

The ring clatters onto the ground, and I sink to my knees, my head spinning. I can't tell if it's the ring or my arm causing the turmoil. I press my palms into the earth, pleading for relief. My bracers glow faintly, and a soothing coolness washes over me, momentarily easing my torment. When the nausea subsides, I grab the ring and stow it in my travel sack. "I don't know why, but it's important. Maybe when we return to the village, Guro can help us figure it out."

Barlan shakes his head, his face etched with worry. "We're going to be late for the Oath ceremony. Maeddes and Cokko will make it in time, and we'll be stuck as neophytes forever."

"Stop with the drama," I snap, picking up my staff and the ring and resuming my slow and painful ascent. The infection in my arm has slowed, but the fear lingers. It nags at me, telling me that the ring has seeped into my very being, tainting me in ways I can't yet comprehend.

The Afternoon's Lull beats down on us, scorching our skin as we trudge through the barren landscape. The air is dry and stifling, and I feel sweat trickling down my back under my hides and leather pauldron. But as we enter the canopy of the old-growth trees, the temperature drops and the air becomes cool and moist. It's a welcome relief, and I breathe in deeply, feeling the refreshing mist on my face.

The relief is short-lived, however, as we soon come across sunken gullies where the streams are nearly frozen. The drastic temperature change catches us off guard, and I shiver as the icy air bites at my skin. It's a stark contrast to the searing heat we just left behind. This is the Hinterlands, the wild and unpredictable wilderness that my father always warned me about. I can now see why he told me to dress in layers.

I adjust the seamed ties under my arms, loosening them to let in some air when it's hot, and tightening them to keep out the biting cold when the temperature drops. It's a constant battle to maintain a comfortable temperature, and I'm grateful for the layers of clothing that shield me from the elements.

Barlan shivers and blows hot air into his clasped hands. "The stories sure don't prepare you for this cold." He lets out a muted laugh.

I mutter something but can't seem to stop thinking about what tied the wraith to the ring and why wasn't it discovered before? Surely, of all the neophytes to take this path over the years, how was I the first to come across that cave? How was I the one to find it?

I can't stop thinking about Neason and the fear in his eyes as he was dragged into the ash. The Defiled Realm seemed so real, like I was there, but somehow I know it was only a vision. But somehow real enough that Neason was stolen from us. A shiver runs down my spine thinking that something from the Rift could penetrate the enchantments of the Isles and rip one of us away and to our doom. My father had said it was impossible for any Forsaken to breach the enchantments of the Isles, but when I get back and tell him about Neason, he's going to have to awaken the forest. The King must be notified.

I stop in my tracks, the realization finally hitting me. I spin so I'm looking at Barlan behind me and state. "We have to tell the King. My father. Guro. Everyone."

Barlan gives me a questioning look, still shivering and blowing air into his icy hands. "But the Oath."

The Oath. I know. But the northern path ahead of me is suddenly barren and desolate and, for whatever reason, a path eastward has stolen my attention. It's like a trail of golden light beckons me eastward, pulling on me unnaturally. I look down at my bracers and wonder; then remember my father told me they'd help me find the path. Could he have meant this?

Barlan looks at my bracers as I study them and steps closer. He leans in and shows me his cloak as if I've never seen it before. It's a tapestry of patched together wolf hides, but as I study it closer, I realize the quality of the stitching and when he moves it, it somehow blends in with the surroundings. He smiles at me, then it suddenly fades. "It was Neason's." He exclaims. "He had taken it off that night he was taken..." Barlan chokes up, then continues. "It was just lying there, so I took it."

"He'd want you to have it." I offer.

He laughs half-heartedly. "He called it the Cloak of the Wilds. Said it was passed down to him by his father and his before him. Told me it had the power to blend seamlessly into the surroundings."

"It suits you, Barlan."

Barlan looks south from where we came then towards the north and finally to the east and huffs. "I'm not coming with you."

"I didn't expect you would."

"I'm also not going to the Lunar Tree, am I?"

I laugh half-heartedly now. "That's up to you, Barlan. One of us needs to inform the King and one of us needs to tell Guro and my father."

Barlan nods unenthusiastically, then strips the cloak off and shoves it at me. "You'll need this more than me."

I shove it back to him and croak. "I never liked Neason." I regret saying it before the words leave my mouth but cannot stop myself.

Barlan winces as if I struck him. "Take it." He shoves it back to me and points to my arm. "Just in case you run into another wraith."

"Wailwraith." I groan.

"Hide this time and don't be a hero."

I take the Cloak of the Wilds from Barlan's outstretched hand and drape it over my shoulders. Immediately, I feel its power flowing through me, like a warm embrace that shields me from harm. It's as if I've been enveloped in a cocoon of safety, and I can't help but let out a gasp of amazement.

"Wow," I say, my voice barely above a whisper. "It's incredible."

Barlan smiles at me, his eyes twinkling with amusement. His boyish charm is not lost on me. He's somehow transformed into a caring, unselfish friend rather than the obnoxious do-gooder I thought he was. "I told you it was something special. How does it feel?"

I take a deep breath, trying to put the sensation into words. "It's like... like I'm one with the forest. The cloak is a part of me, and I'm a part of it. I feel... powerful. And protected."

Barlan nods, his expression serious now. "That's because you are. The Cloak of the Wilds is a powerful artifact, passed down through generations of druids. It's said to be imbued with the essence of the forest itself, and to offer protection to those who wear it." Sadness creeps into his voice. "At least that's what Neason told me."

I nod, feeling a newfound respect for the cloak and the druids who kept it safe all these years. And to Neason as well. "I can feel that power," I say, my voice filled with guilt.

"It's like I'm invincible. But I don't deserve this. Neason would-" But I can't finish the thought.

Barlan smiles sadly. "Neason respected you. He looked up to you. That's why he teased you. He wanted to be like you."

I flinch, like his words sting me.

"The cloak is powerful, but it's not invincible. You still need to be careful out there."

I nod, knowing that he's right. The cloak may offer protection, but it's still up to me to use my wits and my magic to keep myself safe. I think of Neason and all the times we fought as kids and how cruel we were to one another. I can't believe he looked up to me. Then regret washes over me, thinking of how rude I was to him.

"Thank you, Barlan," I say, my voice filled with guilt and gratitude knowing what comes next. "For everything."

He smiles at me, his eyes twinkling once again. "Of course, Faelyn. You need it more than I do. And who knows? Maybe one day you'll be the one passing down the cloak to the next generation of druids."

I smile at the thought, feeling a sense of pride and responsibility welling up inside me. The Cloak of the Wilds may be a powerful artifact, but it's also a symbol of the druidic tradition, and the role that I now have to play in preserving it. My thoughts drift to the Foresaken. To the vicious, hungry way they tore at Neason and I shudder. What other demons will be unleashed on the Isles? Can we even stop them? What if we can't?

"I'll do my best," I say, determination in my voice. "For the forest. And for the druids who have come before me. For Neason."

Barlan nods, a look of approval on his face. "I have no doubt that you will."

Then I step eastward without a goodbye and exhale as I make my decision not to go to the Lunar Grove and instead, embark on a mission to tell of the King that his enchantments are no longer working. I can only assume Barlan will make the right choice and run home to tell Guro that the Ageless Isles are under attack.

12

Surviving the Storm

As the Dusk Ember turns to the Evening's Serenade, I know that I'll need to make camp soon. I scour the area for dry wood, handpicking each piece to ensure that it will burn well. I take several trips back and forth to collect enough to sustain a fire for the night. I'm famished and in need of some meat. The seedcake will not be enough tonight.

Once I have gathered enough wood, I begin the arduous task of trying to light a fire despite the rain that has been falling steadily for hours. At this point, I wish I'd learned a fire enchantment, but scoff because I am no wizard or sorcerer. I strike my flint and steel repeatedly, watching as sparks fly and die out before they can catch onto the wood. But I don't give up. I know how important a fire is for keeping warm and for cooking the snails I scavenged. It's not venison, but it'll sustain me tonight.

After what feels like an eternity, I finally get a small flame going. I carefully add more wood, feeding the fire until it grows into a warm and welcoming blaze.

As the fire crackles and pops, I forage for rare herbs to brew a healing tincture. Anything to relieve the wretched pain within my arm. I carefully pick out the delicate leaves of feverfew, which reduce fever and inflammation, and the sweet-scented woodruff, which is known for its calming and sedative effects. The need for a good night's sleep is bearing on me.

Moving deeper into the forest, I spot the rare pink-flowered fireweed, which will hopefully ease my nausea, while the tall stalks of mullein, with their soft leaves, will undoubtably relieve this dreadful wheezing I picked up probably because of the chaotic temperature change of the Hinterlands.

As I wander further, I find the elusive purple coneflower, used by ancient healers for its antiseptic properties, and the vibrant yellow flowers of St. John's wort, to quell my anxious and foreboding thoughts.

With my arms full of these rare herbs, I return to the fire, where their fragrances mingle and intoxicate. As I add them to the small earthen pot, I feel a sense of gratitude for the healing power of nature, and cast my thoughts into the brew. Just before it boils, I pull it from the fire and set it beside me. The gentle patter of rain ebb and flows, and I lose myself in its rhythm until my tea cools and I down it in one gulp. The healing effects should last for hours and hopefully cure some of my benign ailments. My arm will need an alchemist's attention when I get to Faelyndelle.

As the darkness of the forest deepens, I know I must set up my defenses before it's too late. I reach into my pack and pull out a spool of thick rope, a set of sharp thorns, and a collection of wild root my father gave to me.

I start by scouting out the perimeter of my campsite and identifying any potential entry points for predators. I then carefully weave the rope through the roots, creating a web of sharp, entangling fibers that will ensnare any creature that dares come too close. If perhaps a magical being breaches the wild root, they will immediately dive deep into the earth and draw magic directly from the soil, entangling anything in their way.

As I work, I hear the distant rumble of thunder. The rain, which had been a gentle patter, has now turned into a raging storm. The wind howls. I'm grateful for the makeshift shelter that I've constructed. The dead branches and fallen debris were twisted into a lean-to that will hopefully keep me dry enough, but I know I need to finish quickly before the fire sputters out.

My fingers fumble with the knots as I try to secure the trap to the ground, but the wet earth makes the task difficult. My hair clings to my forehead and rain drips down my face as I work. Before I know it, my icy breath fogs my vision.

Finally, with a sense of relief, I finish setting up the trap. I take a deep breath and survey my handiwork, knowing that it will provide me with some protection as I sleep. The wolves are on the hunt and I hear them howl. I doubt they'd bother me, but I've never been this far east before, so I won't take any chances.

But just as I turn to head back to my shelter, I notice that the fire has sputtered and fades. The rain is coming down harder now, threatening to extinguish my only source of warmth and light.

Without hesitation, I dart over to the fire and shield it with my body, using the last of the dry wood I had collected to revive it. I blow gently on the embers, coaxing them back to life, and eventually the flames begin to roar once more.

I let out a sigh of relief and sink down onto the ground beside the fire, shivering from the cold and damp. Despite the storm raging around me, I feel a sense of peace and safety knowing that I've done everything I can to protect myself. I toss a handful of the snails on the fire and snap a piece of the seedcake in half and chew. When the snails sizzle, I scoop them onto the damp grass beside me and shuffle over to the shelter to enjoy the rest of my meal. When I'm done, I curl into a ball and try to fall asleep.

I toss and turn in my shelter. My eyes are heavy with sleep, but something keeps me awake, then I hear a loud rumble. I sit up and rub the tired from my eyes, hoping it's just thunder. But then I hear cracking wood and realize it's something much worse. I peek out of my shelter and see them - the Forsaken ash demons, trying to breach my wild root trap. I think of Neason and fear grips me. Their eyes burn like a tormented, blazing hot ember. Their faces twisted in a perpetual snarl and their skin is a sickly grey covered in ash and soot. When they move, it's with an eerie fluidity, almost like liquid smoke, as if their bones are sharp yet plyable.

I spring into action, grabbing my blackthorn staff and casting shillelagh to enhance its power. I can feel the magic coursing through my veins as I face off against the demons. They hiss and snarl as they claw at me, but the wild roots of my trap stretch deep into the earth, entangling them with magic, lending me time to strike.

With lightning speed, I leap into the air, swing my staff and strike the first demon, crushing it into oblivion. When the magic of my staff crashes into the magic of the wild root, the demon explodes into a cloud of ash. The second one lunges at me with its sharp claws, but I dodge and counter with a powerful blow to its head. It recoils, dazed, and I take advantage of the moment to cast lightning at it from my staff. Chain lightening erupts from the tip of Shillelagh and blasts through the demon, causing an explosion of soot and a layer of ash surrounds me.

The demons are relentless, but I am determined. I strike back with all my might, hitting them with the full force of my staff and the magic that fuels it. They claw and bite at me, but I am quick and agile. I dodge and parry their attacks, always one step ahead of them.

The battle rages on for what feels like hours, but I refuse to give up. The fate of the Ageless Isles, and perhaps even the Groves, depends on my success. With a last burst of strength, I fend off the demons and escape their grasp. I collapse onto the ground, my breath ragged and my heart pounding with adrenaline.

As I catch my breath, I hear a voice behind me. "Well done, Faelyn. You fought bravely." My heart skips a beat as I turn to see Malvolia, the warlock who killed my mother, step out of the shadows and into the light of my fire, her obsidian eyes fixed on mine. Instinctively, I know it's her from my father's description. She's tall and slender with jet black hair that cascades down her back in loose waves. Her skin is pale, almost ethereal, and her dark eyes seem to glow black, absorbing the surrounding light.

"How did you breach the wild root?" I plea, trying to keep my voice steady.

"I have urgent news," she says, her voice grave. "I have propositioned Malathor," she pauses dramatically, "my better half, to devour the seven sacred groves. And you, my dear, are powerless to stop it." Despite her striking beauty, there's something about her that makes my skin crawl. Maybe it's the way she slides, almost too smoothly, as if she's not quite of this world. Or maybe it's the way her lips curl into a sly smile, revealing sharp canines that seem almost too long for her mouth.

My blood runs cold at her words. Malvolia wants the groves destroyed, and she's using this demon as a tool to do it. "Why?" I snap, reeling with confusion as my mind swirls with questions. Why is she doing this? My mind calms, then it hits me. The better question is, why is she telling me?

Malvolia's lips curl into a sinister smile. "Let's just say I have unfinished business with your mother. And let's also say that her death was just the beginning of what's to come. The destruction of the groves is just the first step." As she speaks, her voice is soft and almost musical, yet there's an underlying coldness to it that sends a shiver down my spine.

I can feel my anger and hatred boiling over at her words. How could she be so callous about destroying something so precious and sacred? "I won't let you," I say through gritted teeth.

Malvolia cackles. "Oh, my dear. You do not know what you're up against. But I admire your bravery. Now, if you'll excuse me, I have other matters to attend to." I can tell she's enjoying this, reveling in the fear and pain she's causing. It's as if she's playing a game, and the lives of the innocent are nothing more than puppets to her.

With that, she disappears into the darkness, leaving me alone with my thoughts. But unexpectedly, I hear a loud snap of her fingers, and my heart drops to my stomach as I turn to see new demons materializing out of thin air. They're massive creatures, with wolflike features made of ash and soot. My muscles tense, and I can feel my hands shaking with fear and uncertainty as I try to grip my blackthorn staff.

As the wolf demons fully manifest before me, their grotesque forms come into focus. Their massive bodies loom large, dwarfing even the largest of wolves. Yet, their features appear as if they've been contorted from some eerie, charred timber and ash, twisted into grotesque shapes. Glowing orbs of amber pierce the dim light where their eyes should be and their teeth glisten with razor-sharp edges. Their fur, coarse and irregular, is marred with patches of burnt blackness, as though they've endured some infernal fire.

Their claws, long and jagged, gouge the earth with every stride they take. Their movements possess an unsettling grace, almost akin to a sinister dance, yet each step is meticulously calculated and precise. The largest among them releases a resounding howl, and I can sense its breath, hot and oppressive, nearly suffocating me with its intensity. It's as though they radiate pure anger and malevolence, their seething rage tangible in the scorching heat that emanates from their monstrous bodies.

As they slowly circle me, their eyes pierce through me, I feel trapped and helpless. Their presence is overwhelming, and I'm not sure if I can defeat them. I'm merely a neophyte after all, and they're something else entirely.

Summoning every ounce of courage, I lift my staff, ready to confront these malicious demons. But when I strike, it's clear they outclass me. They're faster, more agile, and stronger. I quickly realize I can't handle them alone.

Desperate, I try to dodge their attacks, but they come at me relentlessly, their ferocity unabated. My strength dwindles, and I know I won't hold them off for long. With one last surge of energy, I spin my staff, pivot, and strike, but it barely fazes them and only stirs their anger.

In sheer desperation, I wrap myself in the Cloak of the Wilds and dash deep into the woods, aiming to escape their relentless pursuit. I can hear their snarls and growls behind me, but they can't track me anymore. Running for my life, I gasp for breath, my heart pounding so loud it nearly drowns out the eerie sounds of their pursuit. Uncertainty clouds my mind, but I know I have to shake off these relentless demons and get word to the King as soon as possible.

13

The Misty Village

Running through the dark woods, my feet pounding against the earth, my emotions veer between terror and exhaustion. It's been an endless flight, with no respite, and I've lost my rations in the mad scramble to escape the demons. But now, sheer adrenaline keeps me going as I push my limits.

Finally, too tired to even think about making camp, I stumble upon an abandoned hunting encampment hidden within the trees. It's nothing fancy, just a makeshift blind nestled within the fallen log. I crawl inside and, without a second thought about setting traps or eating, I curl into a deep sleep. Time loses meaning, and when I wake, the world outside is bathed in the gentle light of Dawn's Blossom, the birds sing-song is at its peak.

Ravenous and parched, I tear into a seedcake I find in the encampment, savoring it like a famished beast. A nearby bubbling stream calls to me. I rush to its side, drink deeply, and the cold, clear water soothes my parched throat. After drinking my fill, I sit by the babbling brook to meditate, gathering my energy for the journey ahead.

The misty air and pristine surroundings recharge my waning magic. With newfound vigor, I rise, still somewhat rested but far from feeling refreshed, and continue my relentless journey eastward, toward the Capital.

Despite the ever-present fear and uncertainty, the world around me captivates with its serene beauty. Rolling hills stretch far and wide, their sage-green hues shifting with the sun's descent behind me. In the distance, the towering peaks of the High Mountains loom, their snow-capped summits a stark contrast against the sky. I glance at my shoulder, where Moonbeam, remains soundly asleep. Useless in my time of need, he seems lost in some dream or another, perhaps caught between realms.

I glide through a small forest, the air cool and crisp, infused with the fragrance of pine and earth. In the distance, a sparkling stream winds its way through the trees.

Emerging from the forest, I find myself on the edge of a vast plain. Fields of wheat and barley ripple in the wind, their golden waves a breathtaking sight. In the far-off distance, the sprawling Capital city of Faelyndelle beckons, its spires and towers rising above a shroud of mist, a beacon of hope in a world shrouded in darkness.

My hopes are tempered by the reality of the journey, which has left me weary and worn. But as I walk, my thoughts turn toward practical matters, like finding sustenance for the road ahead.

Then, my attention is abruptly yanked back to the present as I spot a traveling merchant on the road ahead. He guides his trader cart with a majestic elk, its antlers poised like regal crowns, lowered as it careens forward. The merchant himself exudes the characteristic appearance and attitude of a High Elf, with his fair complexion and meticulously styled golden hair. He stands with an air of superiority, clad in a robe of fine silk, extravagantly embroidered to accentuate his pompous demeanor. His leather boots, silver chain with a crystal pendant, and wide-brimmed hat all complete the picture of his high regard for himself.

Despite the heavily laden cart filled with various goods, the merchant's Elven disdain seems to outweigh the physical burden. I hasten my pace, eager to reach him and barter for the essential supplies I require for the arduous journey that awaits, even while doing my best to overlook his overbearing presence. I know I'm ragged from the trail, and hopefully, he doesn't mistake me for a vagrant.

"Hello there, young one!" the merchant greets me with an ostentatious smile, as he peers down his nose at me. "What can I help you with today?"

"I need supplies," I respond, my voice laced with a hint of weariness. "But I'm afraid I have no money to trade."

The merchant eyes me with suspicion, his up-and-down appraisal filled with condescension. He even inspects his meticulously manicured fingernails as though their cleanliness is paramount. "No money, you say? Well, that's not unusual for your kind," he comments dismissively. His gaze lingers on my sweaty and dirt-smudged attire, and I can almost taste his disdain. "I suppose I could entertain a trade of another kind."

I reach for the Agate quartz ring, but as my fingers make contact, my mind is instantly overwhelmed by a torrent of nightmarish visions. The raven and a grotesque ash demon tear the Elder Grove asunder, with devastating force and unholy power. Helpless, I watch the destruction unfold, and a revelation dawns with brutal clarity: the raven is not an ill omen, but a guardian protecting the Elder Tree. The demon, known as 'The Devourer,' stands over 20 feet tall, a grotesque fusion of nightmarish elements. The Devourer is an abomination beyond description. Its grotesque form stands over 20 feet tall, a nightmarish fusion of grotesque elements, born from the deepest, darkest pits of despair.

Its obsidian skin exudes an aura of malevolence, its surface marred by protruding gnarled horns, each one a testament to the perversion of nature itself. Jagged, misshapen, and cruel, these twisted appendages create a disturbing mosaic on its body, and they drip with rot and decay.

The eyes of the Devourer burn with fiery, malevolent red light, smoldering like burning coals in a pit of hellfire. These infernal orbs gaze upon the world with a hunger that cannot be sated, promising nothing but torment and annihilation.

From its nightmarish visage extends a set of mandibles that resemble the jaws of some repugnant arachnid, serrated and unhinged, ready to tear through the very fabric of reality. They click and clatter with a cacophonous symphony of doom as they open and close, ever yearning for destruction.

An array of long, sinuous arms sprout from its form, too numerous to count, each ending in cruel, serrated claws. These appendages writhe and slither, independently seeking out their next victim like the malevolent tendrils of some deepwater horror.

Its legs are a nightmare of form, resembling the segmented limbs of a centipede, each section adorned with cruel, thorn-like protrusions. These twisted appendages move with a disturbing, unnatural rhythm, supporting the monstrous bulk of the Devourer as it stalks through the Elder Grove.

As it moves, the very earth trembles beneath its grotesque form, and its monstrous roars echo with a sinister resonance that chills the very marrow of one's bones. The Devourer is a cataclysmic force of destruction, an embodiment of horror, and it stands as a nightmarish sentinel of annihilation, an entity not of this world, but from the darkest depths of a tormented soul.

I somehow glean this information from my vision, as if I'm deciphering a hidden code within the picture itself. Terrified and disoriented, I clasp the Agate quartz ring desperately, yearning to harness its power to halt the cataclysm.

As I leave the nightmarish vision, gasping for breath and shaken to the core, I realize that the merchant has been scrutinizing me with an inquisitive eye. Hastily, I retract my hand, forfeiting the idea of trading the ring. "Actually, never mind," I respond, shaking my head. "I have nothing to trade."

The merchant nods with an air of disapproval, but his gaze remains fixed on the Agate quartz ring. "I see. If you're journeying eastward, there's a coastal village that might be of interest. You can replenish your supplies there."

I offer a curt smile and a nod, refraining from insulting the haughty merchant with my overpowering scent. "How can I reach this village?"

The merchant eyes me with a hint of condescension but eventually provides me with meticulous directions. He explains that the village remains hidden from common eyes, obscured by a shroud of mist. His parting remark about a pure heart needles at my soul, my thoughts consumed by vengeance rather than purity.

The rugged path stretches out before me, treacherous and winding, yet I persevere, driven by an unwavering determination to reach my elusive destination. Inhaling the sea's briny scent, I forge ahead, stepping onto the rocky coast. Towering cliffs, their jagged edges kissed by the relentless sea, dominate the view. The waves crash with thunderous roars against the ancient rocks, sending white plumes of foam into the air.

As I traipse along the coastline, it seems I've arrived at a dead-end. The formidable cliffs stretch unyielding to my right, forming an impenetrable barrier. Despite the initial challenge of the rugged path, I push forward, needing to find rest. Every step brings me closer to the mysterious misty village. The thunderous clash of waves against the colossal cliffs fills the air, an overwhelming cacophony of nature's power.

Trudging along the winding road, the shrouded mist looms tantalizingly in the distance. But my attempts to breach its mystical barrier end in failure. Each time I pass through the misty veil, I'm inexplicably thrust back to the same unwelcoming, rugged coast. It's as if an invisible force veils my efforts, leaving me continually stranded in the same spot, even though I keep walking.

With mounting frustration, I yell, "Let me in." But my scream is muted by the thick mist. I sob and fall to my knees, completely and utterly exhausted. After numerous unsuccessful attempts, I shut my eyes and try to find some kind of resolve, then it comes to me. I meticulously re-call the intricate directions provided by the merchant, the elaborate steps needed to access the hidden village. I cringe as I thought he was pulling my leg, hoping to give his village buddies a laugh as the 'daft' wood elf stands at the boarder of the village acting a fool.

Summoning a deep breath, I focus on the complex in-structions: "Circle thrice with your left hand tracing the sign of the ocean's grace while twirling in place. Whisper the ancient elven phrase for the tides, then, with a heart aligned to the sea, step into the heart of the fog."

Following these cryptic instructions to the letter, I exe-cute the precise gestures, my left hand tracing invisible pat-terns in the air as I spin in place, trying not to get dizzy, the ancient elven phrase for tides whispered in hushed tones. My heart resonates with the essence of the sea, aligning itself to the rhythmic waves.

With a final steadying breath, I step into the shrouded mist. This time, as I breach its boundaries, the world around me undergoes a dramatic shift. The swirling mist wraps around me, unveiling a hidden realm of bustling activity.

Before me lies the elven fishing village, hidden within the mist. The wooden huts, intricately carved with depictions of sea creatures and stories of the deep, stand along narrow, winding boardwalk paths. Wooden totems of fierce sea serpents, graceful merfolk, and playful dolphins guard the entrances to the huts, a testament to the village's deep connection to the ocean.

The lanterns hanging along the pathways cast a gentle, blue light, reminiscent of starlight, but the sight that strikes me most is the marina. There, fishermen and boats line the docks, and enormous sea creatures hang from hooks, their scales shimmering dimly. Merchants haggle fervently over prices, their voices echoing in the salty wind as they inspect the day's haul. The boats, packed to capacity with a variety of fish, sway on the gentle tide.

Dockworkers, with hardened faces and calloused hands, move swiftly and methodically. They load the fish into sturdy wheelbarrows, destined for the village's vibrant markets and stores. The winding paths are alive with activity, resonating with the trundling of wheelbarrows and the hum of voices.

The atmosphere overwhelms me as I take in the sight of the bustling village. I feel out of place amidst the chaos and energy that flows like a tide. Rather than enchanted, I am searching for respite from the commotion that surrounds me. The sounds of clinking tools, animated discussions, and the chorus of the sea are ever-present.

As I navigate the busy streets, I sense a disconnection with the vivacious elven village. It's not the ethereal charm that strikes me but the pulsating life and the fervor of the villagers that leaves me somewhat bewildered. I long to find a quiet corner where I can gather my thoughts and, for a moment, collapse into a restful sleep. My persistence has brought me to this unique place, but instead of awe, I am overwhelmed by the vivid vitality that envelops me.

As the winding path turns yet again, I finally see respite in the distance.

14

The Salty Slug

As I MAKE MY way towards the bustling tavern, my stomach growls in hunger. The wooden sign creaks above the entrance, the paint faded from years of exposure to salt and wind. 'The Salty Slug' is etched in the old wooden sign with an image of a slug foaming from the mouth, holding a mug of mead. Charming. The old building is sturdy and built to withstand the harsh coastal climate, with thick walls made of rough-hewn stone and a thatched roof.

The interior of the tavern is alive with activity. Warm light from the fireplace casts flickering shadows across the worn wooden floorboards. The air is thick with the scent of roasting meat and ale, and the sound of chatter fills the room. The walls are adorned with faded nautical maps and whalebones, and a group of sailors sing sea shanties in the corner.

I approach the barkeep, a burly man with a bushy golden beard, hoping to buy some supper and rent a room for the night. But before I can even speak, a group of High Elves at a nearby table begins taunting me, their derogatory remarks about wood elves stinging like saltwater in an open wound.

"Get out of here and crawl back to the forest where you belong, Wood Elf, your not wanted here," one of them sneers, his voice dripping with disdain.

I ignore their insults, deciding that my best option is to avoid a confrontation. They laugh and clank their mugs, their condescension palpable.

Moonbean, remains snoring on my shoulder, oblivious to the tension in the room. I eye him briefly, wishing he could offer some guidance or protection. He stirs briefly, scratches his ass, and resumes snoring, leaving me to fend for myself.

Taking a deep breath, I turn back to the barkeep, determined to make my plea. But the burly man, too, seems hesitant to serve me, only muttering something under his thick mustache.

I rack my brain for a solution. My last option to secure a meal and a room for the night is to approach the rowdy bunch of elves who harrassed me earlier. I steal a look at them, and now their attention is turned to a game a chance. I see there is betting involved, and with each roll of the dice, one lucky elf collects the winnings on the table. It's a risky move, but hunger and exhaustion leave me with few alternatives. I smile at the barkeep and sweep toward the rowdy table of High Elves.

I approach the table, determined to make my barter, my growling stomach depends on it, and clear my throat. "A wager, perhaps?" I propose. "Can I join your game?"

The High Elves pause, exchanging glances and raising their eyebrows, feigning intrigue but also subtly rolling their eyes. It's apparent that they're not interested in a wood elf joining their game.

"Maybe if you took a bath first." an extraordinarily filthy looking elf says, his face leathered and mouth filled with rotted teeth.

I look down at my soiled leathers, shrug, then wince at his rotted teeth. "Rotted log smells better than rotted fishy breath. Perhaps you're just not up to the challenge." I emphasize the last sentence with a sly smile.

This provokes a few chuckles at his expense, and I've gained their reluctant attention. They lean in closer, still mocking me but with a hint of curiosity. "Alright, Wood Elf, what do you have to wager? And it better be good," one of them challenges.

I slam the agate quartz ring on the table and they all lean in for a better look. After eyeing one another, the one with the rotted teeth smiles a toothy grin and says. "Grove's Gambit," he begins, "is a game of chance and strategy. You wager with whatever you have, and I'll do the same. We take turns rolling a pair of enchanted dice." He produces two beautifully carved wooden dice from his pouch and places them on the table. Their ornate designs shimmer under the tavern's flickering lantern light.

The elf closest to me kicks a chair out from the table and nods for me to sit. The High Elves eye me with a mix of curiosity and skepticism. They're seasoned gamblers, and I'm about to learn the intricate nuances of 'Grove's Gambit.' I settle into the chair, my eyes fixed on the ornate dice set before me. These dice, unlike any I've seen before, are six-sided and filled with mysterious symbols, each carrying a different consequence.

"The rules are simple," the elf with the tattered scorecard explains, his voice laced with a hint of condescension. "Each of us takes turns rolling the dice, and the outcome determines the winner of that round. But there's a twist. The dice have runes etched into them, each associated with a unique power."

He points to the six-sided dice set, each face bearing an intricate rune. "For instance," he continues, "if you roll the Eikthyr rune, it's a sign of favor from the great stag spirit. Your fortune improves, and you win the round." The eyes of his companions narrow with keen interest as they lean in, silently calculating their odds.

I nod, trying to grasp the basics of the game. "Sounds easy enough," I say, keeping my voice steady, hoping to hide my unease.

The High Elves exchange knowing glances, some of them leaning back in their chairs, each silently challenging me to prove my worth. The room is thick with tension, and I sense the disdain that simmers beneath the surface.

The least filthy High Elf leans toward the one with rotted teeth, whispering with a voice loud enough for me to catch, "I could sell that ring for a big bag of coin at the under market."

But their doubt only fuels my determination. I lean in closer, dramatic flair in my tone. "Ah, but you underestimate my ring," I say, allowing a hint of smugness to lace my words. "This ring does more than just adorn my finger. It reveals the future, providing guidance beyond your wildest dreams. So ontop of the supper and room, I require some information."

Their skepticism remains, and one High Elf challenges me, his eyes sharp. "If your ring is as potent as you claim, why do you have to wager for a simple meal?"

I lean in, lowering my voice to a conspiratorial whisper. "Ah, that's the tricky part," I admit, a mischievous glint in my eye. "It doesn't just offer riches; it shows you what it wants you to see. A capricious guide, if you will."

The High Elves exchange wary glances, their curiosity finally overcoming their earlier mockery. The rotten-toothed one with a sly grin says, "Very well, Wood Elf. We'll accept your challenge. But remember, if you lose, your ring is ours."

"And If I win, you tell me some information that will help me on my journey." I retort.

They nod in agreement. The stakes have been set, and I glance at the mysterious Agate quartz ring resting on the table. It carries a powerful enchantment, its true nature still shrouded in mystery. "Agreed," I say with unwavering determination, my fingers reaching for the dice. "I roll first."

The game begins, and the tavern is consumed by the aura of 'Grove's Gambit.' As we roll the intricately carved dice, each face is revealed, and I quickly come to understand their significance. The tension mounts with each roll, and the High Elves grow more competitive, their disdain now wrapped in the allure of the game.

It's in these moments, as the mystic runes unfold, that the heart of 'Grove's Gambit' is laid bare. Several rolls into the game and I produced the Eikthyr rune, and the crowd of onlookers erupts, some in anger and others hoot and hollar, and fortunes shift. The rotted toothed elf rolls the Vyldryn rune, dark and ominous, and he growls in anger, banging his fist on the table. The other's roll, but it's of no significance as the runes carry their unique outcomes, each adding layers of complexity to the game, but none rolled higher than me.

However, 'Grove's Gambit' holds a unique enchantment. When the dice are rolled, they are not passive; they come alive, and the runes etched upon them engage in magical combat. As the dice hit the table, the runes on each die release a burst of mystical energy, causing them to float and circle each other, battling for supremacy. The Eikthyr rune's antlers clash with the Vyldryn's shadowy tendrils, and the Fjelkr rune's jagged peaks stab at the Iskvell rune's icy visage. It's a mesmerizing display that captures the attention of everyone in the tavern, a silent dance of magic.

The mystic battle continues until one set of runes emerges victorious, determining the outcome of the roll. Each roll is a magical skirmish, and the unpredictability of the rune duels adds to the excitement and tension of the game. And once the battle is over, the scorecard magically retallies the score.

"The runes are as fickle as fate itself," I comment as the dice clash with a burst of magical sparks.

"Aye, that they are," the one with rotted teeth replies. "Now, let's see if your ring's guidance can withstand the power of 'Grove's Gambit.'"

As the rounds progress, I find myself adapting to the rhythm of the game. 'Grove's Gambit' isn't just about luck; it demands a strategic mind and a shrewd understanding of the runes. I win several rounds, a sense of satisfaction growing with each victory. The scoring system becomes more apparent, and I grasp how the runes' combinations affect the outcome. Did I mention the dice are fickle, because with each roll, my once high score, is now the bottom of the fish barrel so to speak, and I've lost favor with Eithyr. For seven rounds, we've battled with no winner, and now have reached a precipice the High Elves call a 'Grove Battle'. Apparently, if there is a tie for seven rounds straight, and we have to reroll until a winner is decided.

The tension hangs thick in the air as the dice tumble, and the rotten-toothed elf leans in, his sneer a dagger aimed at my pride. "You've got spirit, Wood Elf," he hisses, "but spirit won't win you 'Grove's Gambit.'"

I meet his taunting gaze with an unyielding stare. "It's not just spirit that'll secure my victory," I retort. "It's skill, strategy, and a bit of luck."

He chuckles, and his voice is a venomous whisper. "Luck's a fickle friend, as you'll soon learn." He rolls the dice, and the runes come alive, clashing in a mesmerizing magical duel. The outcome is in his favor, and a wicked grin forms on his lips. "Looks like Lady Luck is on my side tonight."

I slap the table in frustration and curse. But when the High Elves mock my frustration I regain my composure and quip. "There's still another roll."

The room erupts in laughter, and the tension boils over. The snarky comments and banter now bristle with an electric charge around the table, each placing bets on who will win. To my chagrin, I've gained a few followers who are rooting for me to win. The high stakes have unleashed a primal competitiveness, and we're all caught in its grip.

As the game unfolds, we exchange more heated words with each passing round. The High Elves are determined to outwit me, and I'm equally resolute in proving myself. Laughter and taunts flow freely, and it's a duel of wits and luck, a dance of fate guided by ancient runes.

Finally, we reach the pinnacle, a dramatic showdown that carries the collective weight of our pride. The room is silent except for the soft clinking of tankards and the distant ocean's murmur. All eyes are locked on the dice, their outcome hanging on the precipice of uncertainty. The High Elves, once disdainful, are now consumed by the fiery desire to win, their faces etched with tension. It's a moment where the destiny of 'Grove's Gambit' stands poised to crown a victor, and the air is thick with anticipation.

With a flourish, the dice tumble across the table, spinning and rolling with an almost agonizing slowness. When they come to a stop, the room erupts into collective anticipation. The result is in my favor, and a triumphant grin plays on my lips. The High Elves slump back in their chairs, defeated but not entirely defeated in spirit.

"You've bested us, Wood Elf," the snobbish one grumbles, begrudgingly extending his hand.

I accept the handshake, a sense of satisfaction coursing through me. "A pleasure playing with you all," I say, my voice laced with a touch of smugness. "And now, about our wager."

Before I can finish my sentence, the High Elves burst into laughter, their pride wounded but their spirits lifted by the spirited game. "Well played, Wood Elf," the lanky, pale-skinned elf chuckles, extending an olive branch of camaraderie.

As the barkeep places the succulent meal before us, I can't help but dig in ravenously, my hunger momentarily eclipsing my surroundings. The roasted mackerel is a taste of the sea, and the fresh vegetables are a welcome addition. A hearty tankard of ale quenches my thirst.

Amid mouthfuls of food, I listen to the lively chatter around the table and feel a growing camaraderie with the High Elves. As we indulge in the delicious fare, my curiosity gets the better of me after I hear someone at another table talk about the king's tournament.

"So," I say with a playful grin, "you said you'd give me more information if I won."

An elf with a no-nonsense demeanor, known as Thalion, grunts, "What do you want to know?" Then takes a mouthful of mackerel and chews loudly.

"What's this I've heard about a tournament in the capital? Champions from all around the realms? Sounds intriguing. Care to share more?"

The High Elves exchange knowing glances, their eyes alight with excitement. One of them, a spirited elf named Elowan, leans in, ready to impart information. "Indeed, it's a grand event," he begins. "Warriors, mages, and adventurers from near and far will converge on the capital, seeking glory and riches. The champions, they call them."

Another elf, known as Seraph, chimes in, "The taverns will be flooded with travelers, bringing with them a multitude of stories and opportunities. It's a time of celebration, to be sure."

As they speak of the tournament, I can't help but see an opportunity for my mission. I lean forward, my voice lowered with a hint of urgency. "I've traveled from Willowbrook with a purpose, and the king's ear would be of great help. Can you tell me more about how one secures an audience with His Majesty?"

The High Elves exchange meaningful looks, and their expressions turn somewhat solemn. Thalion turns even more serious then explains, "Gaining an audience with the king is no small feat. The security is tight, and it's known to require a substantial sum of coin."

Their words cause me to pause for a moment, my mind racing with thoughts of my limited resources. But my determination remains steadfast as I tear a piece of crusty bread and dip it in the drippings on my plate, swirl it around and plop it in my mouth. "I see," I respond, masking my concerns with a confident demeanor. "I'll have to find a way. Anything worth achieving rarely comes easy, after all."

We continue our meal, our conversation branching into the King's grand plans for the tournament and the myriad challenges awaiting its participants. Despite the slight unease about the security and costs, I'm resolute in my determination to secure an audience with the king and fulfill my mission.

The night wears on, and my newfound companions and I share stories, laughter, and the bond forged through

'Grove's Gambit.' The initial hostility has given way to genuine friendship, reminding me that common ground can be found even among the most unlikely allies. After a series of tales and laughter, I bid them farewell, ascend the stairs to my room, and, without bothering to light the lantern, collapse onto the bed, drifting into a peaceful slumber.

15

The Ferryman's Herb

I AWAKEN IN THE old elvish tavern, the room bathed in soft, golden light. I sit up, stretching my arms and taking in the unfamiliar surroundings. The woven tapestries that adorn the walls depict scenes from Elvish history, their intricate details hinting at tales of old. A small desk is scattered with parchments, quills, and half-written letters, as if it holds secrets that will never be fully revealed.

I make my way to the window, hoping to glimpse more of the village, but the mist outside is as dense as ever, shrouding the landscape in an eerie haze. I try to clear it away by waving my hand, but the mist only swirls around my fingers playfully before settling once more. Disappointed, I shut the window and turn my attention to the desk.

Among the half-written letters, one in particular catches my eye. It's from a man named the Sylvariel, addressed to his daughter. The letter is short and filled with heartfelt apologies, as if the man is seeking forgiveness for some past transgression. I can't help but feel a pang of sadness as I read the letter, wondering about the circumstances that led to such a rift between a father and his child. I carefully fold the letter and place it back on the desk, my thoughts lingering on the Sylvariel's words.

Hungry and eager to explore the day, I make my way down to the common room, which has transformed since the previous night. The warm light of the hearth welcomes me, and my eyes scan the empty room, landing on an unexpected sight: a human bard, skillfully plucking the strings of his lute. This anomaly in a land of High Elves immediately catches my attention, and like a moth drawn to a flame, I approach him, my footsteps silenced by the plush rug underfoot.

The bard looks up, his hazel eyes twinkling with mirth as he notices me. I find myself drawn to his warm smile, but my eyes flicker to the golden dagger hilt at his belt, causing a momentary unease. "Well, well," he says, setting his lute aside. "If it isn't a fellow traveler seeking adventure. The name's Aiden. Aiden Goldenstring."

My curiosity piqued, I can't help but question the peculiar choice of name. "Goldenstring?" I inquire, my eyes darting from his lute to the golden dagger, then back to his playful gaze.

He nods, still wearing a warm smile. "The one and only. And you are?"

I fumble over my words. "I'm Faelyn. Faelyn Nightsky." I glance around the room, searching for the innkeeper, who seems to be occupied in the kitchen. Then I ask, "I'm looking to get to Faelyndelle."

Aiden's amusement is evident as he chuckles. "Ah, Faelyndelle. The land of dreams, nightmares, and the Tournament of Champions."

"Nightmares?" I question, a bit sensitive about the subject given recent events.

Aiden leans in closer, his expression becoming serious. "Indeed, Faelyndelle is a place of grandeur and beauty, but it's also shrouded in secrets and danger. The shadows conceal more than they reveal." He leans back and plucks a few chords on his lute. "But enough of that. Let's focus on reaching our destination first."

Aiden's words resonate within me, and for an instant, I'm transported back to the stories my mother shared about Faelyndelle. Her tales were not just brimming with intrigue, but they also carried a heavy undercurrent of treacherous politics, where trust was a rare and precious commodity. She spoke of a city that gleamed with grandeur on the surface but was veiled in shadows, concealing the intricate dance of power and deceit that played out behind closed doors. The vivid imagery of her stories reminds me that Faelyndelle is a place where allegiances shift like the tide, and no one can be taken at face value. With my mother's words as a haunting reminder, I mentally prepare myself for the journey ahead, fully aware that danger and uncertainty may lurk in every corner of the capital city.

He watches me quizzically as I'm lost in thought, so I offer. "I've heard of a ferry that can take me there, but my funds are rather limited."

Aiden strokes his chin thoughtfully, his hazel eyes sparkling with mischief. "Ah, the ferry. Yes, it can be quite costly. But fear not, my friend. I have a talent for negotiation, and, well, I also find myself... lacking funds." He speaks with a practiced charm, each word a melody of its own.

I raise an eyebrow, scrutinizing him. "Funny how we seem to be in a similar predicament."

The bard's grin remains, and he continues, "I may have an idea. Theres a job on the message board to collect some rare herbs that the ferryman has requested. If we can obtain some, we might be able to barter for our tickets."

My curiosity is piqued. "Where can we find these herbs?"

Aiden leans in, his voice low and conspiratorial. "There's a garden on the outskirts of the village, said to hold rare specimens. But be cautious; it's guarded by a pack of rabid wolves."

I smirk. "I'm no neophyte. I can handle a few wolves."

The bard raises an eyebrow, not quite understanding the term. "Neophyte? Is that some Elven cult?"

I laugh. "No, I'm a druid in training."

Aiden nods, seemingly satisfied with the explanation. "Intriguing."

I'm still curious about Aiden's knowledge of the village and his presence on the Ageless Isles. "How did you come to know of this place? And why is a human here?"

Aiden's playful demeanor remains, and he continues to strum his lute. "Well, we live in a world full of mysteries and unexpected wonders. I've traveled extensively, and when you journey as much as I do, you uncover whispers of hidden places, secret treasures, and enigmatic villages shrouded in mist."

I can't help but chuckle at his reply. "So, you just happened to stumble upon this village?"

His eyes twinkle with amusement. "Let's just say I have a knack for finding the most interesting places."

Not able to glean anymore information on how he entered the village, I decide to shift the focus back to our mission. "Well, let's go find those herbs. I need to reach the Capital."

Aiden scrutinizes me for a moment, then takes a sip of his ale. "If you're in such a hurry, then lead the way, neophyte."

I look down to his tankard and say. "It's morning you know."

"Aye it is. But have you tasted the water here?" He makes an aweful face.

"No." I admit.

He stands and flicks a coin on the table. "I think they take it straight from the sea." He shakes his head in disgust.

We step out into the crisp morning air, and I take a deep breath. "So, where are these herbs?" I ask Aiden, turning to face him.

He grins mischievously. "We'll need to be stealthy if we want to avoid those wolves. Follow me." And with that, the bard leads me into the mist.

As we meander through the boardwalks of the bustling village, my gaze inadvertently drifts to my shoulder, where Moonbean rests. Aiden, ever observant, notices my repeated glances at my companion and raises an inquisitive eyebrow.

"Why do you keep looking at your shoulder like that?" he asks, genuine curiosity gleaming in his hazel eyes.

I hesitate for a moment, my thoughts briefly dancing around the idea of revealing Moonbean's true nature and think of my mother's warnings. I wrestle with the thought because he technically isn't from the capital, but he is human and I've never met one before, so can he be trusted? Instead, I opt for a more elusive response. "Oh, it's just an elven thing," I offer with a casual shrug, attempting to downplay my own intrigue.

Aiden doesn't let the matter drop, his curiosity clearly piqued. He smirks and playfully teases, "An elven thing, you say? You Elves and your cryptic ways. Come on, Faelyn, we're embarking on an adventure together. We ought to be open with one another, don't you think?"

I stumble over my words, caught between wanting to be honest and not wanting to reveal too much about Moonbean. "My pauldron is too tight," I lie, trying to keep my answer vague.

He chuckles, clearly not satisfied with my response. "Is that so? You must tell me more about these 'elven things' someday. I find your culture fascinating."

As Aiden and I walk through the bustling village, he turns to me and says, "We need fish. Old smelly fish."

I look at him suspiciously and say. "Look around. There's nothing but smelly old fish."

He laughs, then points at an old fishmonger and says. "There. We need a bucket of the stinkiest fish we can find."

"Why?" I question.

"To serve as bait for the wolves guarding the rare herbs." He walks briskly towards the old fishmonger's cart.

I chase after him. "How are we supposed to pay for it? We can't even pay for a ferry ticket and now we have to buy fish?"

Aiden turns to me and grins mischievously. "Leave that to me. I have a way with words."

We approach a gruff-looking fishmonger, his wares displayed on a rickety wooden cart, and the scent of salt and brine fills the air. He eyes Aiden, a human, and me, a Wood Elf, with a dubious gaze that's tainted by prejudice. "What brings your kind and a human to my stall?" he grumbles, spitting to the ground beside him.

Aiden leans in, his eyes twinkling with charm. "We find ourselves in need of some of your finest old fish. You see, these fish are destined for a grand adventure, and we'd be honored to acquire them from a vendor as esteemed as yourself."

The fishmonger remains unimpressed, his prejudice evident in the stern set of his jaw. "Old fish isn't for the likes of you. It doesn't come cheap, especially to your kind. It'll be five silver pieces."

I glance at Aiden, who raises an eyebrow in silent communication. With a sly grin, he reaches into his pocket and produces three silver coins. "How about three silver and a song? A tune to lift your spirits."

The fishmonger squints at Aiden, clearly not swayed by his eloquent words or the promise of a song. "Five silver pieces, and not one less."

Aiden nods to the fishmonger and whispers to me, "watch this." Then turns to the old fishmonger and hands him the three coins and says. "I'll get the rest of your coins momentarily." The fishmonger grudgingly takes the three coins, displaying a reluctant unsatisfied expression as he counts them over several times then holds them up to the misty light, inspecting them further.

With the first part of the transaction complete, Aiden clears his throat dramatically, his lute handled cleverly within his hands. With a flourish, he begins to play a lively, foot-tapping melody, and his voice fills the air with a hearty sea shanty. The fishmonger's stern expression wavers as he finds himself swaying to the rhythm, tapping his foot along with the beat. When he notices me noticing him, he stops and I grin to myself.

Aiden's voice fills the marketplace, rich and melodious, as he weaves a tale of epic adventures and far-off lands. His song beckons curious onlookers, and soon, coins begin to rain into a hat placed at his feet, in appreciation of his alluring music. Even the fishmonger, who had initially eyed us with prejudice, softens as the lively tune washes over the crowd.

As Aiden takes his final bow, there's a brief moment of uncertainty. The fishmonger's face scrunches in thought, and he claps his hands with a toothy grin. "Well, I've heard better songs, but I suppose it'll do. But now the fish is older, so it's ten silver pieces."

Aiden and I both gape at the sudden price hike, our eyes wide with incredulity. "Ten silver pieces?" Aiden protests, a hint of exasperation in his voice.

The fishmonger only smiles slyly as he peers into the hat. "Well, it seems that the ten coins in that hat will do."

Aiden's grumbles, "But I already gave you three."

I scold Aiden and say, "Give him the hat before he decides it's fifteen."

With a grudging sigh, Aiden hands over the hat, and the fishmonger, victorious in his bargaining tactics, kicks over a half-filled bucket of ripe fish, splashing us with pungent juices. I hastily grab the bucket, wrinkling my nose at the unpleasant aroma, and make a hasty retreat from the fish market, Aiden trailing behind me, still grumbling about the unexpected turn of events.

16

A Bargain with a Bard

AIDEN AND I NAVIGATE the intricate maze of alley-
ways, the damp coastal air clinging to our clothes. The
burden of the fish-filled bucket is a shared one, and
we switch its weight when one of us tires, inevitably
creating a splattering mess with each exchange. We steer
our course toward the outskirts of the village, where
quaint cottages line the cobblestone streets and fishing
boats gently sway in the harbor. Yet, the mist hanging
over the village bestows an eerie quality upon the scene,
concealing secrets that the wisest would leave undiscov-
ered.

As we walk further from the village, I hear the distant
sound of waves crashing against the shore, and the occasional cry of a seabird. But aside from that, it's eerily
quiet. The mist seems to dampen any sounds, muffling
them until they are barely audible. We make our way
towards the garden, and I can see the outline of trees
and bushes through the fog.

The mist wraps around us like a shroud, and I can't help but feel a sense of foreboding. What secrets are hidden within this coastal village, and what dangers await us? Only time will tell. I'd heard about sea wolves as a child and shudder. Hopefully, these are only timber wolves and not the larger, more dangerous, waterborne kind.

As we walk, Aiden regales me with tales of his past adventures, weaving in stories of Human history and culture. I listen with rapt attention, eager to learn more about his lands. I'm reminded of my father's version of the history of the humans and their complicated relationship with the dwarves.

"Have you ever heard of the Emerald Reach?" Aiden asks, a glint in his hazel eyes. "It's a kingdom far to the east, known for its lush forests and fertile plains. But more than that, it's a land of riches, with vast reserves of gold and precious gems buried deep beneath its mountains."

I raise an eyebrow, remembering my father's tales. He had said it all began centuries ago, when the humans first discovered the vast wealth hidden deep within the dwarven mines. The humans were amazed by the abundance of precious metals, rare gems, and priceless artifacts that lay within those ancient tunnels. "Riches, you say? That sounds like a recipe for conflict." I smirk thinking of my father's tale of the siblings fighting for desert before they've had their dinner. I imagine Aiden fighting with a stout dwarf over the last pastry and chuckle.

"Indeed it is," Aiden says with a questioning look. "For years, the Emerald Reach has been embroiled in a bitter war with the dwarves, who claim the mountains and all the treasure within as their own. It's a never-ending cycle of battles and skirmishes, with both sides determined to emerge victorious."

Again, I think of my father's tales and wonder how two nations could be so daft and greedy and not be fulfilled by nature's beauty. My father said that as time passed, the humans grew increasingly greedy and power-hungry, coveting the riches that lay within the mines. They staked their claim to the lands around the mines, setting up encampments and fortresses to protect their newfound wealth.

"But why?" I ask, genuinely curious. "Why fight over something so trivial as gold and gems?"

Aiden shrugs. "Greed, perhaps. Or maybe it's a matter of pride. Who knows? But what I do know is that wars have a way of consuming everything in their path. Families torn apart, homes destroyed, lives lost. It's a tragedy, really."

I nod in agreement. "It is. But what about Human history? Surely there's more to it than just wars and battles."

"Of course," Aiden says with a grin. "There are tales of great heroes and adventurers, of mighty kings and queens who ruled with grace and wisdom. There are stories of magic and wonder, of love and loss, of triumph and tragedy. The history of the Humans is a rich tapestry, woven with countless threads of joy and sorrow."

I can't help but think about the differences between Human magic and my own Elven magic. Aiden speaks of Human magic with awe, but I can't help but feel a bit of bias. While Human magic may be powerful, I believe that Elves have a stronger connection to nature, and therefore a deeper understanding of the natural magic that flows through all things. I think of my people's history. Elven druid magic is deeply intertwined with nature, and our stories are full of reverence for the natural world. Human magic, on the other hand, seems to focus more on the manipulation of the elements and the use of arcane power. It's not that their magic is weaker, per se, but I can't help but feel that our connection to nature gives us an advantage.

But as I reflect on Aiden's tales, I realize that there is something admirable in the way that Humans have learned to harness the power of magic to build their kingdoms and civilizations. Their drive for progress and innovation has led them to create things that I could never have imagined. I may have a bias towards my own people and our ways, but I can't deny the ingenuity and creativity of humans. But perhaps it is just my elven pride showing.

Regardless, I am intrigued by Human history and eager to learn more about this land and its people.

"And what role do you play in this tapestry?" I ask, curious about Aiden's own adventures.

The bard chuckles. "Oh, I'm just a humble storyteller, doing my part to keep the tales alive. But who knows? Maybe one day I'll be part of the tapestry myself."

His words are like honey, smooth, and sweet, and I find myself hanging on every syllable. I have to wonder if he's cast his bardic magic on me or if he's just that charming? I try to resist, but I end up giggling like a fledgling, gushing when he speaks. We banter back and forth, trading jokes and teasing each other in a way that feels like we've known each other for years.

As we continue on our journey, I can't help but think about the stories Aiden has shared with me. They paint a vivid picture of a world full of wonder and danger, of heroes and villains, of triumph and tragedy. I think of my village and the surrounding forest and how different it sounds to the farms and mines of the Reach.

Aiden tells me more about the Reach, describing how they have to work hard to cultivate the land and keep it fertile. It's clear that farming is a crucial part of human society and their way of life. Meanwhile, my village has always been deeply connected to nature, and our druid magic allows us to live in harmony with the surrounding forest.

Despite the differences, I can't help but feel a sense of connection to Aiden and his stories. In many ways, our societies and cultures are not so different. We both have our own struggles and triumphs, our own heroes and villains. It's comforting to know that even in this vast world, there are people who share similar experiences and values as me.

Eventually, we arrive at the garden, and sure enough, there's a pack of wolves lounging in the sun streaks that've broken through the mist. I stand at the entrance of the garden, surveying the pack of wolves that lie in wait. They don't notice us yet. Aiden stands next to me, the bucket of fish in his hands. I look down at his golden dagger and smirk, "What, you don't want to use that little thing?"

Aiden doesn't take his eyes off the pack. "It's not the size that counts. Plus, I'm looking to bait them, not skin them." He drops the bucket loudly and I shush him. He looks at me with regret in his eyes and asks, "Do we just leave it here?"

"The fish was your idea." I say with wide eyes.

"Aren't you the hunter. Shouldn't you know how to lure a wolf?" He says picking up the bucket and offering it to me.

I huff and shake my head. "Give me the bucket." I yank the bucket from him and stalk to the edge of the garden, hoping I'm stealthy enough that they don't hear me. But my luck is not with me because the wind shifts suddenly, and now I'm downwind and it's not long before the Alpha raises his nose to the air and within seconds, his eyes are on me.

I'm rudely disturbed by Moonbean, who lets out a thunderous sneeze, then snorts loudly and falls back to sleep. As I'm destracted with my spirit guardian I don't notice that the full pack of wolves are racing towards me.

Suddenly they skitter to a stop and surround us. The largest of them stands at attention, its hackles stiff as bristles as it stares at me. It lets out a low, threatening growl, lowering its head.

I close my eyes and focus, reaching out with my druidic powers to communicate with the wolf. Nature's energy flows from the surrounding forest, through my bracers, calming me further. I send the calming energy to the Alpha and his pack and wait for it to take hold. His pack stands behind him on guard as they growl and snap at me, but I continue to speak to him and then them all, soothing their aggression. Slowly, they begin to calm down, their hackles lowering and their growls softening.

Aiden plays his lute, a soothing melody that complements my druidic magic. As the melody grows stronger, the wolves seem to become more docile, their eyes glazed over with enchantment.

But then, Moonbean suddenly wakes up from his drunken stupor and howls loudly, completely throwing off my concentration. The wolves become agitated once again, snapping and growling, and I struggle to keep them under my control.

Aiden quickly steps in, his fingers moving deftly over the strings of his lute, and he sings, his voice clear and powerful. His bardic magic weaves around mine, creating a stronger enchantment that subdues the wolves.

I seize the moment and start plucking the rare herbs from the garden. Their distinct fragrance is a telltale sign of their potency. I carefully choose only the finest herbs, the ones that will surely catch the attention of the ferryman. As I tuck them into my pouch, I make a mental note to remind myself and be wary of the bard's magic. I did not know it would be so powerful; so mesmerizing.

A sudden cry pierces the air, breaking the tranquility that had surrounded us. The lady, a tough-looking soul with a face as wrinkled as a dried apple, marches out of a ramshackle cottage, her eyes fiery with anger.

"Stop that, you thieves!" she accuses us, her bony finger pointed straight at Aiden and me. Her voice carries a tone of accusation that hangs in the misty air.

Aiden and I freeze, guilt written all over our faces. Aiden hastily stops strumming his lute, and I cease my druidic magic, though the uneasy tension remains.

"We didn't know it was your garden," Aiden protests, his tone apologetic. "We thought it was abandoned."

The lady's gaze remains as sharp as ever, but she calls off her wolves, who sit down obediently, their low growls fading into uneasy silence. "City folk, always assuming they can just help themselves. These herbs are all I've got left."

I'm fuming at Aiden for landing us in this predicament and his carelessness. I hiss at him, "You should've been more careful. You can't just snatch things without asking."

Aiden lets out an exasperated sigh and hangs his head. "I had no idea."

The lady watches us with fire in her eyes, though her stern demeanor shifts when she sees the bucket. "What do you have in that bucket. It stinks to the groves and back."

I answer quickly, showing respect. "It's fish from the market."

She licks her lips and looks down to her pack of wolves and mumbles something to them. She walks around her garden inspecting it, taking account of all we stole. She marches up to the bucket and snatches it, waddling back to her hut. "Get outta here before I sick'em on you." With that, she slams the door shut and Aiden and I look at each other then to the wolves.

We head back towards the village, and Aiden tells me stories of his past adventures. His bardic magic provides a beautiful musical accompaniment to his tales. I shake my head, trying to rid my mind of his mesmerizing words, but I listen with rapt attention, feeling grateful for his help in subduing the wolves and gaining the herbs we need. Together, we make a formidable team, our magic working together seamlessly to overcome any obstacles in our way. Again, I shake my head. Where are these intrusive thoughts coming from? They penetrate my mind as if placed there. I struggle to focus, but am caught in his web of tales.

Exhaust from our adventure consumes us, as we make our way back to the inn and Aiden leads us to the corner of the room where we slump into chairs by the fire. He orders two mugs of ale to celebrate our victory. I can't help but steal glances at Moonbean, who is sleeping on my shoulder in his usual drunken stupor. I wonder what had awoken him and caused him to howl, then suddenly, as if by magic, collapse again into his deep sleep. He hasn't been right since the Wailwraith, if you'd have ever called him right.

I clear my throat, knowing that Aiden has been eyeing my shoulder curiously, but I'm certain he can't see him. "Moonbean is my spirit guide," I say, gesturing towards the sprite.

Aiden looks at me quizzically. "Spirit guide?" He leans back in his chair. "Is this your 'elven things'?" He smirks.

I hold back my smile. "Yes, when I devoted my life to the Druidic Order, I aquired a spirit guide to help me on my journey. Moonbean is... well, he's a bit of a unique case." I feel so open with Aiden and somehow, I'm compelled to hold no secrets from him.

Aiden leans in, and raises an eyebrow. "How so?"

I hesitate, not sure how to explain Moonbean's particular brand of mischief. "Well, he's a bit of a... troublemaker. And he likes his drink. A lot."

Aiden raises his glass. "To Moonbean!"

I shake my head and glare at him. "Don't do that. This is serious."

Aiden slurps his mug and foam covers his smiling lips and my glare softens.

I glance over at Moonbean, who is now snoring softly. "He's a sprite, only druids can see him. But I think something's wrong with him. More than before."

Aiden furrows his brow and squints, trying to see Moonbean. "Hmm, I see nothing. But is that what messed up your magic with the wolves?"

"Yes. He's usually sleeping but awoke suddenly when we had approached the wolves and started howling."

Aiden nods, a look of understanding on his face. "I see. Has anything happened that might have affected him?"

I pause, worrying I'm saying too much. "I fought a Wailwraith during pilgrimage." I blurt out, then regret it immediately.

Aiden leans in. "A Wailwraith on the Ageless Isles?" A worried look steals his eyes from mine. "Like the same Wailwraiths who can only manifest from the Rift?"

I nod. "Yes, the very same ones."

Aiden gulps. The usual whimsical expression muddled with fear. "That means the enchantments of the Isles have failed."

I'm silent as I let the realization set in.

"And your companion has changed since you've seen the wraith?"

"I fought it."

"The wraith?" Aiden exclaims, his face stricken with surprise. "And I was worried about a few wolves." He leans back in his chair taking another sip of ale.

I nod. "But it left me with this." I pull my sleeve up, showing him the scratch just above my leather bracer.

He winces at the sight. "It looks infected."

"I need a healer." I say, but my thoughts are elsewhere. I have so much to tell Aiden, but I've just met him and am unsure of how deep to dig my roots. Do I tell him about the raven, about Malvolia, or how about I tell him about the twenty foot tall demon covered in spikes named the Devourer hellbent on destroying the Elder Grove? So instead I focus again on the simple truth. "It's just that I had this dream about a raven, and I can't help but feel like Moonbean might not be the guide I'm supposed to have."

Aiden raises an eyebrow. "What kind of dream?"

I hesitate, not sure if I want to share the details. "It's silly, really. I dreamt of a raven perched on a branch, watching me. And then it flew away. Several times."

Aiden nods, taking a sip of his ale. "Dreams can be powerful things. Maybe the raven was a sign of something to come."

I shrug, not sure what to make of it. Then think of what my father might say, and how the raven is a harbinger of ill-intent. "Maybe. But for now, we need to focus on getting those herbs to the ferryman and selling them for tickets to Faelyndelle."

Aiden nods in agreement. "Right. The ferryman likes herbs, but there's a catch."

I raise an eyebrow. "What kind of catch?"

Aiden leans in, lowering his voice, but I cut him off. "It better not be like the fish lady." I warn.

He laughs and looks around the room suspiciously, then lowers his voice again. "Let's just say that the ferryman has a bit of a reputation for being... unscrupulous. We'll have to do something mischievous to get those tickets."

I groan. "I'm serious. No more shinanigans."

Aiden chuckles. "I'll fill you in on the details later. For now, let's finish our drinks and get some rest. We've got a big day ahead of us."

17

A Glimmer of Hope

THE MIST-LADEN COASTAL VILLAGE leaves me feeling uneasy as Aiden and I scour the area for the ferryman. The damp fog envelops my clothes, adding a heavy and uncomfortable weight to my leathers, and also shrouds the old Elven buildings, which appear weathered and worn by the harsh sea air. Moss clings to the walls, adding to the sense of decay, creating a hauntingly eerie atmosphere. I peer up at the grey sky and wonder if I'll ever see the sun again.

As we walk by a small fishing wharf, I watch the fishermen prepare their boats for the day's catch. The sound of the waves crashing against the rocks provides a soothing backdrop to their chatter. However, the pungent smell of salt and fish in the air is overpowering, and it makes my stomach churn with a slight queasiness. I wonder how they can tolerate the stench and carry on with their work. The stark difference in our livelihoods makes me appreciate the lush greenery of Willowbrook all the more. The thick mist has covered me in a clammy residue that won't seem to dry.

Despite the thick fog, the coastal village is bustling with activity. As a Wood Elf, I feel the weight of curious eyes following me and my human companion as we navigate through the crowds of High Elves. Their disapproving glances serve as a reminder of the place I hold here. Walking with Aiden, despite his looks and charm, is still a human, and makes it even worse. Making me feel even more like an outsider in my homeland.

However, as we approach the wharf, something diverts my attention. A massive barge has just docked, and a group of rough-looking travelers is disembarking onto the wooden planks. I can't help but feel concerned that their weight may sink the sodden platform. Most of them appear to be warriors, adorned in an assortment of armor and exuding an intimidating presence. Their gear is worn, and their weapons are sharp, giving off a sense of danger that lingers in the air. The sight is unusual for this Elven coastal village, and I wonder if they are here for the Tournament of Champions.

As we make our way towards the ferryman, I can't help but notice the various warriors that have just disembarked from the barge. Some humans are towering over the others, with rippling muscles and battle scars etched into their skin. They carry enormous weapons, including axes and swords, and their eyes scan the village as if they are searching for something.

The dwarves are short but stout, and no less menacing, their beards braided with gold and silver. Some wear golden chainmail armor and carry heavy hammers and axes. I can't imagine trying to leap through the forest in that gear. I look down at my leathers and wonder how I could ever match any of these brutes. One of them catches my eye and gives me a nod, a small smile gracing his lips.

The half-orcs are a sight to behold, towering over even the tallest human with their broad shoulders and powerful muscles. Their skin is a deep olive color, and their beady eyes have a fierce intensity that is both intimidating and captivating. I catch myself staring, unable to look away. The size of their bottom tusks, most ragged and worn, some missing or broken, more than likely a token of battle, seem to dictate the hierarchy between them. As the ones with smaller tusks seem to bow out of the way of the Orc's with larger tusks, even if the warrior is larger.

Yet, a peculiar humanoid creature catches the most intrigue. Under his hood, I can see he has a rich blue skin tone, resembling the depths of the ocean, his long pointed fingers end in razor sharp talons that seem more elegant than functional. His features are sharp and angular, and he stands tall, almost the height of the orcs, but has a regal glide, as if the long legs under his robe hover over the cobblestone rather than press on it. He carries a staff and wears a long robe, made of heavy fabric that has pulsing runic sigils that seem to writhe as he walks. I can sense a power emanating from him that is both unsettling and fascinating. As I approach the man, he turns to face me, and I can see his frosty blue eyes glinting with intelligence and wisdom beyond his years.

Aiden whispers in my ear, "That man you're staring at is a member of the Tal'rahn, a race of powerful mages who are believed to come from the north-east shores of the Isles." I search my memory for a drop of a story or tale of this Tal'rahn, and find nothing. My mother was steadfast about feeding me every bit of information that may help me on my pilgrimage. Why would she leave out a race of beings that live right here on the Isles?

I stand gawking, as the Tal'rahn strides past us, its staff tapping against the cobbled stones of the wharf. I feel a sense of both awe and fear, for I know creatures like it wield immense power, and their motives are often inscrutable. "The north-eastern Isles" I blurt out? "How have I not heard of them before?"

Aiden laughs. "You druids are pretty reclusive. It's a well-known fact."

I scoff. "Maybe to you, loremaster." But inside, unease wells as I feel unprepared for the journey ahead. If I don't even know the inhabitants of my home, what else don't I know?

The warriors are so focused on their own missions that they pay no attention to us as we pass by. But the sight of so many battle-hardened warriors in one place fills me with a sense of foreboding. I've never heard of the King inviting any other races to the Ageless Isles before. This tournament seems ill-fitting to the traditions of the High Elves and the Isles. It's unsettling with everything that's going on with Malvolia, the raven, and the enchantments. I can't help but suspect it's all connected.

"They're here for the tournament." Aiden states, seemingly unphased by the plethora of fresh faces around us.

Moonbean awakens, rubs his eyes and yawns. Then rapidly flings his head from side to side, taking in his new surroundings, obviously flustered. "Izzat the festivus in town? What in the trickster's name tree is all this ruckus about?"

"Your finally awake." I chastise.

Aiden shoots me a startled look. "Is Moonbean talking to you?"

I nod as Moonbean clambers up and stretches his tiny arms before eyeballing Aiden suspiciously, then startling himself and slamming into my neck defensively as if Aiden is about to attack. "Who's that guy? And why aren't we in the Hinterlands?"

I laugh sharply, then whisper to Moonbean so only he can hear. "If you'd be awake more often, you'd know that after the wraith attacked us, the Foresaken breached the enchantments of the Isle, dragged Neason to his death, and I escaped the clutches of Malvolia; her demon Malathor and powerful wolf-demons hellbent on ripping me to shreds. All while you were snoring and scratching your ass."

Moonbean looks stunned and plops down on my shoulder with a tiny thud, releasing a sigh. He removes his top hat and unleashes a knot of wiry white hair and scratches his head. "Well, why didn't you wake me?" He scorns as he rubs the sleep from his eyes. "I'm..." he pauses, then grumbles. "Can't seem to get right."

"I tried, but you were dead to the world. Have been ever since the wraith."

Moonbean hesitates a few times, stopping and starting his words as if he's wrestling with them. "Howling pines and swaying oaks! What kind of elvish tomfoolery is this?" He stands and slaps his tophat back on his head, but it sits crookedly, "I'm Moonbean Flatterwort, for grove's sake.

I'm in a class of my own, one of the oldest guardians of the forest."

I can't help but let out a sharp laugh. "You sure are in a class of your own, all right." My tone is tinged with annoyance, directed at my slumbering spirit guide, who remains oblivious to my turmoil.

Aiden stops and pulls me into an alleyway, letting the crowd rush by us. It's dark in the shadows and with my cloak, I feel almost invisible. "What's the sprite saying?" I almost feel compelled to tell him when Moonbean cuts me off.

"He's weaving his enchantments on ya." Moonbean jumps up, balling his fists as if ready for a brawl with Aiden. "Let me at-em, I'll pop 'im in the nose, I will."

I shake my head vigorously and shoot a questioning look to Aiden as he asks me again what Moonbean is saying, but then I notice it. Sometimes when Aiden speaks, his words seem to take hold and mesmerize me. It's a strange feeling, and I try to resist it, but I can feel myself slipping. Finally, I croak out the words, "Moonbean says you're trying to charm me."

Aiden scoffs, his eyes shift from mine briefly, but it's enough of a tell, a clear sign that he's uneasy. As I wait for his response, he looks away, avoiding eye contact, releasing his grip on my shoulders. His gaze fixes on some distant point in the alley and he turns from me. He's reluctant to answer. Aiden's fidgeting and avoidance lead me to believe that the question I've asked is one he doesn't want to answer, and I feel a pang of frustration at his evasiveness. Has he been charming me the whole time?

"So are you?" I demand.

His face flushes while Moonbean hops around on my shoulder, fists balled and swinging at nothing and causing extensive damage to the surrounding air. "Let me at-em, let me at-em."

I shush Moonbean, then direct my attention to Aiden. "I'll ask once more, then I'm on my way without you."

Aiden looks at me with a guilt washed face then croaks. "I was."

"By the roots." I punch him in the shoulder and replay our conversations since we met. Anger grips me at the thought of him using me. "Trying to sweet talk me into helping you get to Faelyndelle?" I'm fuming and start pacing so I don't pull out my blackthorn staff and thrash him. "You think I am some foolish recluse druid who knows nothing of Capital life, too daft to understand your tricks?"

"It's not like that." Aiden pleas still unable to look me in the eye.

"Then what is it?" I growl, poking him in the chest. "You have one chance at the truth."

Moonbean jump kicks the air, cursing at Aiden, then does an awkward double somersault but lands on his ass, then tumbles off my shoulder and onto the ground with a thud. "I'm alright." he says scrambling up my leg. I grit my teeth in frustration, trying to ignore him as he struggles to climb my leg to get to my shoulder. When it's obvious he's winded himself and unable to climb on his own, I huff and yank him up and plop him back on my shoulder and scold him to sit still.

Aiden watches with a questioning look on his face. I notice how handsome he is standing in the shadows and shake off the feeling, wondering if that's part of his bardic magic. Elves and humans don't mix, I remind myself, thinking of my parents' odd coupling, then of my odd eyes.

"I didn't use you." His cheeks flush. "I thought we could help each other. I've been down on my luck and when I heard about the tournament, I traveled to the Isles, but..."

"But what?" I demand.

He groans. "I have no money. I'm broke. Poor. A vagrant. And I'm used to using my charm to get what I want."

I raise an eyebrow. "So you use me to because you have no money? Can't you sing for your food?"

He chuckles, but without his usual mirth. "That's how I've been buying bread, yes. But I'm stuck here, have been for a while."

"So leave."

"I can't." He shifts his weight, reddening further. "I come from a life of luxury, and living like a peasant doesn't suit me."

"I thought you said you were broke? How can you come from a life of luxury?"

"They threw me out of the castle."

"Castle?"

"Ugh. Must you know everything?" He squirms. "Are you sure it's not you who's the bard?"

"Spit it out." I demand.

He unwillingly explains. "I'm the prince of the Emerald Reach."

I'm stunned, so I just stare at him with a dumbfounded look on my face until he continues.

"I wouldn't marry Grunhilda Ironfist, a dwarven princess from Duunheim. My father arranged the marriage and said and I quote, 'Aiden, you must do your duty and marry the bearded princess. This will end the blasted three-hundred year war between the dwarves and humans,' but I refused."

"What, her beard was nicer than that patchy thing clinging to your face?" I jab, still angry with him.

He almost laughs but refrains and looks hurt. "No. I'm not ready for marriage. So my father banished me from the castle and revoked my titles for time eternal."

"That's harsh." I say. Then I think of the pilgrimage and how they almost banished me for not being able to catch a sprite and I falter. I look at Moonbean and think I would have been better off without him. Although comical, he's been a thorn in my side since I met him. As if knowing that I'm fuming at him, Moonbean whispers to me, letting me know the bard is telling the truth. "I know that Moonbean." I reply.

"Know what?" Aiden questions.

I shake my head and point to my shoulder. "It's just Moonbean." I let out an exasperated sigh and jab my finger at Aiden threateningly. "Do not use your charm against me again."

He agrees with a wry smile.

"I mean it." I warn.

"Okay, I got it. No more charms." He pleads.

Stepping out from the shadows, we merge into the back of a sluggish-moving crowd. I startle a Glimmersprout who appears to be struggling to keep up with the group ahead. He lets out a high-pitched yelp, "Ah! I almost dropped my crescentia!" His delicate, pointed ears wobble as he desperately tries to regain his balance. The tiny gemstones adorning them clank and jingle, appearing to weigh them down with their sparkle. He fumbles several times, trying to keep his crescent roll from hitting the ground.

He wears an intricately embroidered burgundy vest and a pair of loose-fitting sand colored trousers that flap with each of his rapid movements. As he hops around, his voice is high-pitched and musical, a charming and endearing sound. His soft golden shoes come to a point and curl at the toe. A tiny bell hangs on the very tip, adding to the musical jingle of the creature. He's just small, yet his presence is full of life, a sparkling gem amid the misty village's veiled oppressiveness.

I apologize as the Glimmersprout adjusts his tiny spectacles. When he's done, the spectacles have magnified his already enormous eyes to comical proportions. "What brings you here?" His face is heart-shaped, with two large, expressive eyes that glow with a deep, luminescent green hue, and a small, delicate nose that twitches with excitement.

"I'm just passing through, but I couldn't help but overhear something about a tournament," I reply, looking down at the Glimmersprout, who's standing only two feet tall. "Are you here for it too?"

The Glimmersprout nods excitedly. "Yes, the tournament is a grand event that King Eldrin has just announced. He sent a message throughout all the Realms. Everyone has been so excited to come to the Isles for some time. Teams from all over the land will compete against one another."

"Do you know the rules?"

"It's not just one event, but a series of challenges that test the skills of each team member. It's quite an exciting event!"

I listen with interest as the Glimmersprout explains the details of the Tournament of Champions. As he speaks, his tiny spectacles slide down his nose, and he pushes them back up with a delicate finger.

I shake my head. "I'm afraid I know little about it. This is the first I've heard of the tournament. Can you tell me more about the challenges?"

The Glimmersprout's eyes light up with excitement, "Of course! There are a variety of challenges that test unique skills, like archery, swordsmanship, spell-casting, and more. Each team has to work together to overcome the obstacles and earn points. The team with the most points at the end of the tournament wins."

I nod, impressed by the tournament. "Sounds like quite the event. And who is eligible to compete?"

"Anyone can compete, as long as they have a team of four members. It doesn't matter if you're a human, elf, dwarf." He hops into the air, much higher than I expect, and does a pirouette, and lands feather lite. "Glimmer-sprout, or any other race. The only requirement is that you have the skills to compete in the challenges."

I feel a pang of excitement and curiosity rise within me. As a neophyte, I'm skilled in all the categories and have honed my combat skills in the woods. Maybe this is my chance to get an audience with the King.

"I see. And where in Faelyndelle is the tournament being held?"

"It's being held at the Hall of Heroes. The king himself will be in attendance, along with other important figures from across the Realms."

I nod, taking in all the information. "Thank you for explaining it to me. I might have to consider putting together a team to compete in the tournament."

I listen intently, intrigued by the idea of a team event and not a single competition. "How do teams usually form? Are there any restrictions?"

The Glimmersprout thinks for a moment before responding. "Teams are formed by groups of individuals who wish to take part together. There are no restrictions on who can form a team. It's a great opportunity to showcase your skills and compete against some of the best in the land!"

"Best in the land," I say, looking around at all the ferocious-looking warriors. Desperation sets in. I'm out of my element here. Looking around, I'm uncertain there would be enough natural magic for me to draw on here, surrounded by cobblestone and thatch buildings. How can I even compete? And just then, a massive Orc shoves his way by and growls at me. I stumble backward, nearly capsized, but before the Orc can do anything else, a burst of light explodes from the Glimmersprout. I shield my eyes and watch in amazement as light and energy flash from the tiny being.

The Glimmersprout looks at the Orc with a fierce determination as he casts some illumination spell. The Orc, caught off guard, yelps in surprise. His eyes wide as the Glimmersprout's magic surrounds him, lifting him off the ground.

In an instant, the Orc is shot from where he stands, crashing into a nearby apple stall whose produce, that isn't squished, dumps to the ground. The Glimmersprout turns to me and bows, as if to say, "You're safe now." In doing this, his glasses slide from his nose. Awkwardly, he tries to stop them but fumbles and they crash to the ground. He quickly snatches them up, balances his half eaten crescent roll, and scurries away.

I breathe a sigh of relief, and call out to the Glimmersprout. "Thank you," I say, still in shock at what had just happened. A crowd of onlookers has gathered to watch, but as the skirmish ends, they lose interest and merge back into the marching hoard towards the Capital.

"That was odd," Aiden says looking at the half-orc who's glowering at us as he dusts himself off. He bares his teeth and threatens us with a waving fist. "If I see you two at the tournament, you're as good as dead." His deep voice booms as he mocks, cutting his own throat, then stomps away.

"By the roots. I... How do we compete with that?"

"The half-orc is no worries in a tournament, with my charms and your druidic magic-"

"So we're a team now?" I stare at him, arms crossed.

"We just need two more team members and we qualify for the tournament."

"I think the little guy has got some potential." I point to the direction where the Glimmersprout disappeared into the crowd.

Aiden leans against the grey stone wall and plucks an apple from the broken stall. The storekeeper, hurrying and cursing to herself from all the crushed apples the half-orc has caused. She scowls at Aiden, then softens and waves off his feign attempt to pay for the apple, as he gives her his charming smile. I roll my eyes because I know he has no coin and is recklessly using his bardic charm. He finally sets his attention to me and says, "I think we'd be better off partnering with a Tal'rahn."

"Those blue mages?" I question.

He nods. "They say their power is unrivalled."

"Unrivalled?" I say, thinking about the power of Guro, one of the most powerful druids I know.

"They possess an innate and deep understanding of magic and use it to manipulate the elements, control the arcane forces, and bend reality to their will. Their magical abilities are not limited to offensive and defensive spells, but also extend to healing, divination, and teleportation."

"You seem to know a lot about lore."

"I'm a bard. It's part of my job. You called me the lore-master." He smirks at me.

"You have no job, remember?" I snark.

He smiles and takes an obnoxiously juicy bite of his apple and wraps his arm around my shoulder, guiding me towards the ferryman's boat where the massive crowd has gathered.

"My job is protecting you, finding a winning combo of members and adding them to our team. Once we do that, then we win the tournament and a plethora of coin. And once all that is complete, we get an audience with the King."

"We get an audience with the King?" I say with a raised eyebrow. "What do you need the King of Faelyndelle for?"

He gives me a wink. "I can't be a pauper forever."

18

The Ferryman's Curse

As AIDEN AND I approach the crowded square surrounding the ferryman's shack, a sense of anxiety washes over me. A diverse mix of warriors, including humans, elves, half-orcs, glimmersprouts, and tal'rahn, all gather, eagerly awaiting their ferry tickets. The market square is a whirlwind of activity, vendors hollering, peddling their wares, and the scent of fish and spices mingles with the salty breeze.

We navigate our way through the bustling crowd, apologizing as we go, and finally, we reach the ferryman, an old seafarer with a leathered face and a crooked grin that seems to hold a lifetime of stories. One of his ears is merely a stub, a curiosity that catches my gaze. He notices my stare, flicks his ear, and smirks. "Ready to cross or you just fascinated by me ear?" he growls in his rough sea accent, extending his hand for payment.

As I now stare at his face, I can't look away from his unwavering glass eye, that seems to big for his face. He's getting impatient, so I fumble to retrieve the pouch of rare herbs and hand it to him, "You requested rare herbs. Will these suffice?" My voice trembles slightly, trying to maintain composure and willing myself to only look at his good eye.

The ferryman squints as he inspects the pouch. "Better be worth me time," he grumbles, snatching the pouch from my hand.

Driven by curiosity, I can't help but ask, "What happened to your ear?"

The ferryman's face darkens, and he recounts his tale with a snarl, "I was out fishing, and a sea creature bit it off, almost took me life."

An air of unease hangs heavy as the ferryman recounts his tale of terror. Leaning in closer, my curiosity piqued, I probe further, "What kind of creature was it? I've ventured deep into the sea in search of Lunar Seaweed near Willowbrook."

The ferryman takes a deep breath, haunted eyes flickering, and says, "It was a massive sea serpent, one of the fiercest. Twisted and rotted. It had razor-sharp teeth, blazing eyes, and it emerged out of nowhere. Caught me by surprise."

The thought of facing such a monstrous creature beneath the dark sea depths sends shivers down my spine.

"How did you escape?" I ask, curiosity now bordering on dread.

The ferryman's face takes on a grim expression as he continues, "Wasn't easy. Dragged me under, but I used my oar to fend it off, landed a lucky blow to its eye, and made my escape." He pauses, a sense of disbelief in his voice. "I've been fishing these waters for years, never seen anything like it. A true monster."

Aiden and I exchange cautious glances, pondering the lack of enchantments that could have prevented such a gruesome encounter.

"But that ain't the only thing plaguing me," the ferryman continues in a hushed, ominous tone, "I've got a rare ailment, driving me mad."

Intrigued yet uneasy, I inquire, "What ailment?"

The ferryman's voice escalates in frustration, "A cursed rash. It won't leave, no matter what I do." He lifts his shirt, revealing the inflamed, reddened flesh with a scratch similar to the one on my arm.

Recoiling slightly, I acknowledge, "From the serpent?"

He nods, "Take these herbs to the Sylvariel outside the village in Knockwood Forest." He points at us with a gnarled finger. "Don't return without a remedy for my ailment."

Squaring my shoulders, I gaze at the rash with concern. "This rash looks serious. I could make a tincture with calendula and yarrow to ease your pain," I offer, shaking the pouch.

The ferryman scoffs, "I've seen healers, none of 'em worked. I need the Sylvariel, a powerful druid."

Intrigued yet skeptical, I press, "The Sylvariel? I've never heard of him before. Who is he?"

With a mischievous glint in his eyes, the ferryman explains, "A reclusive druid in Knockwood Forest. He's a master of nature, knows herbs, plants, roots, and more. Hard to find, but you're resourceful."

I raise an eyebrow in doubt and retort, "The Druidic Order is from Willowbrook Forest, but I've never heard of this Sylvariel."

Unease sets in as the ferryman responds, "That's 'cause he don't want to be found. He's in hiding but possesses unique powers to cure and break curses."

Aiden joins in with skepticism, "How do we find him? And how do we know he can help with your rash?"

Leaning closer, the ferryman whispers, "There's a clearing deep in the forest. He lives in an illusory hut. It's a perilous journey, and he's a bit of a curmudgeon."

I smirk at the ferryman's description of the elusive druid.

"The forest is teeming with deadly creatures. As for the rash, I trust the Sylvariel. If anyone can cure me, it's him," the ferryman insists.

Straightening up, I assert, "You're in luck because I'm a druid in training, a neophyte. If anyone can find him, it's us. We'll get a remedy for your ailment, and the tickets will be ours." I extend my hand, sealing the promise.

The ferryman grins and shakes my hand. "Good luck, then. Treat the Sylvariel with respect, and he might help you in ways you never imagined." He hands us a tattered map of the area, pointing north to Knockwood Forest. "That's where you'll find him."

Understanding the mission ahead, I nod and state, "We'll do our best to find a remedy for you." Turning to Aiden, who stands beside me, I urge, "Come on, Aiden. We have work to do."

With a sense of urgency, I lead us out of the cramped shack and onto the wharf, where the thick mist obscures the market stalls. Ships of all shapes and sizes line the dock, ready for departure.

Taking refuge beside an empty stall, I slump against the stone wall, my exhaustion weighing on me. As I sit down, my weariness envelops me, and I place my head between my knees. "Nothing is ever easy, is it? First, we need to buy fish for herbs, and that doesn't go well. Now, with the herbs in hand, we have to find a recluse druid I've never even heard of."

Seating himself beside me, Aiden's gaze remains fixed on the ships in the harbor. "Everything happens for a reason," he assures, seeking to offer solace.

"The worst part is that nobody comprehends the danger we're facing," I confess, my voice heavy with oppression. "They consider these dark creatures coincidental with the Tournament. Wait until one of those wolf demons shows up at the gates; then they'll grasp the peril."

He wraps his arm around my shoulder and provides comfort. "That's why we're visiting the Sylvariel, so that doesn't occur."

I lift my head, offering a faint smile in gratitude for his attempt. "Maybe you're right," I concede, though the disquiet lingers. "But we can't linger here. We should leave."

Aiden concurs with a nod, and I retrieve the map the ferryman gave us, unfolding it on my lap. Tracing my finger over the twisting paths and dense forests, I locate Knockwood Forest. "Knockwood forest," I announce. "That's where the ferryman directed us. But I feel an oppressive force here, like it's dampening my magic, my connection with nature." With a sudden urgency, I jump to my feet.

Aiden's expression mirrors my seriousness as he replies, "The Tournament is in two weeks. We need to find the Sylvariel, have him craft the remedy, and get on that ferry."

"Maybe there's a reason for everything," I muse, my thoughts drawn to the mysterious, enchanted ring that grants visions when touched. "Maybe the Sylvariel can help with my arm. Let's go now." With determination, I turn and head north out of the Misty Village, with Aiden following closely.

19

The Sylvariel's Dilema

OUR JOURNEY TO KNOCKWOOD Forest unfolds calmly as we stroll through the wildflower hills. Petals sway gently in the breeze, brushing against our legs. The sun's warmth lifts our spirits as we take in the simple pleasures of the day. We enjoy the sunlight on our skin and the fragrant wildflower scents in the air. It's a serene moment, and we savor the beauty of the landscape as we walk.

But as Aiden and I breach the forest's edge, I feel a shiver run down my spine. The trees are tall and twisted, their branches reaching out like bony fingers. Its dense foliage stifling any of the sun's rays, and the air is thick with the scent of damp earth and decaying leaves. Through my skin, I can feel the forest's enchanting energy. I look down to my shoulder and sigh as Moonbean has again passed out on my shoulder. I can't help but wonder if he, too, is under some sort of spell. My mind drifts to the wraith and my infected arm. There has to be a connection that I'm missing.

We walk in silence through alternating thick brambles and small clearings, taking in the eerie beauty of the forest. As the enchanted energy seeps into my pores, I feel my magic re-energizing. As we stroll, we discuss the tournament we're getting ready for. Aiden suggests adding a dwarven warrior, human ranger, or Tal'rahn to our team, but I believe a Glimmersprout's magical abilities would be more valuable.

I can feel Aiden's gaze on me, waiting for a response. "Why do we need a warrior or ranger?" I ask him. "I can fight Aiden, and I'm one of the most agile Elves I know. Plus, we're going up against other teams with magical abilities. We need someone who can help us counter their magic. What if we're in battle and I can't draw on nature's magic?"

"A warrior or ranger could help us in battle," Aiden counters. "They could take on the physical threats while we deal with the magical ones. My charm only goes so far. If I'm physically attacked and taken down, I'm no help." He points to his golden dagger. "This is more for show, anyway. We need a defender. A 'meat shield' if you will."

I cringe at the term, but he only shrugs. "But a Glimmersprout could use their magic to confuse and misdirect our opponents. They could create illusions to distract them, or even make them see things that aren't there. Plus, they're fast, which could help us in a pinch."

"But Glimmersprouts are notoriously difficult to work with," Aiden says, his voice low. "They're easily distracted and can be hard to control."

I concede that point but ad. "Isn't that what your charms are for? And if we can get one on our team, their magic could be a real asset."

Aiden nods thoughtfully, considering my words. "Okay, I see your point. But we can't rely solely on magic. We need someone who can handle themselves in a fight."

I bite my lip, unsure how to respond. Aiden is right, of course. We need someone who can fight. But I still feel like a Glimmersprout would be more helpful.

We walk in silence for a few more minutes, lost in our own thoughts. Finally, I turn to Aiden. "Let's make a deal," I say. "We'll look for a human ranger or dwarven warrior to add to our team, but if we can't find one, we'll try to recruit a Glimmersprout instead."

Aiden nods, a wry smile on his lips. "Sounds like a plan."

As we wander deeper into the forest, we stumble upon yet another empty clearing. The eerie light in the center of the glade catches our attention. Suddenly, the bushes rustle, and I startle. The Glimmersprout we had encountered in the misty village steps out of the undergrowth, greeting us with a mischievous grin.

"Good morrow, my friends!" he chirps in a sing-song voice, punctuating his greeting with a slight bow. "Fancy meeting you here!"

I startle and look him up and down in frustration. "Hello, Glimmereth." I say trying to hide my sense of unease. How the little bugger snuck up on us with my keen elvish ear on guard, I'll never know.

Glimmereth nods to us, then his expression changes, as if remembering something awful. He narrows his eyes suspiciously and jabs his finger at us. "And what brings you two wandering around in the woods so far from the village?"

I raise an eyebrow. "We could ask you the same."

Glimmereth regards us with a serious expression before his gaze falls on Moonbean, who is snoring on my shoulder. "Why have you got a faery tethered to your shoulder?" he asks, his tone almost accusatory.

I peer down at Moonbean, then clarify. "Moonbean is a guardian spirit, not a pet."

Glimmereth looks from me to Moonbean quizzically, then offers. "Of course, of course. I don't mean to pry?" He pauses for a moment before continuing, "Anyway, I'm on a bit of a mission. The ferryman sent me to find the Sylvariel and retrieve a trinket for his rash. He promised me tickets to the Capital in exchange for my help."

Aiden nudges me with his elbow slyly so Glimmereth won't notice. "The ferryman sent us for the same thing." He crosses his arms and scowls. "I hope we're not getting played.."

Glimmereth's face falls. "I swear I'm not trying to trick you. The ferryman said the Sylvariel's hut is glamoured, and that's why he needed me."

I cross my arms, still uncertain. "Why would the ferryman send all three of us for the same thing?"

Glimmereth hesitates for a moment before responding. "Perhaps he was just being cautious. Or maybe he thought it would be more fun this way!" He winks playfully, and I can't help but grin in response.

His eyes fall to Moonbean again, then he jests, "Your little friend, there could be a big help if he wasn't so sleepy. Why do you keep him enchanted?"

I glance down at Moonbean, wondering how the Glimmersprout can see him when most can't. "How can you see Moonbean?"

Glimmereth giggles. "Glimmersprouts are masters of illusion. We can decipher all forms of glamour magic."

I narrow my eyes, not entirely sure I trust him. "What do you mean, 'keep him enchanted'? Is Moonbean cursed?"

Glimmereth shakes his head. "Not cursed, my friend. Enchanted! There's a difference, you know." He leans in conspiratorially. "I can't tell you much, because the answers are veiled, but I think I know a way to break the enchantment."

My curiosity piqued, I ask, "Really? How?"

Glimmereth grins, his eyes sparkling with mischief. "Ah, now that's a secret. But if you help me with my mission, I'll tell you all about it."

"At your service." I give a playful bow. Somehow, I'm lighthearted around the little Glimmersprout. There's an energy to him that's infectious. I shoot a glare at Aiden and whisper, "Is he charming me?"

Aiden shakes his head. "He's not charming you by force, but his magic is infectious."

"Well," Glimmereth says, rubbing his chin thoughtfully. When he does this, the jewels and beads on his ears jingle. "The Sylvariel's magic is said to have the ability to restore lost magic. If we can find him and convince him to help, Moonbean might break the spell."

Aiden raises an eyebrow. "And how do we find him?"

Glimmereth grins mischievously. "That's the fun part. No one knows exactly where he lives or what he looks like. He's an enigma, a mystery waiting to be solved." There's a glint in his eye as he looks to the center of the clearing.

"I'm in a hurry. We need to get back to the village before the ferry leaves for the Capital."

Glimmereth nods eagerly. "I've heard tales the Sylvariel's magical mastery. He's said to be the guardian of the forest in a clearing much like this one." He waves his arm to show us the clearing.

"He's a druid." I say reciting what the ferryman had explained.

"Not just any druid." Glimmereth beams. "He's the original druid."

I scoff, hurt by this revelation. "I come from the Druidic Order, and I've never heard about some druid named the Sylvariel."

"You wouldn't have. It's said they banished him." He leans in. "Why don't you ask him yourself?" He points to the center of the clearing where the light hits unnaturally. "His hut is right there."

I squint my eyes, trying to make out any details in the distance. "I see nothing but unnatural light," I admit.

Glimmereth frowns, then reaches into his pocket and pulls out a small crystal. He holds it up to the light and whispers a few words. Suddenly, the crystal glows brightly, bending the light around itself and shooting a refracted beam towards the center of the clearing. Without warning, a faint hut outline becomes visible in the clearing.

"There it is," he says triumphantly. "The Sylvariel's hut."

I step closer to get a better look at the old wooden hut in the center of the clearing. It's small and weather-beaten, with a thatched roof that's seen better days. The walls are made of thick, rough-hewn logs, and there are no windows to let in the light. The door is heavy and sturdy, with iron hinges that creak ominously in the wind. Moss and vines cling to the sides of the hut, camouflaging it.

Despite its rough exterior, there's something almost magical about the hut. Perhaps it's the aura of mystery that surrounds it or the fact that it's home to the enigmatic Sylvariel. Whatever it is, I can feel my heart racing as I take a step closer, ready to face whatever challenges lie ahead.

Aiden nods, impressed. "Well, I'll be. You really know your way around this forest."

Glimmereth grins. "I've lived here my whole life. But only recently gained the Truth crystal, that helps me unveil even the most powerful of glamors." He lifts the opaque crystal so when the light hits it, it blinds us. "I've been searching for the Sylvariel for a long time. Now, let's get that trinket."

As we approach the hut, I can't help but feel a sense of unease. The potent scent of herbs engulfs me, making me dizzy. There's something about this place that doesn't feel quite right. But before I can voice my concerns, Glimmereth steps forward and knocks on the door.

There's a rustling sound from inside, then the door creaks open. A tall, sturdy figure stands in the doorway, dressed in a long hooded cloak. His face hides in shadow.

"Who are you?" he demands.

Glimmereth steps forward, holding out his hand. "I've come on behalf of the ferryman. He sent me to fetch a trinket called the Lunar Infuser."

As the Sylvariel steps out of the hut, my eyes lock onto his weathered face. "How did you find me?" the Sylvariel asks, his voice gruff.

There's something familiar about his features I can't quite place, but his gruffness overshadows it. His face is covered in intricate druidic tattoos, which seem to have taken on a life of their own. Raven trinkets dangle from his cloak, which is made from a white wolf pelt. But what stands out most are his piercing eyes, which seem to see straight through me.

Then I freeze, because his eyes are exactly like mine. One emerald green eye and a piercing blue eye glare at me.

"What are you looking at?" He growls. The surrounding air is heavy with the scent of herbs and plants, and the shelves behind him are cluttered with jars and bottles. It's clear that this is a man who has spent his life in communion with nature and the spirits that inhabit it.

I step forward, my hands shaking. "We ask for your help," I say, my voice barely above a whisper. "The ferryman in the misty village has a cursed rash, and we've been told that you're the only one who can cure him." I show him the pouch of herbs Aiden is carrying.

The Sylvariel studies us for a moment before nodding. "I may help you," he says, his voice softening. "But first, you must prove yourselves worthy."

Aiden and I exchange a nervous glance. We do not know what we are getting ourselves into, but we will do whatever it takes to get to the Capital.

The Sylvariel's piercing gaze settles on me, and I feel a shiver run down my spine. "What do you mean by prove ourselves?" I demand, trying to anchor my roots.

The Sylvariel leans in closer, his eyes locked onto mine. "There is a grove deep in the forest that has been corrupted by dark magic. The creatures that once lived there have turned malevolent and violent. If you can cleanse the grove of its corruption and restore balance, then I will consider helping you."

My heart sinks at the thought because I know which grove he's talking about. And I know I don't want to go there. I have to warn the King, not go back to the Grove. "The Lunar Grove." I say.

The Sylvariel offers a gruff smile. "Your quick young neophyte."

He knows I'm a neophyte. He must know of Willowbrook then. "Why are you not in Willowbrook with the Druidic Order?" I question.

The Sylvariel's expression turns somber. "I have been exiled from the 'Order', as you call it. It is not the same as it once was. But that is a story for another time. Right now, you must focus on the task at hand." He turns and disappears back into his hut, leaving us to contemplate our next move.

"Does this dark magic have anything to do with Malvolia?" I blurt out.

Aiden shoots me a warning look. "Faelyn, we don't know this guy," he says, his voice low.

But the Sylvariel seems to ponder my question. "It's possible," he says finally. "Malvolia's influence is strong, and it wouldn't be the first time her dark magic has seeped into the Isles. But be warned, the corruption in the Lunar Grove is not to be taken lightly. I've foreseen a veiled darkness."

I feel a knot form in my stomach at his words, but I know we can't back down now. He knows of Malvolia, so he must know more. "I was on pilgrimage for the Oath before Malvolia breached the protective enchantments of the Isles." I say with trying to glean more information.

His eyes flash to me and he rasps. "She's already here?" He stalks to the table, fills his satchel with several vials and herbs from his cupboards and says. "We need to set off at once. May the moon guide our steps."

20

Into the Forest

As I STRIDE FORWARD, I take in the thick forest and flow-ered meadows that surround me, completely captivated by the stories the Sylvariel has told me. My mind races as I learn more about the ancient Druids, the first to live in and guard the seven sacred trees, and how they only recently moved away from the groves they had protected for centuries. The Sylvariel's explanation that the Druidic Oath wasn't always so formalized leaves me in a state of bewilderment.

Aiden and Glimmereth's bickering echoes through the tranquil sounds of nature, distracting me briefly from the surrounding beauty. They continue their heated debate behind me, with Aiden siding with the humans of Emer-ald Reach and Glimmersprout standing firm in his belief that they cannot be trusted. The two argue with passion and detail about the rightful guardians of the mines in Du-unheim, with Glimmereth insisting that only the dwarves have the right to them.

I try to tune out their argument, piecing together bits and pieces, but my attention is quickly stolen away by the stunning golden sunset ahead of us. The light cascades through the tall grass of the meadow, casting a magical glow across the land. The air is thick with the sweet aroma of blooming flowers, and the distant chirping of crickets creates a symphony of natural music. My favorite time of day is between Dusk's Ember and the Evening's Serenade. I am in awe of the enchanting landscape around me, lost in my thoughts of the Druidic Order and the beauty that surrounds us.

I approach the Sylvariel with fascination, still trying to wrap my head around what he's telling me. "So you're saying the Druidic Oath wasn't always so formalized?" I ask, eager for more knowledge.

He chortles faintly. "It's not as straightforward as that. The Oath is earned through pilgrimage, but the Order have overly simplified the rituals and theories surrounding it, including your mother."

I freeze at the mention of my mother, my heart rate picking up as I try to process this new information. "What about my mother?" I ask, my voice betraying my unease.

The Sylvariel turns away from me, his gaze fixed on the setting sun. "Your mother loved the setting sun. It was her favorite time of day."

"How do you know so much about my mother?" I question, unease setting in.

"You look so much like her," he says wistfully. "I miss her."

My mind races, wondering if this is some kind of trap or trick from Malvolia. I grip my blackthorn staff tightly, my Elven senses on high alert as I consider my options.

But then the Sylvariel speaks again, his voice now soft and reassuring. "There's no need for that, Faelyn. You have nothing to fear from me. I am your grandfather." He turns to me, unveils his hood revealing his features in the golden light of the setting sun. His ashen white hair is the same shade as mine. His eyes, and now I'm noticing his other features, remind me of my mother. I gasp.

I stand there, dumbfounded and overwhelmed by the series of events that have led me here. First my pilgrimage was interrupted, then I was sent on a quest by the ferryman, and now I face the revelation that this old recluse is my banished grandfather, and now I've gone full circle and am headed back to the Lunar Grove. "I don't understand," I mutter, feeling lost and confused.

Even the surrounding birds seem to sense the gravity of the situation, their songs trailing off into silence.

The Sylvariel looks around and declares, "This is a tale that deserves a fire and a meal." He walks towards the edge of the forest and sets camp. As I watch him set a wild root trap with precision and direct Glimmereth to gather wood for the fire, I can't help but feel like I've been thrust into some kind of ironic storybook.

As I stand there in shock, Aiden approaches me with a worried expression. "You look like you've seen a ghost?" he coaxes.

I can't even bring myself to look at him as I try to wrap my head around the revelation that the Sylvariel is my grandfather. "I think I have," I whisper in response, my voice barely audible.

Aiden's eyes shift to my shoulder. "Is Moonbean dead?" he asks, sensing my distress.

I shake my head in response, still processing the weight of the news. "No. The Sylvariel is my grandfather," I finally say, the words sounding surreal even as they leave my lips.

"What?" Aiden's shock mirrors my own, and we stand there in silence for a few moments, trying to process this unexpected turn of events.

"I'll let the old man tell his tale," I say finally, breaking the silence. "In the meantime, I'm going to go gather some berries and see if I can snare something for supper."

As I walk away, I try to steady my breathing and clear my mind. This journey has taken so many unexpected turns, and I don't know if I'm ready for any more surprises. But as a neophyte, it's my duty to listen and learn, to keep an open mind and heart. And so I root myself for the tale that awaits, even as my mind races with questions and doubts.

SMALL SMALL

Sitting by the warmth of the fire, and at the request of the Sylvariel, I listen to Aiden's melodic voice as he plays his lute and sings the tale of our adventures. My heart swells with pride as I hear the bard's song, and I marvel at how he came up with it so quickly.

> (Verse 1)
> In the Misty Village's morning haze,
> Strolled Faelyn, her eyes a radiant blaze,
> A druid skilled, heart pure, spirit light,
> Setting out with dawn, on a quest so right.

(Chorus)
Faelyn, Aiden, and
Glimmereth in tow,
A trio forging bonds,
as they boldly go,
From village mists to
woods so deep,
Their journey's se-
crets they'll unlock
and keep.

(Verse 2)
Amidst the outskirts,
the wolves did bay,
Faelyn whispered,
brought the wild at
bay,
Aiden's charm, en-
chantment of a kind,
Faelyn's hawk-eye
scouted, dangers to
find.

(Chorus)
Faelyn, Aiden, and
Glimmereth in tow,
A trio forging bonds,
as they boldly go,
From village mists to
woods so deep,
Their journey's se-
crets they'll unlock
and keep.

(Verse 3)
Moonbean woke
drunk, with a fishy
dream,
A cure needed for
the ferryman's rash, it
seemed,
Off they ventured,
through woods and
strife,
Seeking the Sylvariel
to mend a life.

(Chorus)
Faelyn, Aiden, and
Glimmereth in tow,
A trio forging bonds,
as they boldly go,
From village mists to
woods so deep,
Their journey's se-
crets they'll unlock
and keep.

(Verse 4)
In a humble hut, the
Sylvariel did dwell,
Weathered face, gruff
voice, his story to tell,
As they conversed,
kindred spirits they'd
win,
Faelyn's heart swelled,
as their journey did
begin.

(Chorus)
Faelyn, Aiden, and Glimmereth in tow,
A trio forging bonds, as they boldly go,
From village mists to woods so deep,
Their journey's secrets they'll unlock and keep.

(Verse 5)
With the Sylvariel by their side, they stand tall,
Facing darkness, hearts open, ready to enthral,
Faelyn, Aiden, and Glimmereth, strong and true,
Together they rise, to see the quest through.

(Chorus)
Faelyn, Aiden, and
Glimmereth in tow,
A trio forging bonds,
as they boldly go,
From village mists to
woods so deep,
Their journey's se-
crets they'll unlock
and keep.

Before Aiden sings the final chorus, both Glimmereth and the Sylvariel are stomping their feet to the
beat and humming. When Aiden begins the final chorus, they are both signing in tune with the bard. I clap
and join in for the finale.

As the round of applause finally gives way, Aiden sets
his lute beside him and sets his eyes on the Sylvariel and
says, "Now it's your turn."

The Sylvariel finishes his sage tea and sets his earthen
cup beside his dusty boot and leans towards the fire
warming his hands; the glow highlighting the intricate
tattoos on his face.

II sit silently, listening as the Sylvariel recounts the story of the beginning of the Druidic Order. He speaks of a time when things were more organic and natural, before the world became corrupted by the darker forces at play. He even goes on to say that the name 'Druidic Order' goes against the principles of the ancients.

"Long before the rise of cities and kingdoms, there was a time when the world was untamed and wild. It was then that the Elder tree, the mother of all life, first sprouted and spread her roots across the land. From her roots grew the seven sacred groves, where the first druids would commune with nature and learn her secrets." When the Sylvariel's hands are warmed, he leans back and continues. "In those days, the first of us lived in harmony with the land and all her creatures. We listened to the whispers of the trees and the songs of the birds, and we used our magic to heal and protect the natural world. Ravens were not seen as ill omens, but as messengers between the spirits of the land and the first druids who tended to them." His raven adorned necklaces jingle as he speaks.

When he finishes the sentence, as if on purpose, a lone raven caws. We all startle and look at the surrounding forest. I think back to my vision of the raven and the Devourer, Malathor battling at the Sacred Groves and wonder; was it a vision of the past?

The Sylvariel has a twinkle in eye before he continues. ""We were the ones who founded the ancient natural magic and gave ourselves the name The Elder Druids because we lived within the Elder Grove-"

"My mother was not a dark force." I interrupt, suddenly irritated.

The Sylvariel looks at me with sorrow in his eyes. "Your mother was not dark like Malvolia, you're right." He pauses, suddenly stricken. "But she was guarded against the teachings of the ancients. She veiled herself from the truth of the sacred groves and, because of that, the darkness clouded her mind."

"My mother was not clouded." I growl. "She taught me all that I know."

The Sylvariel nods, the sorrow turning to regret. "Instead of embracing the teachings of the Elder Grove. She moved our clan away from the Elder Grove and instead founded Willowbrook. She believed the druids should use their magic to control the land, rather than work within it. Your mother saw the ravens as omens of death and destruction, rather than the messengers of the spirits. She sought to change The Elder Druids' teachings, to make it more about power and control."

"She may have been strict, but she respected the forest and the groves." I say, both Aiden and Glimmereth stay silent, their wide eyes darting from me to the Sylvariel and back again.

"Respecting and listening to the groves are two distinct actions, Faelyn. The Sacred Groves emphasize balance and harmony, while control and fear, particularly towards any of nature's special creatures, contradict the teachings of the Groves." The Sylvariel leans down to pour more sage tea from the pot and into his earthen cup. "The decline started when she began directing neophytes to the Lunar Grove instead of seeking the natural wisdom of the Elder Grove."

I cross my arms, trying to decipher whether or not to believe this old man. Memories of my mother flash through my mind. Her teachings weighing against what the Sylvariel is saying. And for whatever reason, what he says rings true, and it's shaken the roots of my world.

As if knowingly, the Sylvariel pauses and finishes his tea before continuing, letting his tale soak into my mind. "We argued and fought, and in the end, she had the ear of the others like her and banished me from the groves if I wouldn't comply." He smiles softly looking into the fire as the light and shadows play on his features. "And I was too old in my ways, and couldn't change. But she changed the ancient ways, and the druids used their magic in unnatural ways to corrupt the forest. The balance of the world was disrupted, and the land suffered. And I was powerless to stop it."

I feel a pang of sadness in my chest, knowing that the Order that I have grown up with is not what it once was. "What can we do to restore the balance?" I ask the Sylvariel, hoping for some guidance.

The old druid smiles at me. "You are already on the right path, Faelyn. You have a connection to the land that is rare among our kind. You listen to the spirits and seek balance. Instead of following the path the Lunar Grove as instructed, you chose your own path and found me. That is what the Druidic Order was meant to be."

I feel a sense of pride at his words, but also a weight of responsibility. "But what about the Druid's Oath?" I ask, remembering the vision I had of the Elder Tree and the Oath I was meant to take.

The Sylvariel nods, "The Druid's Oath should come naturally, Faelyn. It is a commitment to the land and the spirits, a promise to uphold balance and harmony. It cannot be forced or manipulated. It must come naturally."

"But how can I do that alone? And I left pilgrimage to warn the King and I can't even get there."

The Sylvariel nods in understanding, "You are not alone, Faelyn." He turns to Aiden and Glimmereth with a knowing smile. "The spirits have shown me a vision of your

Druid's Oath, and it will bring together those who seek balance and harmony. It will come naturally to you when the time is right. And together, you will save the Elder Tree and restore the balance to the land."

I'm shocked by his words, feeling a sense of awe and wonder and fear. "How can you be sure that this vision is true?"

The Sylvariel smiles, "I have learned to trust the spirits and the ancient teachings of the Groves. And I have faith in you, Faelyn. You are the key to restoring the balance and healing the land."

A sense of determination is growing within me, as I know that I have a duty to fulfill. "I will do my best to honor the true meaning of the Druid's Oath and restore balance to the land." I look to my shoulder and wonder if the Sylvariel can see Moonbean, my half-dead, ill-enchanted sprite.

The Sylvariel seems to sense my thoughts and gently touches my shoulder. "Moonbean is under the control of Malvolia," he breathes, "but I don't think he knows it. He was somehow chosen to become your spirit guide, not to guide you, but to sabotage you."

My heart sinks as I look at Moonbean with fresh eyes, realizing that he's never seemed right. "Can you fix him?"

The Sylvariel nods, "I will do my best. It won't be easy, but with your help, we can break the enchantment and restore Moonbean to his true self." He turns to Glimmereth and hands him a small glowing orb.

With outstretched hands, Glimmereth can't seem to contain his excitement. "The Lunar Infuser!"

"Help us banish the darkness from the Lunar Grove and the trinket is yours." The old druid looks at Moonbean and says, "We will use it to heal Moonbean."

I watch in amazement as Glimmereth takes the Lunar Infuser and holds it up to the light.

"What does it do?" I ask the Sylvariel.

"The Lunar Infuser is a powerful artifact that can harness the energy of the moon," he explains. "It can remove enchantments and heal the spirits of the forest. With it, we can restore Moonbean to his true self."

I feel a glimmer of hope and gratitude towards the Sylvariel. I'm amazed by the story of my family's history. It's strange to think that the man sitting in front of me was the original druid, and that my mother exiled him from the Druidic Order.

The Sylvariel's voice breaks me from my thoughts, and he speaks with a sense of reverence. "Things were different back then," he begins, his words carrying the weight of ancient memories, "but now we must focus on the present.

The realms are in danger, and we must do all we can to save them."

My curiosity intensifies, and I lean in, absorbing his words. "What do we need to do?"

The Sylvariel raises a weathered hand, pointing toward my shoulder where Moonbean rests. "We need to break the spell on Moonbean," he states, his eyes locking onto the tiny guardian spirit. He then turns to Glimmereth, who hands him the Lunar Infuser, a delicate and intricate artifact that shimmers with celestial magic.

We gather around, creating a circle in the heart of the moonlit clearing. The forest holds its breath as the Sylvariel raises the Lunar Infuser high. An ethereal, radiant energy surrounds us, humming with an otherworldly power. The trees' leaves rustle in response, creating a soft, eerie melody.

The Sylvariel begins to chant in a language I've never heard before, the words weaving a tapestry of magic that envelops us. His voice grows louder and more urgent, resonating with the very spirit of the forest. I feel a deep connection with the natural world around me, as if the ancient trees themselves are listening.

Moonbean stirs on my shoulder, his tiny body quivering as the enchantment is challenged. He grunts and moans as if in pain, his tiny form wracked by the spell that has ensnared him. My heart races, and I'm unable to move, gripped by a mixture of fear and hope.

The fire flickers, casting dancing shadows upon the clearing. The world around us blurs, leaving only the Lunar Infuser in sharp focus, an anchor in the mystic storm. The ritual consumes my senses, and I become acutely aware of each breath, each heartbeat.

A brilliant burst of moonlight radiates from the Lunar Infuser, bathing the clearing in a celestial glow. It's an awe-inspiring sight, like witnessing a piece of the moon itself. Moonbean's agony intensifies, and he releases a piercing scream that shatters the stillness of the forest.

Time seems to blur as I watch in trepidation, questioning whether the ritual is unraveling the enchantment or worsening Moonbean's plight. The Sylvariel's unwavering incantations, however, serve as a soothing balm to Moonbean's torment.

As quickly as it began, the ritual ends. Moonbean falls silent, his once tumultuous body now motionless. Panic surges within me as I hold my breath, fearful of what's to come. Yet, against the backdrop of my dread, I detect a gentle rise and fall of Moonbean's tiny chest. With a triumphant chirp, his eyes regain their spark, and his body vibrates with newfound vitality.

Relief washes over me, tears of joy threatening to spill from my eyes. Moonbean's healing is swift, showcasing the power of Sylvariel's ancient magic. It highlights the unbreakable bond between a guardian spirit and the everlasting enchantment of the forest.

Moonbean hums with happiness, dancing on my shoulder as if a great burden has been lifted from his tiny form. I can't help but feel an overwhelming sense of gratitude toward the Sylvariel for his help. While I watch Moonbean's joyful dance, our connection deepens, moving beyond mere words to a profound understanding that resonates in my very soul. Memories of one of Moonbean's earliest communications flood my mind: 'I haven't been captured in a thousand years; I dance my days away in the forest.' Now, I can see the truth of his words as he gracefully sways on my shoulder, completely lost in the moment of pure bliss.

The Sylvariel places the Lunar Infuser back into Glimmereth's waiting hands and turns to me, his face serious. "We have much to do, Faelyn. The darkness is spreading, and we must work quickly to stop it. Are you ready to continue your journey?"

I take a deep breath, feeling giddy at what just happened, but for whatever reason, the Sylvariel doesn't allow me this joy. "Yes, I'm ready."

"There is something you must know, Faelyn," he says gravely. "The darkness that threatens our land is not just a force of nature or the result of some malevolent being. It is something far more insidious, something that has been growing for years right under our noses."

My mind races as I listen to his words, wondering what kind of dark force could have been lurking in our realm for so long, with no one noticing. My thoughts drift to Malvolia, but he knows about her already, so I ask. "What is it?"

The Sylvariel takes a deep breath and looks me straight in the eyes. "It's the Druidic Order, Faelyn. They have been corrupted by the very power they swore to protect, and now they seek to use it for their own gain. They are the ones behind the darkness, and they will stop at nothing to achieve their goals."

I stare at him in shock, unable to believe what I'm hearing. The Druidic Order, the very organization that I had always thought of as my family, my heritage, my legacy. Is now the enemy?

"Your mother was right to exile me," the Sylvariel continues. "She saw the signs of corruption in the order and knew that I would never stand for it. Now, it falls to you, Faelyn, to stop them. You are the only one who can."

With those words, he turns and disappears into the forest, leaving me with the weight of his words and the knowledge that the enemy I must fight is the very organization I had always thought of as my own.

I stand there, stunned, trying to process everything the Sylvariel has just told me. The Druidic Order, my family, corrupted? Despite seeming impossible, I trust the Sylvariel had a valid reason for saying such things.

Aiden places a comforting hand on my shoulder as we stare at the forest's edge. "What are we going to do?"

I take a deep breath, rooting myself for what lies ahead. "We have to keep moving," I say firmly. "We can't let them succeed in their plans. And somehow along the way, we must heal the ferryman and warn the King before Malvolia can get to the Lunar Tree."

"What about the Tournament?" Aiden asks looking down at his shabby clothes. "If we win, we can ask the King for anything. I bet there's a handsome reward."

"Coin is useless if we're overrun by demons and a corrupted Druidic Order." I think of what the Sylvariel said and how the order may be connected to Malvolia. But my mother banished her—how is it all connected?

Glimmereth nods in agreement, his determination shining through. "We have the Lunar Infuser, and with it, we're..." he sniffs it. "SO POWERFUL."

Then, something unusual happens in my mind, not conveyed through words but emotions. I glance at my shoulder, where Moonbean continues his joyful dance. Without any spoken communication, he conveys to me the idea of venturing into the forest to find the Sylvariel, while instructing the others to rest.

I acknowledge Moonbean's unspoken advice with a determined nod. "Let's take a break before we set out."

Aiden and Glimmereth make themselves comfortable near the fire, lying on some old leather hides. Meanwhile, I venture into the forest in search of the Sylvariel.

21

The Ancient Way

I FOLLOW THE SYLVARIEL into the forest, my heart pounding with anticipation and fear. The darkness looms, and I know I must do everything in my power to stop it. I'm just uncertain how. I see a glimmer of light ahead, and know it's the Sylvariel, meditating under the trees.

As I approach, I see he's surrounded by a glow of fireflies, their wings fluttering softly in the night. Even as I near, the fireflies don't seem to care. The forest is alive with the sounds of crickets and the rustling of leaves, and I can smell the earthy scent of the trees carrying in the breeze. I think back to the day I left Willowbrook and how Guro and my father had us release the fireflies and I have mixed emotions. Is what the Sylvariel is saying true or is he full of troll dung?

I approach the Sylvariel, and he greets me with a serene smile, his eyes glimmering with ancient wisdom. "Welcome, Faelyn," he says, his voice carrying a mystical undertone. "Are you prepared to let go?"

Although I have been meditating for years, his offer intrigues me. I nod hesitantly, wondering what secrets the Elder's meditation holds that I have yet to uncover. The Sylvariel seems to sense my apprehension and re-assures me with a gentle smile. "The way of the Elder's meditation is not just different, Faelyn, it's a gateway to the very essence of the Groves themselves. Letting go will connect you to the elements in ways you have never imagined."

As he guides me through the meditation, I realize he was right. This is unlike anything I have ever experi-enced. With each breath, I connect more deeply to the earth, the trees, and the sky. Roots stretch from my feet and anchor me to the soil, and I'm enveloped in a radiant white light, pulsing with ancient power.

As I delve deeper into the meditation, I see things that were previously hidden from me. The forest fairies, once mere glowing orbs, come into sharp focus, and I can see their intricate features and the magic they weave. The leaves of the trees come alive, rustling with secrets that only the ancient forest can tell. I feel interconnect-ed with the forest, it is intertwined with my being. It's like the 'spirit sight' of the Order, but I didn't have to meditate for four straight days to see it. And what I'm seeing now is more vibrant, more real.

While we meditate, the Sylvariel imparts a profound understanding of the original druidic magic, the ancient power that has existed in our world since time immemorial. His words weave a vivid tapestry of knowledge, unraveling the secrets of the magic circles and their practical applications.

"These circles are not just ancient; they are vessels of immense power," he begins, his voice carrying the weight of countless generations. "Bestowed upon us by the Groves in the dawn of time, these circles are the conduits to nature's primal forces, to the very essence of the elements."

He proceeds to illuminate the distinct purpose of each circle, articulating how they can harness the intrinsic power of nature.

He first introduces the Circle of the Sun, a ring of magic that taps into the life-giving energy of the sun. "This circle," he explains, "channels the sun's radiant power, embodying warmth, light, and vitality. With it, you can heal, invigorate, and strengthen. It rejuvenates and breathes life into all it touches."

As he tells me about each circle, I delve deeper into meditation. My breath slows and my roots deepen.

Then, he proceeds to the Circle of the Moon, where the magic connects with the celestial body's energies. "The moon," he elucidates, "is the realm of intuition, wisdom, and enigma. This circle attunes us to the moon's energy, enhancing our intuitive capabilities, deepening our wisdom, and linking us to the mystical aspects of the cosmos."

He follows with the Circle of the Stars, attuned to the brilliance of distant celestial bodies. "The stars," he describes, "represent guidance, hope, and wonder. With this circle, you can draw on the star's energy, seeking guidance in the darkest of times, igniting hope, and fostering a sense of wonder."

To my surprise, he goes on to reveal three more circles of magic. The Circle of the Land channels the power of the earth, forging a connection with the natural world. "This circle," he clarifies, "draws on the earth's energy to cultivate crops, heal the land, and commune with the creatures dwelling within. It forges a profound bond between druid and nature."

Then, the Sylvariel introduces the Circle of the Witherbloom, a powerful yet perilous circle that balances the forces of death and rebirth. "With 'wither' and 'bloom' intertwined," he warns, "it is a circle that demands caution and prudence. However, it signifies the eternal cycle of death and rebirth. Through decay and dissolution, new life emerges. This circle initiates change, transformation, and the release of the old, paving the way for fresh beginnings."

Finally, he speaks of the Circle of the Infernal Grove, a circle that weaves connections to the inferno and the underworld. "This circle," he solemnly concludes, "establishes a bridge with the spirits of the infernal realm, allowing us to harness their formidable but perilous powers. Yet it must be invoked with great care, for the infernal forces are not to be trifled with."

As the Sylvariel's teachings unfurl, I begin to comprehend the profound nature of these circles, their capabilities, and the immense responsibility that comes with wielding such ancient, elemental magic.

Then it hits me, so I ask. "Why does the Druidic Order only focus on the circle of the land now and not all the magic circles you speak of?"

The Sylvariel smiles tenderly and nods, understanding my question. "The Druidic Order once focused on all the circles of magic," he begins. "But over time, as the world changed and the darkness grew stronger, the focus shifted towards the circle of the land. It was deemed the most practical circle in the fight against the darkness." He pauses for a moment, his expression turning serious. "But I believe that it's important to remember and understand all the circles of magic, Faelyn. The different circles complement each other and can be used together to achieve greater results. The circle of the land may be the focus of our efforts, but it's not the only circle that holds power."

I nod, understanding his point. The power of the Druidic Order lies not just in the mastery of one circle of magic, but in the understanding and use of them together.

"The circles of magic are ancient, but are not static," the Sylvariel continues. "They can evolve and adapt to new situations, and it's up to us to explore and experiment with their potential. The future of the Druidic Order may lie in the rediscovery and mastery of the other circles of magic." He breathes deeply, then adds. "But what do I know? I'm a relic who spends most of his days listening to birds in my hidden hut."

I snort, and he lets out a chuckle.

When we finish laughing, I remember the question that had been lingering in my mind. "Sylvariel, can you tell me more about the significance of ravens in druidic lore?" I ask tentatively. "I keep seeing a white-headed raven and am wondering what it means." At that, several ravens suddenly leap from their perch and fly into the night, their shadows exaggerated by the full moon.

He looks at me with a twinkle in his eye. "A white-headed raven, you say?"

I nod.

The Sylvariel's expression becomes solemn as he thinks about my question. "Ravens have a long and storied history in druidic lore," he begins. "They were sacred birds and often associated with the goddess Morrigan, who was known for her prophetic abilities and her connection to death and rebirth." He takes a deep breath before continuing. "Your mother, Faelyn, was a powerful druid, but she also had a fear of death and the unknown. She believed that ravens signaled the approach of death or tragedy, and this fear colored her perception of these birds."

I feel a pang of sadness as I think about my mother and her fears. "Is there more to the story of ravens in druidic lore?" I ask, wanting to know more.

The Sylvariel nods. "Yes, indeed. Because of this fear of death, and her possessive love for you, she banished the ancient ways and only accepted the more conservative views of druidic magic."

"So, because of me, the way of the Druidic Order was tarnished?"

"It's not your fault." The old druid sighs. "A mother's love is a powerful thing. And when you have a powerful mother, with a powerful love, she would pull the roots from the Elder Grove itself if it would protect you."

It's like my whole reality shatters in a matter of hours. From surrounding the fire and listening to the Sylvariel talk about the ancient order, to Moonbean, and now my mother.

I sense my grandfather patiently waiting for me to digest this latest revelation about my mother before he continues. I can sense he's about to reveal something larger. "Ravens were also associated with the concept of transformation and change. They were thought to possess the ability to guide lost souls and to act as messengers between the world of the living and the dead. In some cultures, they were even considered shape-shifters, able to take on different forms and travel between worlds." He looks at me, his eyes shining with a knowing wisdom. "The truth is, Faelyn, that the meaning of symbols and signs is not always clear or straightforward. It's up to us to interpret their messages and meanings based on our own experiences and understanding."

Speaking of messages reminds me of the ring. Fear grips me because I know that when I grab it, I'll unleash whatever vision it has in store for me so I instead tell my grandfather about the ring, and how I found it fighting a Wailwraith, and how we tried to use it in a healing touch ritual but somehow botched it. Then I ask, "What is it?"

The Sylvariel's eyes sparkle as he hears about the ring. "The ring is a portal to the Defiled Realm, Faelyn," he says, his voice wise and knowing. "It allows you to see what is coming, like a messenger. It is not a bad thing, but a warning."

I draw back, expecting a very different reaction.

The Sylvariel notices my surprise and explains further. "The Defiled Realm is a place of darkness and corruption, but it is also a place of immense power. It is said that those who can harness the magic of the Defiled Realm can achieve incredible feats of transformation and shapeshifting."

"That's dark magic." I say, fear setting in.

"Not if used with good intention." He pauses for a moment before continuing. "In fact, the ring is likely connected to a ritual that can help you learn shapeshifting, Faelyn. It is a difficult and dangerous practice, but one that has been mastered by many druids throughout history. And if properly done, can wield powerful results."

This new information leaves me with more questions, so I ask, "But where did the ring come from? How did it end up guarded in a cave with a Wailwraith?"

The Sylvariel's face grows thoughtful as he considers my questions. "It's difficult to say for certain, Faelyn, but I believe it was placed there intentionally by someone within the Order. The Wailwraiths should not be able to manifest on the Ageless Isles, so it's likely that someone summoned it there specifically to guard the ring."

"So I'm dealing with a summoner." I pause and suddenly realize I only know one summoner. "My father." I exclaim.

He pauses again, his expression growing more serious. "Your father is a good man. I knew him well. He would not do this. Not willingly, anyway. As for why someone would want you to find it, that is a question we may not be able to answer. But whoever left it there must have had a reason, and it's up to us to determine what that reason might be."

"So, can you shapeshift?" I ask tentatively.

His response is an uncanny flash of moonlit luminescence within his eyes, a subtle glint reminiscent of the moon's glow, and a sly wink. My heart quickens in anticipation of his answer. Yet, before words can form in reply, an extraordinary transformation overtakes him.

The body of The Sylvariel undergoes a transmutation, transforming into a stunning white-headed raven, radiating beauty under the moonlight's shimmering glow. As he extends his newly formed wings, a rush of wind brushes against my face, carrying with it the scent of freedom, as he effortlessly soars into the nocturnal sky. As I observe his ascension into the inky abyss, the realization dawns on me with startling clarity.

Could it be? Was this grand, mystical creature the very same white-headed raven whose presence had graced the woods of Willowbrook, foretelling the impending changes? The connection to my father, the cryptic message, the enigmatic circumstances—everything appears intricately woven, and I am at the epicenter of it all, with the Sylvariel as my guide.

22

The Unexpected Savior

As I MAKE MY way to camp, Dawn's Blossom turns to Morning's Call and brings a pink hue to the sky, casting a blanket of color throughout the meadow. Butterflies are taking their early morning flight, the baby birds are calling for their mothers and I even spot several ravens and I wonder if one isn't the Sylvariel.

Glimmereth yawns and stretches his tiny arms, giving his head a shake awake, his jeweled ears jingling and his golden curls shaking. He stamps out the fire and heads off into the forest in search of a patch of berries he said he spotted yesterday.

Aiden calls out as he packs the bedroll into his travel pack and slings his lute onto his shoulder. "Where have you been?"

Aiden listens intently as I recount my conversation with the Sylvariel and the revelation about my mother's past. He nods thoughtfully as I describe the history of the ancient druids and their mastery of the different circles of magic.

"Wow, that's incredible," he says, his mouth agape. "And the ring is a portal to the Defiled Realm? That's some powerful magic."

I nod, still processing all the information I learned. "He told me druids can shapeshift. He said there's a ritual, but I never thought that was possible."

Aiden looks at me, a mix of curiosity and excitement in his eyes. "Shapeshifting? That's amazing! What did he say about the ritual?"

"He didn't go into too much detail, but he mentioned it involved connecting with the spirits of nature and the animals, and using their power to help me transform," I reply, trying to recall everything the Sylvariel had said.

Aiden grins, his fingers tapping eagerly on his lute. "That sounds like something I would love to see. I bet you'll be a little white wolf. When do you think we can start?"

Just as I open my mouth to reply, a sudden flutter of wings interrupts us. I look up to see a raven perched on a nearby branch, its eyes fixed on us with a piercing gaze. As I watch, the bird floats to the ground and suddenly transforms into the form of the Sylvariel, his ancient face creased with a smile. "Greetings, young ones," he says, his voice carrying on the morning breeze. "I trust you slept well?"

Aiden and I exchange surprised glances before greeting the Sylvariel in return. "I did, thank you," Aiden replies with a grateful smile.

Now that the Sylvariel is back, I ask my question. "Was it you in the forest that day I hunted for the sprite?"

The Sylvariel nods solemnly. "Yes, it was." He says. "I was trying to warn you, but the dark magic that surrounds you prevented me from reaching out to you."

I feel a pang of guilt for not listening to the warning sooner, then I realize something. "Wait. When we first met, you acted like you didn't know us?"

The weight of the Sylvariel's hand on my shoulder grounds me in his presence. "Do you think you'd have listened to me if I told you from the getgo that I was your grandfather, young Faelyn?"

I shake my head but am annoyed he didn't tell me sooner. I reflect back to all the times I asked questions, and he revealed hints of who he truly was.

He then tells us that before we venture into the Hinterlands, he must heal my wound and remove the dark magic from the ring. "I have gathered the special herb we need for the ritual," he says. "We will use the Lunar Infuser to cleanse the ring and your body."

Aiden and I nod in agreement. "Thank you, Sylvariel," I say gratefully. "We are in your debt."

The Sylvariel grins warmly. "Think nothing of it, my dear," he says. "That's what family is for."

With that, he walks northward towards the Hinterlands. He calls back, "We have a day's walk before we reach the edge of the forest. There, we'll stop and perform the ritual before moving through the forest."

As we journey northward, the atmosphere is one of enchantment and wonder. The sun is shining high in the sky, casting a warm glow over the rolling hills and bubbling streams we pass by. The air is fresh and fragrant, filled with the sweet scent of wildflowers and the earthy aroma of the forest. My step is buoyant and I dash ahead of everyone else, merrily scattering the resting butterflies in my wake. Glimmereth leaps and bounds trying to catch one, and Aiden guffaws as he swallows one, claiming it may have ruined his voice. But I only laugh and dance, mirroring Moonbean, who is now doing the jig on my shoulder.

We trek through sunken valleys, where the sides are steep and green, and the ground is covered in a carpet of spongy moss. Water trickles down from the top of the cliffs, creating a peaceful background noise that blends with the chirping of birds and the rustling of leaves. The sound of the water echoes around us, creating a natural orchestra.

The Sylvariel talks about the Elder Druids and their connection to the spirit world. He tells me it is not natural to tether a spirit guide to oneself, and that it is not the ancient way to do so. When he removes the dark magic from my arm and the ring, it is my choice to release Moonbean from his duties. He explains that the Druidic Order did that to ensure a connection to the spirit world, but it is forced and not natural. "The ancient way of connecting to the spirits of nature and the animals is through patience, respect and communication," he says. "It is not about control or tethering them to us. It is a mutual partnership."

I nod, taking in his words. "I understand," I say. "But what about my mother? She was a druid, and she had a spirit guide."

The Sylvariel sighs. "Your mother was a powerful druid, but she was also misguided," he says. "The Druidic Order has lost its way, and it is up to the younger generation to rediscover the authentic way of the druid."

As we emerge from the valley, we find ourselves in open plains, where the grass stretches as far as the eye can see. The wind rushes through the tall blades, creating waves that ripple like an endless sea. In the distance, we can see herds of deer grazing tranquilly, their gentle forms silhouetted against the golden sun.

The peaceful atmosphere is interrupted by Aiden and Glimmereth's argument. Aiden argues the dwarves are the ones responsible for the war in Emerald Reach, while Glimmereth believes humans are to blame and that the dwarves deserve the gold and riches they have claimed. I roll my eyes because I've heard this argument a hundred times. Their voices grow louder and more heated as they continue to argue, and I can feel the tension rising between them.

Suddenly, the Sylvariel speaks up. "Young ones, listen to me," he says in a calm and measured tone. "Let me tell you a story, a Tale of Two Brothers."

We all fall silent. I'm intrigued by the Sylvariel's words but both Aiden and Glimmereth stand with their arms crossed with questioning looks on their faces. "These two brothers lived in a beautiful kingdom, where gold and riches were abundant," he continues. "The older brother was a dwarf, and he loved nothing more than to mine for gold and jewels. The younger brother was a human, and he was a skilled craftsman, creating exquisite items from the treasures his brother mined."

Aiden interrupts, "Humans and dwarves are not related. The women have beards." He shudders.

The Sylvariel smirks. "I listened to your love song for Faelyn and even sung the last chorus. The least you could do is pay me enough respect to listen to my tale."

Aiden flushes and mutters under his breath, but won't make eye contact with me.

The old druid smiles and continues. "For many years, the two brothers lived in harmony, sharing the wealth of their kingdom. But one day, the older brother felt that he was entitled to more. He believed that because he was the one who mined the gold, he should have a greater share of it. The younger brother disagreed, believing that they should continue to share the wealth equally. But the older brother was stubborn, and his greed clouded his judgment. He took more than his fair share, hoarding the gold and jewels for himself."

"You're just recounting the current war between the two nations but adding that they're siblings." Glimmereth interrupts.

The Sylvariel smiles, "Indeed, young one. The story may sound familiar, but it holds a valuable lesson nonetheless."

Glimmereth scoffs. "We don't have siblings, so we Glimmersprouts are without war."

"Are you not at war right now?" The Sylvariel corrects.

Glimmereth glares at Aiden and steps further away from him. "He's not my brother."

"Is he not your brother in arms?" The Sylvariel chides.

Glimmereth huffs. "Fine. I won't interrupt again."

The Sylvariel nods. "As for the Glimmersprouts, you may not have families in the traditional sense, but you are still raised with a unique bond to your surroundings. You are taught to respect and care for the forest, and to use your abilities to help protect it. You are raised to understand that you are a part of something much larger than yourselves, and that your actions can have a significant impact on the world around you."

Aiden nods in agreement. "It's a shame that dwarves can't seem to understand that same principle," he snarks.

Glimmereth snorts in disagreement. "It's not just the dwarves, humans have been pillaging the earth and claiming it as their own for centuries. The dwarves were just defending what rightfully belongs to them."

The Sylvariel holds up a hand to quiet the argument. "You both have valid points, but you are also both in the wrong. The truth is that no one owns the land. We are all merely stewards of it. The land, the trees, the animals, they were all here long before any of us, and they will be here long after we are gone. We must learn to live in harmony with it, to respect it and care for it, and not see it as something to conquer or own."

We all fall silent, taking in the Sylvariel's words. The wind continues to rush through the grass, and the herds of deer continue to graze undisturbed. It's a moment of stillness and reflection that I know will stay with me for a long time.

The Sylvariel breaks the silence just at the right moment and continues his tale. "The younger brother was hurt and angry, feeling that his hard work and craftsmanship were being overlooked. He plotted his revenge, determined to get back what he believed was rightfully his. Eventually, the two brothers went to war, each fighting for what they believed was their birthright. The kingdom was torn apart, and in the end, neither brother could claim victory. They both lost everything, including their brotherly bond."

The Sylvariel's words hang heavy in the air as we all contemplate the tale. It's clear that Aiden and Glimmereth have been foolish to argue over who is to blame for the war in Emerald Reach. Both sides have their grievances, but in the end, everyone loses.

The Sylvariel continues. "It's easy to assign blame and point fingers, but it's much harder to come to a peaceful resolution. We must learn to listen to each other and work together, even when it seems impossible. Only then can we truly find peace."

Aiden and Glimmereth nod in agreement, and the tension between them dissipates. I think of Neason when I look down and my cloak blends in with the field grass, camouflaging me as I walk. We were so rude to one another, as we battled our way to the Lunar Grove. But in the end, it was Neason and Barlan who stayed with me while I was at death's door. I owed him better than that. We continue our journey through the Ageless Isles, the Sylvariel's words weighing heavily on our hearts.

The vast plains gradually yield to dense woodlands, where colossal trees reach for the heavens themselves. Our journey continues along a clearly marked path that meanders through the woods, the tree branches overhead converging into a verdant canopy that offers welcome respite from the sun's warmth. The harmonious rustling of leaves plays like a soothing melody, accompanied by sporadic snaps of twigs succumbing underfoot, forming a symphony of nature. I now chuckle at Moonbean, not because of his drunkenness, but because of his mirth and the sheer delight his dancing brings him. It becomes increasingly clear that his dances are intricately entwined with the natural world, as if his movements possess the uncanny ability to converse with our immediate surroundings.

As we enter the meadow, the Sylvariel suddenly stops in his tracks, his eyes scanning the horizon. "We're approaching the edge of the Hinterlands," he says. "Be on your guard, for danger lurks in these woods."

I scoff at his words. "I've been through the Hinterlands before on my own. I can handle whatever comes my way," I say confidently.

The Sylvariel's expression turns grave. "Yes, but at that time, you were veiled, and therefore protected from the dangers that lurk in the Hinterlands. Now that the veil has been lifted, you are vulnerable to the dark magic that permeates these woods. And with Malvolia's influence growing stronger, the danger is greater than ever."

I shrug off his warning, remembering my promise to Barlan and to Neason. "I'll be fine," I say dismissively. "We've wasted enough time. I need to tell the King about the evil so we can stop it."

The Sylvariel sighs. "Very well, but remember what I said. The Druidic Order's way of tethering the spirit guide is not the ancient way, and the protection it offers is false. You must be careful."

With that, we continue on our way, walking deeper into the Hinterlands. The atmosphere grows more ominous, with the trees growing darker and the air growing colder. My bravado fades, and I feel a sense of unease. I glance over at Aiden, who looks just as on edge as I am. I lament,

"Maybe we should be cautious, like you said." I plea to the Sylvariel.

"We must cleanse the ring before it can befoul you again." The Sylvariel commands.

"Why didn't you say so earlier?" I cry.

"This is your path Faelyn. I am only here to advise you."

Aiden rushes to my side. "Something doesn't feel right. You should do it now." He looks to the ever darkening skies as Glimmereth catches up to us.

"There is dark magic here." He exclaims, pulling at my trousers and scouring the surrounding forest.

"Fine. Let's do it." I say.

The Sylvariel points to a clearing ahead of us. "There in the clearing. Follow me."

As we round a bend in the path, a figure materializes before us. It's the wraith that I had encountered before, its form writhing with dark magic. I draw my staff, ready to defend myself, but the Sylvariel steps forward and raises his staff. "Return to the Infernal Gateway!" he commands in a booming voice, and the wraith recoils, unable to withstand the power of the Sylvariel's magic.

I stare at the Sylvariel in awe, realizing for the first time the true extent of his power. He turns to me, a stern expression on his face. "This is the danger that I warned you about," he says. "That ring is like a beacon to the Foresaken."

I feel a mix of embarrassment and frustration. "But I banished the wraith already," I protest. "With echoes of the ancients, it should be gone."

The Sylvariel shakes his head. "The Wailwraith is bound to the ring. Unless I cleanse it, the wraith will continue to stalk you. You must learn the ancient ways, Faelyn, and not rely on the false protection of the current Druidic Order."

I nod, absorbing the magnitude of the situation. "I'm sorry. Let's cleanse the ring."

The Sylvariel nods approvingly. "Good. You have potential, Faelyn. But you must be careful, for the darkness in these woods is strong, and it can easily corrupt even the most powerful magic."

With a heavy sigh, I try to regain my composure, preparing for the arduous task ahead. A whirlwind of emotions churns within me - anger at my gullibility, fear for what lies in store, and a profound sense of sorrow. The knowledge of being ensnared by deceptive druidic teachings plagues me, as it feels like a cruel illusion to have spent a lifetime learning them. My gaze narrows at Moonbean, whose ceaseless dance on my shoulder serves as a constant reminder of my past folly, a sorrowful testament to the time when he was nothing more than an ill-tempered, intoxicated sprite. And now, as a blissful dancing idiot, what purpose does he serve me other than my own narcissistic pursuit of my Oath?

The Sylvariel shifts his focus to Glimmereth, his eyes filled with a glint of urgency. "Glimmereth, can you work your magic to veil us from the wraith's sight?"

Glimmereth responds with a resolute nod, his incantations resonating with power as his hands trace intricate patterns through the air, seamlessly weaving his illusions into existence.

Aiden takes out his lute and plays a haunting melody, his voice adding to the strength of the illusion. As I watch in amazement, the world around us shimmers and distorts, creating a new reality that conceals us from the wraith's sight.

Once the illusion takes full effect, the Wailwraith screeches with rage gliding around us, searching for its lost prey. The illusion won't last forever because already the wraith has caught our scent and is circling us, trying to discover a weakness of our charm.

The Sylvariel takes out the Lunar Infuser, and I hold out my arm, feeling a tingle of magic as he removes the darkness from my wound. I watch as the ring glows with a bright light, and I feel a sense of relief as the darkness is lifted from it as well. But as the ritual ends, there is a sudden shift in the air.

The illusion falters, and a heavy, ominous atmosphere settles in as the wraith's presence intensifies. "We have to leave," I shout, but the Sylvariel shakes his head.

"I have to lift the curse," he says, his voice tense.

I feel a chill run down my spine as the wraith appears before us, its eyes glowing with malevolent energy. We are trapped, with no escape from its wrath.

Aiden steps forward, his nimble fingers strumming the lute. "I'll switch songs and try to charm it rather than strengthen the illusion," he says, his voice trembling slightly.

Glimmereth calls out as his intricate illusion crumbles around us. "I can't hold it." The wraith turns its gaze on us, and I feel a surge of fear.

The Sylvariel raises his staff, his eyes blazing with power. "Stand back," he commands, and we move away as he unleashes a torrent of magic at the wraith with one hand while lifting the curse with the other. But it's not enough.

The wraith's dark energy seems to swallow up the Sylvariel's magic, growing stronger with each passing moment. Aiden's song falters, and Glimmereth's illusion dissolves like a mirage.

We find ourselves exposed and achingly vulnerable. The wraith, a specter of malevolence, readies to strike. It's a breathless moment, the air thick with anticipation, when suddenly, from the very shadows that threatened to engulf us, a cloaked figure emerges. A sense of déjà vu washes over me; I've seen this enigmatic figure before, but this time, with the snap of her fingers, she radiates a searing brilliance of energy, slamming the wraith backward, a symphony of rage and torment. In that piercing light, the figure steps forth, unveiling a face that's been our greatest dread—Malvolia herself.

Her voice, smug and chilling, slices through the tension. "Fortunate, indeed, that I arrived just in the nick of time," she sneers, her smile bearing the weight of ancient grudges. "But make no mistake, this is no act of benevolence. You and your pitiful companions remain staunch enemies of the state, and my intervention is merely a matter of convenience. Cross me, and you shall still taste the bitterness of my wrath."

I exchange a bewildered glance with the Sylvariel, who mirrors my astonishment. Rescued from certain doom by our most formidable adversary, I can't help but tremble under the weight of the unknown price she wants in return.

23

Faelyn's Oath

A SINISTER CHILL SWEEPS through the air as Malvolia draws near. The darkness thickens around us, a smothering cloak of malevolence. Her eyes shimmer with an ominous energy that sends a shiver racing down my spine. It's evident that she wields immense power, and she flaunts it with a mere flick of her fingers. The Hinterlands' forest edge quivers with dread and trepidation. Trees twist and extend their gnarled limbs like nightmarish talons, and impending danger looms with an eerie swiftness.

My heart skips a beat when Malvolia addresses the Sylvariel as 'Father.' The revelation staggers me. The Sylvariel's reaction mirrors my astonishment, his eyes narrowing at her.

"You have no right to call me that," he retorts, his voice chilling and his posture rigid. His age shows more now than ever.

Malvolia's laughter ripples through the forest, a haunting resonance. "Oh, but I do, dear father," she taunts, punctuating 'father' with a malevolent grin. "Or have you forgotten that I am the fruit of your liaison with a demon?"

The Sylvariel's features twist with anger, but he holds his tongue. The tension between them is palpable, the weight of their shared history casting a pall over the once-illuminated woods.

"She was a succubus who deceived me. Why are you here?" the Sylvariel demands, his voice low and bristling.

Malvolia's expression turns solemn. "Oh, dear father," she lingers on 'father.' "Do you not love me? Your infidelity made me the one and only Auroriel, and it's a rather lonely existence." Her intricate silver jewelry glimmers in the moonlight, each piece adorned with a unique symbol etched into it, some featuring obsidian the shade of her eyes.

The Sylvariel winces at her words but remains silent. Abruptly, he shouts at her, his voice filled with pain and anger. "You're an abomination, and the day you killed your sister, both of my daughters perished."

Malvolia's smirk vanishes, replaced by an austere demeanor. "I've come for what's rightfully mine," she declares, her eyes gleaming with avarice. "The power of the Lunar Grove. I've lured you here, dear father, to wrest it from your grasp."

I gasp, my realization of the looming danger cutting through the tension in the air. Malvolia, my mother's banished sister, seeks not only revenge but also the annihilation of the Groves. My worried glance finds the Sylvariel, and in our exchange of looks, we both share an unspoken question: How will we stop her?

Malvolia's eyes dart toward me, and her lips twist into a wicked grin. "And has this naïve little rat realized you're her grandfather yet?"

The Sylvariel steps forward, positioning himself protectively in front of me, shielding me from Malvolia's gaze. His gaze, however, stays locked on her. He whispers to me, his voice a hushed plea, "Leave now and don't look back."

I retreat a step, my heart racing. This is the same aunt my mother never spoke of, the one whose name was whispered only in the darkest corners of our family's history. And now, she stands before me, emanating an icy darkness that seems to swallow the very forest around us. The hairs on my neck bristle, and a chill snakes down my spine, but I won't flee. I can't leave the Sylvariel to confront her alone.

"Moonbean, protect us," I implore, but he either doesn't hear or doesn't care as he continues his unending jig on my shoulder.

Suddenly, Malvolia springs into action, her hands morphing into jagged claws as she lunges toward the Sylvariel.

He counters her assault just in time. An inferno blade materializes just beyond his outstretched hand and propels towards Malvolia like a flaming arrow. But with a flick of her wrist, it bursts into a cloud of ash, harmlessly dissipating. She cackles, "Is that the extent of your abilities, old man?"

The Sylvariel's eyes flare with fury, and he raises his staff, invoking the power of the forest. A lightning bolt crackles through the air, colliding with Malvolia's chest amid a deafening burst. She staggers backward, surprise flashing in her eyes, briefly rendering her vulnerable. But then, she utters Darkwyrds, and a tempest of ash erupts from the ground, enveloping her. When it disperses, inky blackness has devoured her eyes, as she releases the Curse of Exhaustion on the Sylvariel. I watch in horror as a tide of dark energy engulfs him, sapping his strength and vitality. The Sylvariel's body quakes, and he clutches his chest, gasping for breath. His complexion turns ashen, his eyes, once full of life, now appear dull and lifeless.

The trees around us mournfully groan, their leaves rustling in a lamenting chorus. Malvolia's curse seems to infect the very heart of the forest, darkening its core. The Sylvariel wavers, his legs trembling as he fights to remain upright. His once-steady hands tremble with fatigue, and his staff falls to the ground with a dull thud. Fear becomes visible in his eyes, and I realize that we are in grave peril.

Malvolia's malevolent smile deepens, and she takes a step forward, her power tangible. She is like a predatory creature meticulously toying with its prey, awaiting the opportune moment to strike.

Aiden unslings his lute and prepares to strike a chord, but Malvolia fixes him with a sinister glare and laughs. "Foolish boy, you're no match for me." She flicks her wrist, and Aiden is sent hurtling, crashing into a tree with a sickening thud. His lute tumbles to the ground beside him, and in a disconcerting transformation, his lips and mouth vanish, leaving only smooth skin. He has been silenced. His eyes betray terror as he thrashes uncontrollably on the ground.

I am torn between helping Aiden or the Sylvariel, but Glimmereth is already at Aiden's side. Rage envelops the tiny Glimmersprout, and he propels himself toward Malvolia, cursing her in his native tongue. Landing before her, he conjures an illusion, momentarily causing Malvolia to stumble back, swatting at something that isn't there. However, she quickly regains her composure, swiftly clapping her hands together, causing Glimmereth to be engulfed in ash. He rubs his eyes frantically, struggling to clear his vision, but to no avail. Running in circles, he stumbles and falls, his fate mirroring Aiden's as he is rendered powerless.

Before I can decide, the Sylvariel hobbles in front of me. The air hums with energy as Malvolia unleashes another surge of dark magic. I close my eyes, bracing for the inevitable impact, but then I feel a warm energy enveloping me. Upon opening my eyes, I find the Sylvariel standing protectively in front of me, arms outstretched, eyes locked on the impending blast.

A shimmering green shield appears before us, intercepting the onslaught with a thunderous explosion. The shield flickers and crackles but remains steadfast, safeguarding us from the lethal attack.

I watch in awe as the Sylvariel's druidic magic courses through the shield, siphoning the shadowcraft away from us and into the earth below. His face contorts with exertion, sweat cascading down his brow, but he stands resolute, determined to shield me from harm. The wrinkles on his ancient face deepen, and the longer he holds the shield, the more he seems frail. The curse still courses through him. I need to act.

Placing my hand on the Sylvariel's shoulder, I summon the forest's strength to augment his magical shield; I look to the clouded sky and plea for light, reinforcing it with vitality and vigor. As the enhancement takes hold, I feel the dark magic pummel us, and I collapse, unable to sever my connection. My focus rests on the forest, drawing its energy and channeling it toward the Sylvariel.

He turns to me, his eyes dull. "Are you okay?" he inquires, his voice laden with worry, his stance faltering. Malvolia's curse has taken a heavy toll. He appears pallid and emaciated, drained of life.

Malvolia's triumphant gaze finds mine, filling me with dread. I realize that the battle is far from over, and she is consumed by a relentless determination for revenge. Her eyes penetrate mine, and I become ensnared in a malevolent magic I cannot see.

Once more, she utters Darkwyrds, and the crushing pressure of her words ensnares me, clouding my thoughts with relentless and violent visions. I am unable to shake them. Grief and confusion muddle my mind. I cannot comprehend what is happening, and a sense of helplessness consumes me.

Abruptly, the shield vanishes with a soft pop, and the Sylvariel collapses. I crawl toward him, my movements slow and labored. Malvolia advances on the fallen druid, and I am powerless to stop her. I cry out, paralyzed, barely able to move, my gaze locked on the unfolding tragedy.

Malvolia raises her hand, unleashing a formidable blast of black magic that hurtles toward the Sylvariel. I scream in terror, but before I can reach him, the Sylvariel raises his hand, and a radiant green shield materializes before him. The blast strikes the shield, rebounding harmlessly and dissipating into the air.

For a moment, it seems as though the Sylvariel has a fighting chance, but Malvolia acts swiftly. She amplifies her dark magic, causing the shield to splinter under the strain. The Sylvariel clenches his teeth, his face etched with determination as he struggles to maintain the shield, but it proves futile. The barrier shatters into a million fragments, and the dark magic blast hits him squarely in the chest.

The anguish and agony in his eyes is palpable as he is propelled off the ground, writhing and convulsing in pain. Malvolia relishes his suffering, her eyes gleaming with a sadistic and twisted delight. The Sylvariel's body collapses to the earth, his eyes closed and his chest still. In that moment, I know he has been claimed by a vengeful daughter.

Malvolia approaches me, ready to utter Darkwyrds, when Moonbean leaps into the air, forming a brilliant bubble around me. The radiance blinds Malvolia, who screeches in agony and vanishes into the night. Moonbean's top hat settles as he dances lightly on my shoulder once more. I am left alone beside my fallen grandfather. Desperate attempts to revive him prove futile, and the darkness that surrounded us has claimed him.

As I kneel beside him, a sense of defeat washes over me. I realize my responsibility, a solemn Oath to uphold the memory of the Sylvariel and safeguard the Lunar Grove, as well as all Groves threatened by encroaching darkness. I will stop at nothing to thwart Malvolia's ambitions and protect those I hold dear. The battle may be lost, but the war is far from over.

As if preordained by fate, the words of the Sylvariel resound in my thoughts, a binding and solemn druidic Oath emerging organically, a testament to our unending struggle against the encroaching shadows.

24

The Tribute and the Troll

I'VE BEEN CRYING ALL night, through the Moon's Blessing and into the Dawn's Bloom, while Moonbean flutters on my shoulder, a tiny beacon of happiness amid my grief. His playful dance seems out of place in this solemn moment, but I can't bring myself to release him. We've been through so much, surviving the darkness that has claimed so many others.

Aiden kneels beside me, a silent comfort as I weep for the Sylvariel. The pain of my loss is a heavy weight on my chest, making it hard to breathe. When Malvolia fled into the night, she left a trail of destruction and heartache in her wake.

Aiden places his hand on my shoulder and mumbles something, but cannot speak. Aiden's touch on my shoulder is a small anchor in the storm, and I wipe away my tears to give him a sad smile. I try not to stare at his shapeless mouth, muted from Malvolia's shadowcraft.

Glimmereth calls over from the makeshift campfire beside us, "We should eat and be on our way."

I shake my head. "I have to honor him. Send him off proper."

Glimmereth shuffles over and offers. "We Glimmersprouts honor our dead by song and dance and offerings."

I nod. "We Wood Elves do the same." I look around for a proper resting place, and then I see hundreds of ravens perched on a lone tree standing in the meadow on the outskirts of the Hinterlands.

"I think I've found the perfect spot," I say, pointing to the tree. "The ravens can carry him to the afterlife."

Aiden nods in agreement, and we gather offerings to place around the Sylvariel's body.

As we gather the offerings, I feel a deep sadness welling up inside me. Losing the Sylvariel is not just a personal one, but a loss for our entire druid community, even though he'd been banished. He was a wise and respected elder, and his passing leaves a void that can never be filled.

I search through my belongings, hoping to find something special to offer as a tribute to his memory. After rummaging through my pouch, I find a small acorn that I had picked up during our night of meditation. It had reminded me of the Sylvariel's deep roots and love for nature.

I gently place the acorn beside his body, feeling a small sense of comfort that I have contributed something special to honor his memory. We continue to gather more offerings, ranging from flowers to feathers, and small trinkets that held personal significance to each of us.

As we place the offerings around the Sylvariel, Glimmereth sings a haunting melody, his voice filled with sadness and grief. Aiden joins in, his voice lost but his heart full of emotion. I join in too, my voice choked with tears, as we continue to sing and dance around the Sylvariel, paying our respects and sending him off to the afterlife with love and honor.

As we finish our tribute, the ravens gather around us, their dark feathers contrasting with the morning glow of the sun. Moonbean flits over to the Sylvariel and whispers something in his ear, before dancing his way back to me.

"It's time," I say, and we watch as the ravens pick up the Sylvariel's body and carry him up into the sky. We watch as they disappear into the distance, our hearts heavy with grief and loss.

But as we turn to leave, I can feel the Sylvariel's spirit hovering around us, his presence reassuring and comforting. And I know that even though he's gone, he'll always be with us, guiding us on our journey and protecting us from the darkness that surrounds us.

I turn to Moonbean and say. "You're free to go, my friend. I release you. The Sylvariel said it was unnatural to have you tethered to me, so you are free to go." I shoo him away playfully but with sorrow as a tear streaks down my face.

Moonbean hops off my shoulder and hovers in front of me, looking at me with his bright blue eyes. He gives me a bow before flying off into the forest, free at last. Aiden and Glimmereth exchange skeptical glances as they watch Moonbean disappear into the trees.

Aiden mumbles something, raising an eyebrow. I can't make out much, but it sounds a lot like, "Are you sure that was the right thing to do?"

Glimmereth mocks Aiden, "Aren't familiars supposed to stay tethered to their masters?"

I feel a pang of sadness as I realize my companions don't understand the Sylvariel's wisdom, so I explain, "Moonbean was never meant to be bound to me. The Sylvariel said it was unnatural. Moonbean is a guardian of the forest, and he deserves to be free."

Glimmereth nods in agreement but Aiden still looks unconvinced. But I know in my heart that I made the right choice. As we walk away, a sense of peace washes over me. I know that the journey ahead will be difficult, but with the

Sylvariel's spirit watching over us we have no choice but to move forward.

I sweep ahead northward, intending to stop Malvolia.

Aiden races beside me and points to his mouth area and mumbles something inaudible. I assume he's asking me to break the spell, but all I can do is shrug. "I do not know how to remove a dark spell that's made you mute."

Glimmereth speaks up, "I've heard of a rare flower that grows in the mountains said to break any silence spell. It's called the Whispering Bloom."

I turn to Glimmereth, surprised at this new information. "There are mountains northeast of us."

"It's dangerous in the mountains," he warns. "But if we're going to stop Malvolia, we'll need Aiden to speak again."

I nod in agreement. "Then we have no choice. We have to find this Whispering Bloom."

Glimmereth points to distant grey mountains on the horizon. "I bet there's Whispering Bloom in those mountains."

I squint my eyes, searching for answers in the mountains' depths and nod in agreement. "Those are the mountains I was talking about. The Grey Mountains."

We march for a day and night before reaching the foothills of the Grey Mountains. The landscape of the foothills is barren, with only a few sparse trees and patches of yellow grass dotting the rocky terrain. The ground is rough and uneven, making our journey slow and difficult.

Glimmereth points to a worn mountain path and says, "Whispering Bloom will grow on high ground or in dark places. Let's follow the path to higher ground."

As we climb higher, the air grows thinner, and the sky darkens. We hear the distant howls of wolves and the occasional screech of an owl, but other than that, the mountain is eerily silent. Aiden and Glimmereth grow increasingly nervous as we move further into the highlands.

Suddenly, we hear a loud rumble, and the ground shakes beneath our feet. Glimmereth gasps, "An avalanche!" and we scramble for cover, hiding behind a massive boulder as rocks come tumbling down the mountain.

When the rumbling subsides, we emerge from our hiding spot, shaken but unharmed. We continue up the mountain path, that is now covered in a layer of rubble, wary of any other dangers that may come our way.

As we approach a bend in the path, I notice a strange smell in the air. It's a sickly sweet scent, like decaying flesh. I tighten the grip on my staff as I realize that something is not right.

Holding my hand up to stop the others, I whisper, "Do you smell that? Something's not right."

We cautiously move around the bend and come face to face with a dark and rotted wooden frame leading into what appears to be an abandoned mine. The stench is even stronger here, and I can see a trail of black, sticky goo leading into the mine.

My hands shake as I say, "We should turn back. This place gives me the creeps. Last time I went into a cave, I was attacked by a Wailwraith."

But Glimmereth hops excitedly and says, "That's where we can find the Whispering Bloom flower. It also grows in dark places."

Aiden looks at me with desperation, his eyes pleading with me to help him. He mumbles through his closed lips, "I'b nothig 'ithout by boice." I can see the pain and frustration etched on his face, and my heart breaks for him. I remember my Oath to protect the Lunar Grove and the creatures who live there, and I know that if Aiden needs his voice to save the Grove, then I must help him get it back.

I take a deep breath and creep into the mine, full of renewed vigor. As I turn the corner, I stumble to a stop, frozen in fear. Suddenly, we hear a muffled gurgling sound coming from deep within the mine. Glimmereth whispers urgently, "That sounds like a Rocktroll. We'll have to be careful."

My heart races as I whisper through gritted teeth, "Rocktroll!" I peek around the corner and see a massive Rocktroll snoring loudly. Beside it are smoldering embers set in the center of the cavern. The air is thick with the stench of death, and scattered around the cavern are bits of bones and carcasses of long-dead animals. My eye is drawn to the corner of the cave where I see a strikingly blue flower emitting a gentle glow. It's the Whispering Bloom, and aside from the embers, it's the only light in the cavern.

Thinking quickly, I look down at my cloak and when I do; it blends into the rock wall beside me. "I have an idea," I whisper to Glimmereth. "Stay here." And with that, I creep further into the cave. I hope to sneak by the Rocktroll and pluck the Whispering Bloom flower in the corner of its cavern.

As I make my way towards the Whispering Bloom, I step tentatively, trying not to rattle the bones scattered on the floor, and my hands tremble with anticipation. The blue petals glow with an eerie luminescence against the dim red glow of the embers, casting an otherworldly aura around it. The scent of the flower fills my nostrils, overpowering the stench of decay, and I'm overwhelmed by a sense of awe at its beauty.

Suddenly, I hear a deep rumble, and the ground shakes. My heart leaps into my throat as I realize that the Rocktroll has awoken. With a thunderous roar, it rises from its slumber, and I freeze in place, hoping against hope that it won't notice me. Its massive frame fills the cavern, and its rough, rocky skin glistens in the faint light.

I hold my breath as the troll sniffs the air, and its beady, golden yellow eyes shoot open, searching for the disturbance. My heart races as it lumbers towards me with a menacing growl, revealing a cavernous maw jutted with razor-sharp teeth that glimmer like knives in the dim light. Its skin is rough and scaly, resembling the texture of weathered rock. The creature's massive arms sway heavily at its sides, rippling with muscle, and I know that I'm in trouble.

In a desperate attempt to defend myself, I reach out with my magic and summon a gust of wind. The embers of the fire swirl around the cavern, and the troll howls in pain as they burn its face. Its massive arms swing blindly, pounding the surrounding walls, and I take advantage of the distraction to grab the Whispering Bloom and make a run for it.

Bones and debris scatter under my feet as I sprint towards Glimmereth and Aiden. The troll's heavy footsteps echo behind me, and I know that we're not safe yet. I can hear its ragged breathing and the thudding of its footsteps getting closer and closer. But then I see a faint glimmer of light up ahead, and I push myself even harder.

As I burst into the daylight, I hold up the Whispering Bloom triumphantly. "I got it," I say, gasping for breath. "Let's get out of here before that troll catches up to us."

With Aiden and Glimmereth leading the way, we race down the mountain path. My heart pounds in my chest as I glance over my shoulder, expecting to see the Rock-troll chasing after us. When we reach the bottom of the path, we race north, putting as much distance between us and the troll as we can. Finally, when I'm certain that we're far enough away, I skid to a stop and catch my breath.

"That was a close one." Glimmereth declares.

I nod in agreement and hand him the Whispering Bloom. "How do we cure Aiden with this?"

Glimmereth takes the flower carefully and scrutinizes it. "It's said that the petals must be ground into a powder and then brewed into a tea. The drinker will then speak their true name and their voice will return."

Aiden looks hopeful as Glimmereth prepares the tea. I watch as he carefully grinds the petals and boils the water. "That's like a tincture I make from the Yarrow." I say.

Glimmereth nods. "We Glimmersprouts and you druids have a lot alike." As he adds the petals to the boiling water, the aroma of the Whispering Bloom fills the air. It smells sweet and delicate, with a hint of spice.

Aiden watches intently as Glimmereth stirs the tea and pours it into a small cup. "Here you go, Aiden," Glimmereth says as he hands him the cup. "Drink this and speak your true name."

"True name?" I question.

Glimmereth nods. "This is a powerful concoction."

I turn to Aiden and realize something, then I blurt out. "He has no mouth. How's he supposed to drink this?"

All three of us stare at one another.

Glimmereth scratches his head, his golden curls bouncing as he does this. He looks down at the cup in Aiden's hands, then back at me. "I'm stumped."

"What if we rub it on his..." I look at his lipless mouth and say, "where his lips used to be?"

Glimmereth shrugs. "Could work."

I dip my finger into the hot tea and rub slowly rub it onto Aiden's smooth skin. We lock eyes and I lean in closer. I'm lost in his gaze for far too long, and then it happens. Suddenly I'm lost in blackness, unable to move or speak, and then images appear before me. I see the Sylvariel, but only much younger, he's with a beautiful woman and they're locked in an embrace. She's cooing in his ear and looks like Malvolia, only different, older maybe. It must be her mother, the succubus.

Something is wrong and her form changes and morphs, but my grandfather doesn't notice. He's captivated by her. She writhes on him, her hips seductive and suddenly her form changes, and the woman on top of him looks like my mother but only older. I try to focus but I can't, and then it hits me; the succubus is pretending to be my grandmother. The realization sets in. My grandfather had two daughters with two women. And he didn't realize it.

The vision is suddenly gone, and I collapse to my knees. Glimmereth and Aiden are both by my side and I hear them calling out to me. I hear Aiden calling out to me. I look to my side and Aiden is there with a wide smile. "That was amazing." He points to his fully formed, beautiful mouth, his voice musical, then he turns solemn, "Are you okay? What happened?"

I dive at him and try to hug the life out of him. We crash to the ground and roll several times until I'm on top of him and we share an embrace. "I missed your voice."

He stares up at me, obviously shaken, unable to speak.

"This is the first time you've been speechless without the help of magic." I tease as I rub my finger against his lush bottom lip.

Glimmereth clears his throat. "Uh, you're welcome for brewing the potion."

I remember Glimmereth and push myself up, red in the face. "Sorry. I'm not sure what came over me."

Aiden brushes himself off and stands beside me, his face flushed and he has trouble making eye contact. "You collapsed again. Another vision?"

I look down at my travel sack where the ring is buried and know that it wasn't it that gave me the vision. My grandfather had cleared it of dark magic. "Malvolia's mother was a demon. A succubus that tricked him into thinking she was my real grandmother. They had a baby out of wedlock and that was Malvolia."

Aiden walks over to his lute and snatches it up from the dirt and strings it on his shoulder. "This is like one big, weird family reunion."

"What does it all mean?" Glimmereth says, leading the way northward, up and over several heavyset boulders anchored on the mountain.

Suddenly, Aiden clears his throat and speaks, "My name is Aiden Moonwhisper."

I march over to Aiden. "I thought your last name was Goldenstring?"

"I know." Aiden declares, a look of both worry and confusion setting in. "But that isn't right."

Glimmereth shuffles over to us. "It's the Whispering Bloom. I said it's powerful stuff. Clears all kinds of clutter in the mind."

"But why is his name suddenly changed? What does that have to do with anything?"

Glimmereth thinks for a minute before answering. "It's a calling, not an actual name change. It reveals purpose, if you will."

Aiden taps his lute restlessly. "I happen to like my name." He wraps his knuckles on his lute. "It was the perfect name for a bard who plays the lute." He raises his eyebrows as if that will change things.

Glimmereth wags his finger at Aiden. "Don't look at me like that. I just helped you get your voice back and gave you new skills."

"New skills." Both Aiden and I ask.

"Yeah." Glimmereth says haughtily. He swipes the cup of tea from Aiden and takes a swig. "Whispering Bloom unlocks hidden potential. If you have any talents not yet declared, they present themselves to you and boom. You have a subclass."

"A subclass." I scoff. "A druid is a druid. I'm not going to change into a druid bard, am I?" My voice squeaks.

Glimmereth laughs. "Not unless you have a hidden talent for singing." He looks at me sympathetically, "Which you don't."

Aiden chuckles.

"We need to move. Let's walk and talk." I say, ignoring their joke.

As we walk, Glimmereth explains the Whispering Bloom potion some more and tells me that my visions were the first hidden talent to present themselves, and that although Aiden's presented itself as a name change, the talent would probably make itself known soon enough.

"So, what's your hidden talent?" I ask Glimmereth.

He sniggers. "I'm not sure yet, but it might take some time for us Glimmersprouts. We have a very strong immune system and things don't affect us like it does with you elves and humans." He falls behind and continues talking to himself, explaining the history of Glimmersprouts, their heightened immune system, and how they don't really have a nation and are more prone to wander the lands looking for adventure.

Aiden walks beside me and whispers. "What happened between us back there?"

I flush. "I was just happy to hear your voice." I lie.

He shoots me a questioning look. "So we're good then?"

I nod and hurry my steps, hoping the conversation will end. "Maybe it was the vision or the Whispering Bloom or a combination of everything that's happened so far." I try to explain my outburst away.

"Your right. We need to focus on the Grove." He nudges my shoulder and grins. "I've heard about the others in lore but have only seen the Witherbloom Grove. Are they all the same?"

"You've seen a sacred grove?" I exclaim, surprised that he's seen one.

"Of course. The Witherbloom Grove is on a small island south of my castle in the Emerald Cove. We used to travel to it all the time. We'd have picnics there."

"Blashphemy."

"It is not." He scoffs. "We respected the grove. We just don't think of it the same way you do."

"Well, when we get to the Lunar Grove we will not have a picnic."

25

A Deceptive Melody

THE SERENE PINE FOREST engulfs us, the towering trees filtering the sunlight to create a dappled effect on the soft bed of pine needles crunching underfoot. The sweet aroma of pine and damp earth fills my senses, and the distant babbling brook adds to the peaceful ambiance. But the calm is short-lived as Aiden and Glimmereth's argument reaches a boiling point, and I can feel my patience waning.

We bicker about the best plan to safeguard the Grove, and I assert that my magic is the strongest. I explain I will summon the spirits of the forest and the ancient guardian of the grove to aid us, and with Aiden's charm and Glimmereth's illusions, we can create a convincing distraction that will allow me to strike a deadly blow against Malvolia and her demon army.

However, Aiden and Glimmereth strongly disagree. "Absolutely not," Glimmereth counters. "I hate to brag, but I am definitely the most powerful one here."

Aiden scoffs. "I could make you think you're a rabbit, hopping around the forest all day." Before Glimmereth can retort, Aiden sings a hypnotic tune, and Glimmereth mindlessly smashes into a nearby pine tree.

I growl, "Enough! Stop it, both of you!"

Glimmereth leaps to his feet and storms over to a laughing Aiden, who raises his hands mockingly, as if he fears the tiny Glimmerspout. "Ooh, don't flash a bright-ish light in my eyes, making me mildly unconfortable, you tiny imp."

Glimmereth glares at Aiden and rolls up his sleeves as his eyes bulge and a tiny vein throbs on his forehead, threatening to burst.

Aiden backs away, almost tripping himself up, a sudden fear stricken look taking hold. "Woah, easy now, big guy."

In one smooth motion, and in a flash, the tiny Glimmersprout grows ten feet and morphs into a massive Rocktroll and roars at Aiden, covering him a torrent of sticky slobber. Aiden falls on his ass and tucks into the fetal position and screams. "Don't eat me!"

I stumble back, grab my staff and cast Shillelagh. The end of my staff hardens like ironwood. "Back off, you troll." I gasp.

Suddenly the massive Rocktroll shrinks back into the tiny Glimmersprout and he stumbles around, mumbling to himself.

Aiden and I exchange surprised glances, then I say. "Are you alright Glimmereth? Is that really you?"

He nods as he places his tiny hands on his head and says, "Oh, my aching head."

"Are you a changeling?" Aiden asks as he stands and dusts himself off. He grabs his lute and slings it over his shoulder.

Glimmereth shakes his head no, then it turns to a yes and back again until he's just bobbing his heart-shaped head in circles. "Stop it, you're going to make yourself sick." I say.

He walks over to me and leans on my leg. His hand just over my knee. "That Whispering Bloom is powerful stuff."

"Can you change into anything you want?" Aiden asks with genuine curiosity.

Glimmereth shakes his head, then can't seem to stop his whole body from trembling. His knees are rickety, then with each passing second they knock together more vigorously until he falters and tumbles over.

I bend down and sooth him. "Just lay for a while." I brush his golden curls from his forehead.

He nods and closes his eyes. Within minutes, his eyes flash open and he bounds to his feet and I stumble back but steady myself immediately. "That was fast."

Glimmereth gives a wide smile and shakes his ears so they jingle. "My hidden talent presented as acute transmorphation."

Aiden scoffs. "A cute what now?"

Glimmereth annunciates. "Acute trans-morph-ation."

"Meaning?" I ask.

"I'm able to transform into shapes or beings that I've recently come into contact with. But with a price." He rubs his forehead, "As you just saw, the transformation takes a toll on you, and from what I've heard, side-effects may include physical exhaustion, temporary loss of memory or identity, and a heightened vulnerability to certain types of magic."

"So you're a changeling, like I said." Aiden brushes by Glimmereth, shaking his head, and stalks off northward.

Our progress is slowed by both Aiden and Glimmereth, who are not as agile as I am. My keen eyes and nimble feet easily navigate the debris and fallen logs, but Aiden is clumsy and Glimmereth small and unable to scale the rugged terrain as easily as I can. Glimmereth's constant chatter behind us explaining how he's not actually a changeling, but sort of is, grates on my nerves so I hurry along and scout far enough ahead that his chatter is only a whisper.

As we move through the rocky terrain, my mind wanders to the upcoming battle. We need a plan to take down Malvolia and her army of demons. The rocky terrain turns to lowland forest, and then suddenly I'm blasted with an icy coldness that engulfs the forest. Snow's falling and crunching under my steps. I still can't understand the weather patterns of the Hinterlands.

As I march northward, I'm finally at peace, and able to think because the constant chatter from Aiden and Glimmereth has ceased. I glance back to make sure Glimmereth and Aiden are still following me, but they are nowhere in sight. They're probably stopped up, arguing again. I call out to them, but there's no answer. I storm back with balled fists, ready to thrash them when I find them, but when i storm far enough that I should see them, panic sets in as I realize we're alone in enemy territory. What if something has happened to them?

I grip my staff tightly and run, hoping to glimpse them unharmed.

As I sprint through the icy forest, icy sweat drips from my forehead. The ground beneath me is uneven, and I stumble over jagged rocks and upturned roots.

My breathing becomes ragged, and my muscles ache with exertion, but I keep running. Suddenly, I hear a noise up ahead. I slow down, and crouch behind a tree and peek through the leaves. I see a group of demons marching in single file, their eyes glowing red with malice. These differ from the others. They have leathery wings and razor-sharp claws and are covered in a hellish, smoldering fire. As they walk, they burn the ground beneath them, leaving a trail of cinder and smoke. I watch as they pass by, staying hidden until they're out of sight.

I leap from the bush and I continue to run, my mind racing with thoughts of how to fight a demon that smolders with hellfire. One touch and I fear my leathers would either melt or go up in flame. My thoughts are interrupted as I hear a loud growling sound. I pivot and see a massive demon looming over me. It's covered in black, matted fur, blending into the surrounding shadows, and its skin looks tough and leathery, as if it's been exposed to constant battle. Its eyes glow with a malevolent red light, seeming to look straight through me. The creature's mouth is filled with razor-sharp teeth that gleam menacingly in the dim light. It snarls at me, saliva dripping from its jaws. This is some kind of massive Shadow Beast.

I prepare to fight, but suddenly, I hear a high-pitched laugh. I see Glimmereth appear, perched on the demon's shoulder. Aiden is nowhere to be seen. With a wave of his hand, Glimmereth transforms back into himself, the

Shadow Beast disappearing. "Had you scared for a second."

I falter but stay silent, still reeling from the encounter.

He tells me he had to transform into one of them to hide from the Hellfire demons marching a circle around the Grove, and that the forest is teaming with all kinds of demons. "Aiden is scouting ahead, looking for a way to flank the enemy."

I shake my head, frustrated with their lack of caution. "I could have killed you Glimmereth. You need to be more cautious." I pull him behind the tree and whisper urgently, "Shh, we need to stay hidden until we find Aiden, but we have to keep moving." Glimmereth nods, still looking confused. We move again, creeping deeper into the forest and away from the Hellfire demons. But with Aiden missing, I know our plan to protect the Grove is doomed to fail. We need to find him, and fast.

As we continue through the forest, I keep an eye out for any sign of Aiden. But the dense foliage, snow storm and ever growing drifts, make it difficult to see very far ahead. Glimmereth stumbles behind me, so I slow my pace to help him along. "Are you okay?" I ask him, concern lacing my voice.

He nods weakly. "I think so. Just a little dizzy. Do you think Aiden is okay?"

"I don't know," I admit. "But we have to keep moving. Where did you last see him?"

Glimmereth points to where we came from, determination in his eyes. "He scouted ahead when the fire demons marched by."

"We should have found him already," I say, and we continue on through the forest. But the longer we search for Aiden, the more hopeless it feels. The sun is setting, Dusk's Ember turning to the Evening's Serenade, but something is wrong. The forest is eerily silent, as if it's holding its breath in anticipation of what's to come. My stomach growls with hunger, and my legs ache with exhaustion. Just when I'm about to give up, I hear a faint sound in the distance.

It's the sound of a lute being played. My heart leaps with hope, and I run towards the sound. Glimmereth follows close behind me. As we get closer, I can see Aiden sitting on a fallen log, snow piling on his tussled brown hair, strumming his lute and singing softly to himself.

He looks up as we approach, a surprised expression on his face. "What are you guys doing here?" he asks, his eyes dull and grey.

"We've been looking for you," I say, out of breath.

"I've been here the whole time." He says with a blank look on his face.

Glimmereth and I exchange worried looks. I pivot several times, scouting the surrounding area, scrutinizing for a trap or an ambush but find none. I cautiously pad over to Aiden to get a closer look at him.

As I approach him, I notice something off about him. His eyes are glazed over and unfocused, and there's a strange energy emanating from him. "Aiden, are you okay?" I ask, placing a hand on his forehead. "You're burning up."

Aiden's unsteady steps lead us deeper into the forest, his erratic movements growing more pronounced. The air thickens with foreboding, as if the very atmosphere resents our presence. Glimmereth leans into me and whispers, "Something's wrong with him."

"I can see that," I retort, my heart hammering in my chest. A chill races down my spine, an unshakable unease tightening its grip on my core. The forest feels like it's closing in on us, its ancient trees now lurking giants, their branches menacingly outstretched.

"Maybe he's leading us to what hurt him," Glimmereth suggests, his voice trembling with concern.

"Maybe it's a trap," Glimmereth's worry tugs at my trousers. I brush him off and rush to Aiden's side. Each step feels like a descent into an abyss of dread, the weight of uncertainty growing heavier with each passing moment. I grip his shoulder and twist him to me and plea. "What is wrong with you."

Aiden's convulsions intensify, and I leap back, unable to tear my eyes away from the nightmarish transformation. His body contorts, twisting, and bending in grotesque ways. It's as if his very essence is being consumed by darkness. The forest, once a sanctuary, seems to moan in sympathy, its towering sentinels bearing witness to this unholy metamorphosis.

Glimmereth and I, unprepared for such a horrific sight, fumble for our weapons, our breaths ragged with fear and disbelief. Aiden, or what used to be Aiden, is now a demon of pure malevolence.

The demon's body is a grotesque tapestry of nightmare, its form twisted and misshapen. Its eyes, once warm and inviting, now radiate malevolent energy that pierces through the dim forest. The demon's gnarled hands end in elongated claws, its skin sickly and covered in veins that pulse with dark magic.

The very ground beneath us quakes with the weight of the moment, as if nature itself mourns the loss of our friend. Glimmereth's voice trembles as he whispers, "What in the name of the ancients has happened to him?"

I have no answer, for my own heart is heavy with a sense of impending doom. The transformation we witness is a chilling revelation of the twisted power that Malvolia wields, a power that has turned our friend into a creature of the abyss. We've found Aiden, but the cost is a chilling discovery—a new and terrifying threat lurking in the heart of the Hinterlands.

26

Forged in Ice

As THE ICY DEMON writhes as if in pain, a torrent of emotions surges through me. My heart races with fear and disbelief, and a profound sense of loss grips my soul. Aiden, my friend, who was once full of warmth and laughter, now stands before us as this grotesque manifestation of darkness. My eyes lock onto the demon, and I struggle to come to terms with the nightmarish transformation that has overtaken him.

I cry out in a voice laced with anguish, "What is this thing?" It's a question that reverberates with the weight of our shared horror and the sinking realization that our reality has been irrevocably altered. I can barely stand to look at the abomination before us.

The ice demon is a horrifying sight to behold. It looms over us like an ancient nightmare, its towering frame reaching at least ten feet in height. Its body is a twisted amalgamation of flesh and ice, and its very presence chills me to the bone. Razor-sharp claws extend from its fingers, poised to rend us apart, and its jagged, icy teeth gleam with a malevolent hunger.

The demon's skin is a deep, otherworldly shade of icy blue, encased in a layer of frost that glistens ominously in the faint light. Its eyes are piercing and hypnotic, like twin abysses that threaten to consume all that is good and pure. An aura of sheer malevolence exudes from it, hanging heavy in the air, as if the very world recoils from the darkness it embodies.

Glimmereth's voice, heavy with dread and knowledge, reaches my ears as he answers my question. "It is an ancient creature, born of the coldest, darkest depths of the world." His words only deepen the despair within me, as I realize the enormity of the foe we now face.

The demon's leathery wings, tattered and frayed, bear the scars of countless battles. I can see its powerful muscles rippling beneath its thick hide, a testament to the strength of the evil that has overtaken it.

Then, with a sickening lurch of my heart, the demon charges at us with lightning speed. Its claws slash through the air, a terrifying symphony of death. I dive to the side, narrowly avoiding its leathery wings, but the reality of the situation is inescapable. I must confront Aiden's transformation head-on, a friend turned into a nightmarish creature of the abyss. Glimmereth's desperate spells erupt in a cascade of light, but they merely dance impotently against the demon's impenetrable icy hide, angering the creature further.

In the face of this horror, my inner struggle intensifies. How can I bring myself to harm someone who was once a cherished companion? How do I find the strength to combat this malevolent entity and save what's left of my friend? All the while my heart aches with sorrow and my mind reels from the shock of it all.

My instincts take over as my mind reels. I dodge another ferocious attack from the ice demon. Fear and desperation grow like black knot, defiling my soul. How can we possibly defeat such a monstrous creature? Its sheer size and strength are intimidating, and that our magic seems useless against it only adds to the mounting sense of dread.

During our relentless skirmish with the demon, its malevolent aura intensifies, suffocating us like an ominous storm. Its eyes, like twin voids, bore into my soul, and I sense my focus slipping away, as if lured into a hypnotic trance. Each of my movements becomes an arduous chore, and my thoughts grow clouded, enshrouded in an unsettling haze. I duck and dodge it's strikes, but each one coming closer to taking my head off, and somehow, it's luring me to allow it.

As the demon's nefarious charm ensnares my senses, I teeter on the brink of surrender, lured by its sinister temptation. I inch forward, lowering my guard, falling deeper under its spell. It strikes again, and its claws graze my pauldron, knocking me to the ground. The world around me fades, and I nearly succumb to its beguiling embrace, poised to abandon myself to its malevolence.

Yet, before it leaps on me, a surge of realization pierces the ensnaring fog. I shake myself from the demon's bewitching grasp, my heart pounding with newfound clarity. An instinctive jolt of terror courses through me and I roll away violently before it's knee smashes into the ground where my head once was, missing me by a raven's feather. The demon's hypnotic cry threatens to enslave, to transform me into a puppet of its desires.

With gritted teeth and steely resolve, I pull away from the brink of capitulation, resisting the allure of malevolence. I vault into the air and strike it with my blackthorn staff, but it only dazes the creature fleetingly. As it regains its bearings, it swings at me with a torrent of violent strikes, but as I dodge and sway, my cloak, as if fueled by the surge of evil, wraps itself around me, defending me from the demon's fury. As I parry and roll, the cloak camouflages me, encapsulating me in its protective grasp. This angers the demon and it cries out in rage and the forest floor rumbles in its wake.

"Glimmereth, we need to be careful. This demon can charm," I shout, my heart pounding in my chest.

Glimmereth nods, his expression tense and focused. "I'll try to shield us from its charms with a barrier spell. But we need to be agile and stay alert," he replies, unleashing a burst of magic that envelops us in a protective barrier.

As we continue to fight, the demon's attacks become more ferocious and unpredictable. Its claws and teeth seem to be everywhere at once, it's strikes a blur of frosty shadow, and I can feel my energy waning with every passing moment. But then, just as it seems like all hope is lost, I notice a glimmer of weakness in the demon's defenses.

"Glimmereth, its hide is weakest around the joints! Aim for the knees!" I shout, pointing to a vulnerable spot on the demon's leg. "We need to break through its defenses," I say, panting from the exertion. It emanates a cold, otherworldly energy that bites at my skin. I can feel its icy touch devouring my mind, trying to persuade me to give up and surrender to its will. I know I must be careful, that I cannot let my guard down for even a moment, or it will be all over.

Glimmereth nods in agreement. "I'll try to confuse it with illusions while you focus on attacking its weak points."

As the demon charges towards us again, I summon the power of the earth and vines to ensnare its limbs. Glimmereth takes advantage of the opening and casts an illusion and another demon, one identical to the Shadow Demon, morphs into view and starts swinging at the original demon. Confused, the original demon lashes out, swinging at the illusion. I leap behind the demon, swing my staff with all my might and strike the demon's knee, shattering it into a thousand pieces.

Collapsing, the demon yanks out the entangled roots from the ground and stumps towards me as a grotesque clawed foot grows out of the shattered knee. I stumble back, raise my staff and summon the power of the winds to create a fierce gust that blows like a storm, slowing the demon in it's pursuit. Glimmereth unleashes a blinding flash of light, causing the demon to stagger.

"Now's our chance!" I shout.

I channel the fiery essence within me, invoking the power of flames that surge forth to enshroud the demon. The ice demon's chilling visage contorts with anguish as it howls in torment, its frigid veneer crackling and melting away in the searing inferno. Yet, even as it writhes and shrieks in pain, its malevolent core endures, unyielding to the scorching blaze.

In retaliation, the colossal demon pounds its massive claws into the earth, eliciting a violent tremor that reverberates through the very ground. From the epicenter of its furious strike, a barrage of glinting ice shards hurtles toward us. Glimmereth and I are caught off guard, thrown into a frenzied dance of evasion, narrowly avoiding the deadly hailstorm of razor-edged ice fragments.

With unyielding tenacity, I crawl over to Glimmereth who wheezes vigorously. "I'm running low on magic,"

"I'll cover you," I reply, clawing to knees.

Glimmereth nods, his expression twisted with a fierce determination that mirrors the intensity of our struggle. He hurls a relentless barrage of spells aimed at the demon's towering knees, each magical assault striking with searing force. The relentless fury of his magic causes the demon to stumble and falter, agony etched across its face. The scorching heat of Glimmereth's spells sears my skin as I surge forward, my battle cry ripping through the battlefield, borne of anguish and determination.

With every ounce of strength, I swing my staff, invoking the power of fire and earth to conjure a cataclysmic explosion that consumes the demon in a roaring conflagration. The very ground quakes beneath me, the earth's lament mingling with the inferno's deafening roar. The wails of the dying demon pierce my soul as the flames consume it, every fiber of my being aflame with anguish and fury. Pouring my entire reservoir of magic into the cataclysmic onslaught, I witness the demon's slow dissolution, its malevolent presence finally vanquished and extinguished, leaving behind only ashes and the anguished echoes of its torment.

Glimmereth and I collapse onto the ground, exhausted but victorious.

"That was Aiden." I whisper, my voice trembling as tears stream down my cheeks.

Glimmereth pants, "I can't believe he's gone."

We lay in silence for a moment, trying to come to terms with what had just happened. Aiden, our friend and ally, was just killed by the ice demon, or was the ice demon, I'm uncertain. It's hard to believe that someone I've become so close to is now gone. And I'm to do what now? Keep going?

"We have to keep going," Glimmereth says, breaking the silence. "We can't let his death be in vain."

"But how do we fight something that can take control of us and turn us into a demon at will?" I ask, thinking about the ice demon's ability to control our minds. "And could the ice demon charm us because Aiden was a bard?"

Glimmereth shrugs. "I'm not a demon scholar, but it would appear so. It seemed to harness his abilities. Maybe we can use some kind of barrier to protect ourselves from her Warlock magic."

"I know nothing of Warlocks magic." I admit, still trying to regain my breath.

Glimmereth's eyes twinkle with a hint of knowledge. "Warlocks, from what I've heard, strike pacts with high demons, gaining their dark powers in exchange for servitude or some other favor. These pacts twist and corrupt the magic within them, often allowing the warlock to wield spells that are both powerful and sinister."

I listen intently, wanting to understand more. "But what kind of magic are we talking about here? I've seen her snap her fingers and summon demons and disappear at will."

Glimmereth ponders for a moment. "Warlocks often dabble in curses, summoning malevolent spirits, and manipulating shadow and fire. It's said that they can twist the elements to their will, using them for both destruction and control."

I shudder at the thought of such dark magic and the formidable foe we face. "So, Malvolia's powers are derived from this demonic pact?"

Glimmereth nods solemnly. "It would seem so, and her powers may be unique to her particular alliance with the demon she made a pact with. We need to be cautious and learn as much as we can about her abilities to stand a chance against her."

"She mentioned her better half, Malathor." I explain.

Glimmereth sits up stark straight. "That's not good. That is the highest of High Demons."

We both stand up, determined to avenge Aiden's death and protect our world from Malvolia's wrath. But the weight of his loss hangs heavy over us. Two companions are dead in such a short amount of time. Fury grows in my belly and I'm worried it will consume the light.

"We head north. I'm certain the Lunar Grove is over the next ridge." I say.

Glimmereth nods in agreement and we set off, moving swiftly through the forest. The moon is high in the sky, casting a pale glow over the trees. The air is crisp and cold, and I shiver despite my layers of clothing.

As we approach the Lunar Grove, we see another ice demon standing at the entrance, its eyes locked onto us. But something is off. Its posture is different, less aggressive, and its eyes seem almost...sad? "Glimmereth, do you see that?" I whisper, pointing to the demon.

He nods. "It's almost as if he's waiting for us."

We cautiously approach the demon, ready for a fight, but he doesn't make a move. Instead, he speaks, his voice soft and almost...apologetic? "I'm sorry for what I've done," he says, bowing his head. "I was under a curse, and I had no control over my actions. Please, forgive me."

Glimmereth and I exchange a look, unsure of what to do. Could this really be the same demon that killed Aiden and attacked us earlier? But his words seem genuine, and his posture is submissive. Slowly, cautiously, we approach the demon, ready to defend ourselves if needed. But as we get closer, the surrounding ice melts, revealing a figure inside. It's Malvolia.

My heart skips a beat as I recognize the warlock. She steps out of the melted ice, her eyes cold and calculating. "You fool," she sneers, "did you really think I would let you get away with what you did to me?"

Glimmereth steps forward, his tiny fists balled and at the ready. "You're the one who cursed our friend into a demon," he accuses. "Why would you do such a thing?"

Malvolia laughs, a chilling sound that sends shivers down my spine. "Why? For power, of course. And revenge. Revenge against all those who have wronged me."

I feel a surge of anger and determination within me. This is it. The last battle. The fate of our world hangs in the balance. With a fierce battle cry, Glimmereth and I charge towards Malvolia, our weapons at the ready.

27

Chaos in the Grove

THE GROUND TREMBLES BENEATH us as Malvolia raises her hand, and the earth convulses violently. Trees are wrenched from their roots, and boulders tumble down the hillside. We stumble and fall, desperately struggling to keep our balance as the world tears itself asunder. Just as suddenly as it began, the shaking subsides, but the grove has already been scarred.

I look up to see Malvolia's calm expression twisted into a maniacal grin. "You do not know the power I possess," she cackles, her voice dripping with venom. "And you have no chance against me." With a flick of her wrist, she summons a legion of demons, who materialize from the shadows. Glimmereth and I stand our ground, determination etched on our faces as we brace for the battle of our lives.

Ash demons of all kinds rise from the ashen earth, taking shape before our eyes. Malvolia, with a snap of her fingers, vanishes into thin air. In the distance, I glimpse the towering Lunar Tree bathed in the moon's ethereal light. It's surrounded by seven smaller Willows, a stark contrast to the once-peaceful grove now ignited by a chaotic, raging battle.

The demons surge towards us, and Glimmereth and I charge at them, blades flashing and magic crackling. The Lunar Grove is our destination, and we strive to reach it as swiftly as possible. Glimmereth, a brilliant ball of light surrounding him, thwarts any demon foolish enough to approach. I follow in his wake, and together we carve a path to the Lunar Grove.

"Watch out." I call out to the glowing orb that is Glimmereth, but before he can adjust his path, a large ash demon swings a clubbed hand with a gnarly spike right into Glimmereth, but his light repels it and the ash demons clubbed fist bursts into a cloud of dust. It rages and roars in pain. I race by Glimmereth's side and slide on my knees towards the enraged demon. With a swift, precise strike to its knees, my staff comes alive with the power of the moon. Moonlight courses through it, and as my staff slices through the ash demon, it bursts into white fiery flames. The demon collapses with a violent crack, consumed by the intense lunar fire, leaving nothing but a smoldering pile of ash in its wake.

Glimmereth stands by my side, his luminous form pulsating with approval, and together, we continue our relentless charge towards the Lunar Grove, determined to protect our sacred sanctuary from the demonic onslaught.

When we arrive, my eyes widen in astonishment. A horde of demons encircles Guro, the Oathkeeper, who stands his ground, his staff a blur of motion as he defends the grove. I grip my blackthorn staff tightly, and race to his side. As I draw nearer, I witness Guro's grace and precision as he battles the demons, twirling his staff and unleashing bursts of energy. I hope the Sylvariel was mistaken about Guro, because I don't know if I could defeat him in battle.

I signal to Glimmereth to charge the demons surrounding Guro, and he does so with a flourish. He races around the center of the grove, his glimmering Truth crystal flashing, driving back the demon hordes. Reaching the base of the Lunar Tree, he calls out to me, pointing at a lump at the tree's trunk. "Faelyn, it's Aiden!"

I spin around to see Aiden tied to the Lunar Tree, unconscious and bound by vines. Glimmereth and I rush to his side. Vines entangle Aiden, holding him upright, but I swiftly slash through them. Aiden stirs, and within moments, his eyes suddenly wide with panic as he scans the chaos in the grove. When he recognizes me, he clings to me and exclaims, "I thought I was lost."

"I thought so too," I admit. "But we'll catch up later." With a swift spin, I slam my staff through a demon's head, attempting to ambush us. "For now, we must protect the Grove."

Aiden nods and stumbles to his feet. After several attempts to catch his balance, he leans on the Lunar Tree, unstrings his lute and plays a hypnotic melody, like a half-drunk maestro on a chaotic stage, desperately trying to enchant the vile and ravenous demon horde. He falters and fumbles, his usual nimble fingers struggling to pluck the strings. I call out to him, "Are you okay?"

He winces as if in pain and nods. "I'll be alright. Just stiff and sore from the thrashing I received from your warlock friend." It's only then that I realize how utterly battered he is. His eyes are swollen and blackened, his nose, once proud and straight, now bends to one side and it too is swollen. Blood streams from his mouth, and his neck is bruised, as if someone with abnormally large hands had been strangling him.

Despite the challenges, he stumbles upon the perfect melody, captivating a few of the demons. Nevertheless, Aiden's music alone cannot pacify the multitude of them. I leap into the fray, my staff aglow with the Lunar Tree's power. I unleash a potent burst of white energy, reducing a group of demons to ash. But as I turn to face another wave of attackers, I'm blinded by the cloud of ash and debris. I cough and gasp, struggling to regain my vision.

Through the dissipating ash, I see Guro regarding me with a quizzical expression. "Where are the other neophytes?" he asks, his voice muffled by the chaos surrounding us.

I gasp for air and reply, "one of these demons dragged Neason into the Defiled Realm. Barlan was supposed to warn you and my father, and I don't know where Maeddess and Cokko are."

Guro moves swiftly, striking at an unseen foe behind me. When I finally regain my sight, I see him swinging his staff fiercely, and he questions me through the tumult. "What do you mean, the Defiled Realm?"

Struggling to be heard above the chaos, I bellow, "They breached the Isles, and I saw the Rift. Neason got dragged there, and we need to find him."

Guro roars a battle cry as demons close in. "Defend yourself, young neophyte!" he bellows.

I struggle to my feet and assert, "I am a druid now. I follow my grandfather's teachings, the ancient way."

Guro lowers his staff, the embers on the tip dimming. "Faelyn, your mother only sought to protect you. To protect us all. That is the only way."

I shake my head, steadfast in my resolve. "My grandfather, the Sylvariel, has shown me a different path. He's taught me that the raven is not to be feared, but is merely a messenger. It may bring bad omens at times, but not all messages are ill-intentioned."

Guro growls. "The Sylvariel's ways were no longer relevant in our world. If he had his way, we'd still be taking the Wildshape forms and turning into ravens and other beasts."

I look at him and see what my grandfather preached about. I can see how ensnared he is with fear. "Your ways are corrupted. My mother led you astray."

But Guro counters, "Your mother only wanted to shield you. To shield all of us." Then he pauses and looks at my shoulder. "And where is your spirit guardian?"

"I freed him." I say plainly. "The Sylvariel said it's unnatural to have a spirit guide tethered against their will."

"Blasphemy!" Guro roars. But before he continues, two shadowy figures emerge from the chaos, heading straight for Glimmereth, who somersaults and evades three wolf-demons, hellbent on devouring him in a single gulp. He cunningly morphs into a wolf-demon, perplexing them. In the ensuing chaos, Glimmereth strikes one, and the wolf-demons start fighting amongst themselves.

With my staff poised, I prepare to strike the shadowy figures, only to realize that they are Maeddess and Cokko, the missing neophytes. It's a dual-edged surprise, as I want to pummel them, but at the same time, we need all the help we can get.

"What took you so long?" I rasp, dashing toward them. "Where have you been?"

Maeddess smirks, malice in her eyes that stops me in my tracks. "We've been here the entire time. The real question is, where have you been? You almost missed the grand spectacle." She waves her hand, displaying the destruction and chaos in the grove, as if she takes credit for it.

I'm lost for words, but Guro steps in and demands, "Explain yourselves, neophytes." He punctuates his words by striking his staff on the ground, creating a threatening tremor.

Cokko glowers at us and strides forward. "Calm down, old man, before you hurt yourself. The King has ordered us to eliminate your order. You stand in the way of his plans for this land."

Guro and I exchange puzzled glances, and at that moment I now know it was Maeddess and Cokko who sabotaged the pilgrimage. But why would they betray our sacred order? My rage roars in my belly, spreading to my chest. I heave for breath with the realization. "We will never let you destroy us." I charge towards them, my staff glowing with moonlight. "We are the guardians of this land."

Glimmereth joins me. At least I assume it's Glimmereth, morphed into a demon-wolf, and when he's running beside me, he growls, "Raiju."

"What?" I ask as I duck a vicious strike from Cokko. I then leap into the air, somersault over him and when I land, swing my staff, taking out his legs from under him. He curses me as he crashes to the ground.

"These wolf-demons are called Raiju." Glimmereth declares, snapping at Maeddess, who is doing an impressive job of keeping him at bay.

"How do you know?" I ask as I parry a flurry of Cokko's strikes.

"When I change into one of them, and take their form, I know what they know." He snaps at Maeddess, who dodges his bite, then slams her staff onto his back. He yowls in pain, his knees buckle and he topples to the ground. Shortly after, he morphs back into his original form of a Glimmersprout. As he groans on the ground, I'm left to deal with both Maeddess and Cokko, who've now flanked me. As I dodge and weave their coordinated strikes, my cloak whips around me, acting like a shield when I need it to.

Guro slides into the battle beside me and growls. "What is this madness?"

"Cokko and Maeddess sabotaged the pilgrimage." I huff, then call on the entangling power of the earth, ensnaring a group of rabid Raiju. We are back to back as Maeddess and Cokko circle us like hungry Raiju, hungry for the kill and savoring our vulnerability. Before too long, the ravenous pack of once ensnared Raiju bite their way through the vines and stalks us on the outskirts of our battle, taking opportunities to snap at us when we turn our backs.

Amid the chaotic battle, a second pack of Raiju charges toward the demons circling us, diverting their attention momentarily. I glance toward the Lunar Tree, where Aiden, his fingers dancing deftly on the lute's strings, skillfully weaves a mesmerizing melody into the air. His music seems to possess an otherworldly quality, and it's clear that he has mastered the art of charming the demons, turning them into his puppet-like minions.

Before I can even applaud Aiden for his newfound talent, I'm spiraling backwards, slamming onto my back. My staff rolls away from me, and I can hear an explosion in the center of the Grove. A flash of blinding light sears my eyes, followed by a deafening clap of thunder, and robs me of my hearing.

As I struggle to my feet, I'm met with a nightmarish scene — the once-beautiful grove lies in utter ruin. The Lunar Tree, a symbol of life, is now a smoldering sentinel, its branches consumed by relentless flames. Trees that once stood tall are cruelly uprooted, the earth scorched and littered with ash and debris. Amidst this desolation, an ominous figure emerges, her silhouette a stark contrast against the chaos she's wrought. Her jet-black hair billows in the wind, an emblem of darkness itself: Malvolia. The forest's very breath seems stolen, as if her presence has devoured the once-fresh air, leaving behind only a suffocating void.

"What have you done?" I shout, my voice hoarse and ears ringing from the explosion. "How dare you come into our sacred grove!"

Malvolia merely smirks and spreads her arms wide. "Oh, little druid," she says in a mocking tone, "you really think I care about this little grove?"

Rage runs through me. I know Malvolia is a powerful sorceress, but I had no idea she was capable of this. "What do you want?" I roar.

Malvolia laughs, a cold, sinister sound. "What do I want? I want what every warlock wants: power. And I know just where to find it."

I take a step forward, brandishing my staff. "I'll die before I let you take it."

Malvolia just smiles, her eyes gleaming with malice. "We'll see about that, won't we?" She glares at Maeddess and Cokko then says, "Off with you. Give the King my regards." With a flick of her wrist, both Maeddess and Cokko disappear in a puff of smoke, leaving us to face Malvolia alone with her Raiju in the shattered remains of our once-beautiful grove.

Malvolia's arms reach into the sky, and suddenly, an eerie vortex of dark magic swirls around her. It's as if the very life force of the grove is being siphoned away, a vile spectacle of nature's corruption. Shadows converge, forming grotesque shapes that dance within the inky maelstrom. Each tendril of this sinister miasma writhes with malevolence, threatening to consume all it touches. The air grows heavy, laden with a sickly, sweet stench, a putrid storm of death and decay.

28

Battle in the Lunar Grove

I RAISE MY STAFF high, channeling the power of the Lunar Grove into my blackthorn staff, a shimmering barrier forming to shield my companions from the malevolent onslaught of Malvolia's dark magic. The once tranquil grove now burns with an eerie, flickering light under the full moon, casting an unsettling glow on the surrounding chaos.

"You think you'll get away with this, Malvolia?" I shout, desperation coursing through my veins. My voice is a battle cry, laced with raw emotion. "This twisted magic of yours has no place in our sacred grove."

A swirling vortex of darkness envelops her, like a tornado of twisted soot. Malvolia's face appears from the torrent. She bares her teeth in a snarl, launching herself toward me. But Guro, ever selfless, leaps in front of the attack, taking the full force of her malevolence. He crumples to the ground with a sickening thud, his skin and bones deteriorating before my disbelieving eyes, leaving me in stunned horror.

As Guro's lifeless form lies before me, Malvolia's wicked cackles fill the air. She hurls another malevolent blast of dark magic, which I narrowly evade, responding with a searing surge of lunar energy that crashes into her chest and sends her tumbling to the ground.

"Your corrupt and vile," I declare, my words echoing in the grove.

On her knees, Malvolia digs her hands into the earth. Her eyes shine like the black of night. "You've awoken the wrath of the Moonshadow Alpha, Zeraxxus."

Suddenly, the ground shakes, and a massive wolf demon made of ash materializes from the soot. Zeraxxus is imposing, with deep black fur that seems to absorb all light. Its eyes glow with fiery red intensity, and its snarling jaws are filled with razor-sharp teeth.

Aiden jumps into action and performs his concert for the demons, his voice hypnotic and enchanting. I watch as the lower Raiju become entranced by his song. Their bodies move in unison, like puppets on a string. He looks at me with fear in his eyes, but his song does not waver.

Zeraxxus snarls and lunges at me, but I'm ready. As the ash demon's jaws snap shut just inches from my face, I dodge to the side and strike his neck with a blast of elemental magic. Zeraxxus growls in pain, confused by my sudden speed and agility. The Cloak of the Wild has activated, and I feel its power flowing through me more than ever before. I'm here, there, and everywhere. Zeraxxus cannot keep up, nor see me. Somehow the Lunar Grove has awakened the cloak, and I am now a shadow among shadows.

But the alpha wolf is not one to give up readily. With a howl that shakes the very ground beneath my feet, Zeraxxus sends me flying with a powerful tremor that reverberates like a torrent of waves that eventually crash into me. I hit the ground hard, my arm aching from the impact. I look down and see that my arm is broken. Luckily, my hand that wields the staff is unharmed. I make a makeshift sling using the ties of my pauldron and lock my arm into place, grimacing through the pain.

As I struggle to get back on my feet, I see the Raiju pack closing in on me. Aiden scrambles behind the pack, and I realize his enchantment has broken. Their snarls and hot breath steal the air from the grove, bringing a stench of sulfur, making it hard to breathe. I snarl fiercely at them, ready to defend myself, but then Glimmereth crawls to me from the fray, and hands me the Lunar Infuser and croaks, "Use the power of the grove to summon Garm, the Guardian of the Lunar Tree."

I snatch the Lunar Infuser in my good hand. I raise it into the air and call upon Garm, the Lunar Grove's Alpha, to battle Zeraxxus. Suddenly, the light of the moon streaks through the Infuser and gathers around the burning Lunar Tree, dousing the flames, and when all the flames are gone, the light morphs into a massive white wolf, slightly smaller than Zeraxxus, but just as ferocious.

Garm's fur is a pristine white, shimmering with a faint silver aura, and his massive paws are adorned with razor-sharp claws. He casts a protective glare around the grove, his eyes shining with a fierce determination, and they finally settle on me. We stare at one another for what seems like an eternity. The battle rages on around us, but I hear him speak to me, not in words, but telepathically. He thanks me for summoning him, filling me with the white light of encouragement. Then his muscles ripple with a coiled tension of the ages and he leaps towards a charging Zeraxxus.

The two massive wolves clash, their thunderous roars echoing through the grove. The ground trembles at my feet as they battle, making it impossible to stay upright. Their jaws snapping and their paws pounding the earth as the battle rages. Garm is faster than Zeraxxus, but size is with the black wolf and he has a malice to him that sends a shiver down my spine.

As I watch the two alphas fight, I know that this is the only chance we have to save the Lunar Grove. I grit my teeth and raise my staff, channeling my magic into a powerful blast of elemental energy. With one last burst of strength, I race to Garm's side to take down Zeraxxus once and for all.

Malvolia crawls to the center of the grove and leans against the trunk of the Lunar Tree, her breath ragged, and digs her hands into the earth. She speaks Darkwyrds, summoning some vile magic that swirls around and engulfs her. I look between her and the two wolves and decide to thrash her instead.

When I reach her, she's weakened and vulnerable but looks up at me and smiles maliciously, her neck defenceless to a dagger strike. I unsheath my dagger, but before I can thrust, her eyes turn black and a sooty cloud erupts out of her gapping mouth in a wave of horrifying terror knocking me asunder. Her black eyes, vengeful and hungry, she leaps to her feet and stalks to me. The blackness swirls around her and culminates into a vile ball at her hands. Then she unleashes it at me. I scramble to my feet and just before it reaches me, I slam the butt end of my staff into the ground and call on the protective roots of the earth to shield me. A tangle of massive, writhing roots erupts from the ground, safeguarding me from the assault. But as her fury rages on, the blackness grows more powerful, and I falter. I crash to one knee, and when I do, some of the blackness penetrates the roots that guard me, searing me like a runaway ember.

I can't hold much longer and I look to my sides where both Aiden and Glimmereth lie helpless, and realize I have to make a choice. Protect Aiden and myself, or Glimmereth, who's just far enough from us, that my shield cannot hold this size for much longer. If only I could drag him closer and still hold the barrier. "Why does it always have to be so damn hard?" I plead.

I tremble under the fury of her hate, and before I can choose, a crack appears in my blackthorn staff, and suddenly, the protective barrier of the roots shrinks, covering only Aiden and me. I scream as the vile dark magic eats away at Glimmereth, just as it stole Guro, leaving nothing but ash and soot.

Terror and pain violently grip me, and the wave of darkness abruptly stops. Time slows, and the ancient knowledge of the forest blesses me. I see a vision of myself soaring from a bird's-eye view, and unexpectedly, in a moment of desperation, I transform into the Wildshape of a raven.

Flapping my wings with newfound grace, I launch into the air, ascending rapidly, and circle the warlock defiantly. The lunar energy courses through my avian form, empowering me with every beat of my obsidian wings. I know what the raven knows. The world becomes a tapestry of shadow and moonlight from above, and I dive with unerring precision.

As I plummet like a living bolt of night, my beak sharp as an obsidian dagger, I zero in on Malvolia. The raven's instincts guide my attack, and I strike with a vengeance. With uncanny accuracy, I aim for her malevolent eyes, a direct assault on the very essence of her power. I peck with the relentless determination of a creature deeply connected to the ancient forces of the grove.

Malvolia's desperate attempts to evade my strikes are futile, her warlock defenses crumbling under the relentless assault of my Wildshape. I taunt her, my raven's voice echoing with a haunting mix of defiance and triumph, "You can't catch me now."

Meanwhile, on the ground below, Garm, the guardian of the Lunar Grove, engages Zeraxxus, the malevolent alpha Raiju. The two colossal wolves collide again with an earth-shaking impact, their roars echoing through the grove, and their snarling jaws lock in a deadly duel. The air crackles with the elemental tension, and the ground quivers beneath their mighty struggle.

In the pivotal moment of the battle, Garm's indomitable strength prevails. With a surge of primal power, he pins Zeraxxus to the ground, his massive jaws clamping around the alpha Raiju's throat. The force of the death-strike is cataclysmic, a crescendo of nature's fury. As he bites down, a white light flashes through the grove, scattering the darkness.

Zeraxxus shudders, its fiery red eyes wide with a final realization and breath. The jugular succumbs to the relentless pressure of Garm's jaws, and the massive Raiju erupts into a swirling tempest of ashen particles. Garm stands tall and extends his jaw to the moon, belting out a triumphant howl that fills the air.

Garm, radiant in his lunar power, gazes around the grove, ensuring its safety. His gleaming white fur and wise eyes show the battle's end, but not the war. Steadying his gaze on Malvolia, he charges into the fight.

He joins my struggle against Malvolia, along with Aiden, as we collectively strike, claw, and use our charms with all our might. The battle relentlessly rages on, with Malvolia feverishly defending and countering our onslaught to no avail. Between strikes, when I'm circling from above, I hear it. The voice of the Lunar Tree guides me, not with words, but through ancient wisdom. It's a sound like no other. No music or words do it justice. It's as if the very roots of the world are speaking to me, and it's only in my Wildshape form that I am able to hear.

Suddenly, I comprehend the ancient way, and can dispel her.

I drop to the ground and, before landing, shift back to my human form. I slam into the earth, creating an eruption that sends a shockwave through the grove. On one knee, I drive my hand into the soil, drawing forth the earth's power. With this energy, I shape a brilliant, silvery ball of crackling light, pulsing with electric intensity. It's as if all the earth's elements merge into one powerful entity. Fully formed, I launch it at Malvolia, and it streaks toward her like an arrow. Upon impact, she howls in agony as the magic courses through her, weakening her dark powers. Her defenses waver, and we seize the moment, striking her with all our might. As the light displaces the darkness, fear fills her eyes, realizing her defeat.

"I'll send you to the Defiled Realm where you belong," I say firmly, my eyes flashing white.

Malvolia resists, but she is no match for the power of the forest. The ground beneath her feet opens up, and a swirling vortex of dark energy consumes her. As it pulls her into the abyss, she lets out a chilling scream that transforms into a wicked cackle, taunting me. "You might have bested me for now," she sneers, "but remember your dear father you left so long ago. Your precious home? It's already crumbling, and you can't do anything about it!"

Malvolia's words send a shiver down my spine, and a wave of fear washes over me. However, before I can re-act, Garm steps closer to me, and his voice resonates in my mind with unmistakable clarity. "Faelyn," he com-mands, "the protection of the groves is your paramount duty. Accept this Amulet of Renewal. It shall bolster your resolve in this battle."

I take the amulet, and as soon as it touches my skin, I feel a surge of energy coursing through my body. It's as if the power of the forest itself is flowing through me, giving me strength and courage. I look down at my broken arm, and somehow, the pain ceases. It's still broken, and will need time to heal, but it feels as if the bone has reset itself. Garm's words ring in my ears, and I realize the gravity of the task ahead.

Her words linger in my mind like a haunting refrain, and a gnawing fear for my father and my cherished home takes root within me. I pause for a moment to take in the heart-wrenching devastation that Malvolia has wrought upon the Grove. Trees stand uprooted, their branches broken, and the air is heavy with the stench of decay. But I stand resolute, unyielding.

With a gentle touch upon the amulet, I channel the very essence of the forest into a healing spell, an ancient wisdom guiding my hand. It's as though the spirits of the woods themselves are aiding me.

The spell takes hold, breathing life back into the wounded land. The scent of fresh growth replaces the foul odor, and Aiden watches in awe. The true power of the amulet, a gift from Garm, becomes unmistakably clear.

Renewed, I work tirelessly to mend the harm that's been done, weaving protective spells and casting enchantments previously unknown to me. Glowing orbs of white light dance in the air as I weave them into a protective web, unseen yet potent. As I do, I understand that Garm's words were not mere advice; they were a vision of the future that awaits.

Convinced that the enchantments are secure, I race toward my home, Garm's amulet radiating a calming energy. The fear that Malvolia's warning invoked remains, but I push it aside, focusing on the task ahead. For my father, my home, and the sacred groves must be protected, no matter what perils lie ahead.

29

Fire and Ashes

FEVERISHLY, AIDEN AND I sprint through the Hinterlands, our footfalls echoing the urgent beat of our hearts. We race on, fear fueling every step, dreading what we might find in Willowbrook. Though Aiden falters, his tenacity compensates for his lack of agility. A human amid the haste of an elf, he pushes on, each stumble outweighed by his boyish charm and his newly discovered humility. It suits him. I understand his limitations, halting occasionally for a sip from a creek or a stolen breath. Then, like a relentless specter, I resume the chase.

As we trek, dense forests surround us, and the air carries the enchanting scent of earth and pine. We burst forth into meadows, the swaying grass caressing our legs as the wind plays havoc with our hair. Yet, the scenic respite vanishes as we reenter the embracing woods, nimbly sidestepping densely packed trees and hopping over the gnarled, uneven terrain.

The transition from open plains to familiar forest leads to the clenching of my stomach. As we near Willowbrook, I dread the harrowing truth that awaits us. Did Malvolia speak the truth? What happened to my village? Is my father still alive?

Racing through the woods, we reemerge in a familiar clearing. But the once-thriving village of Willowbrook has metamorphosed into a landscape of fire and ashes. My heart plummets to my gut as tears prick my eyes. Aiden's bridled gasp and hand on my shoulder offers little consolation. We stand amid the ruin, taking in the desolation. Tears streak down my face now and I can't seem to catch my breath.

"Survivors." Aiden's voice is an urgent plea. "Let's search the ruins."

Wiping away my tears, I nod, and together, we comb through the wreckage, our voices calling out for anyone still alive. The grim task weighs heavy on our hearts as we uncover lifeless bodies one after another. Desolation surrounds us, the starkness of death in every direction, with no signs of life to be found. Our search for survivors becomes a harrowing ordeal, and the overwhelming silence of the once-vibrant village amplifies our sorrow.

Willowbrook, once teeming with vitality, has now transmuted into a hushed graveyard. The lingering silence casts an eerie pall, unbroken except by the gentle murmur of wind through the leaves. Time seems suspended, ensnared within this moment of ruin and desolation.

Thoughts turn to my father, and then a voice slices through the silence. "Faelyn, over here!" Barlan's voice echoes through the woods. We dash towards the source, only to find him crouched beside my father, clinging to a fragile semblance of consciousness.

"Thank the groves you're here," Barlan sighs with a sense of relief, but his weary eyes betray him. "Your father." He bleats.

I kneel beside my father, my mind racing with questions. "What happened? Who did this?"

Barlan's eyes convey a mixture of fury and sorrow as he explains, "The King's soldiers came in the night seeking you. Your father fought them off as best as he could, but they overpowered him."

The piercing knowledge of my father's solitary battle to shield me cuts through me like a sharp sword, igniting a kaleidoscope of emotions within. As I kneel by him, tears cascade freely down my cheeks. "I'm so sorry, Father. I wasn't here to stop them."

Weakly, my father grips my hand, a faint smile forming. "Faelyn, you mustn't blame yourself. You are destined for greatness, to accomplish what no one else can. And now, with the Amulet, you possess the means to do so."

I'm taken aback and grasp the Amulet of Renewal. My father's words echo as I place my hand over his heart, conjuring healing energy.

"How did you know about the Amulet?" I inquire.

He smiles softly, his strength waning. "Your mother, she spoke of a powerful amulet offered by Garm but declined—"

"My mother spoke to Garm?" I interject.

My father nods, weakly. "When we moved from the Groves to Willowbrook, Garm foretold a time of darkness. Your mother would often speak to him. It was there she made her Oath." His gaze falls upon the Amulet, as though he's known it for all his life.

"But at what cost, Father?" I ask, my voice trembling. "How many more innocent lives will be lost? How many more homes will burn to ashes?"

"Sometimes sacrifices are necessary," he murmurs, his eyes closing. "But you're not alone. You have allies who will fight alongside you."

I realize the Amulet's purpose transcends our needs; it serves the Groves. My heart aches as my father's grip on life weakens, and I know time is running out. I turn to him, my voice quivering with emotion. "We need to leave, Father. And then, I must confront the King."

My father's eyes flutter open, and his smile fades, his voice a mere whisper. "Protect the groves, Faelyn. Save our people."

With those words, he breathes his last, his eyes closing for the last time. I cradle his lifeless body in my arms, the weight of his sacrifice heavy on my heart. Tears stream down my cheeks as I delicately lay him back on the scorched earth. He looks peaceful now, freed from the pain that had gripped him.

Aiden places a comforting hand on my shoulder, but there are no words to ease the grief that engulfs me. My father is gone, and I'm left with a profound sense of loss and a burning determination to honor his memory. The Amulet of Renewal, warm against my skin, seems to pulse in tandem with my heartbeat, a reminder of the responsibility that lies ahead.

"We will rebuild Willowbrook," Barlan says, his voice filled with resolve. "And we'll make sure your father's sacrifice was not in vain. But you need to go. The groves are in danger."

With renewed strength, I stand, tears still glistening in my eyes, and look at the village that was once our home. Now it's a smoldering ruin, a stark testament to the cruelty of the King and the price my father paid to protect me. My heart is heavy, but I know that the battle is far from over. The Amulet of Renewal, a source of power and hope, serves as a constant reminder of the journey that lies ahead.

Without a goodbye, I march out of Willowbrook, heading east towards Faelyndelle.

30

The Ferryman's Debt

UNDER THE EERIE MOONLIGHT, Aiden and I approach the misty village. My heart sinks as we reach the Ferryman's hut, and a pang of dread fills me as I see him lying on his cot, groaning in pain. The rash has spread all over his side, and I fear we may be too late.

"We need to act fast," I say to Aiden as we pull out the Lunar Infuser and the rare herbs we collected earlier. "The Ferryman's life may depend on it."

We perform the ritual with intense concentration, mixing the herbs and chanting the incantation. As the mist clears, the light of the moon amplifies through the Infuser and into the concoction. The Ferryman drinks the potion, and the rash gradually subsides.

"Thank you, young ones," the Ferryman says, sitting up and rubbing his now-healed side. "You have saved my life, and for that, I owe you a debt. Here are your tickets to Faelyndelle." He gets up, shuffles over to a cabinet behind the counter and hands them to us. "You can take the ferry from the dock by the river."

"Thank you, Ferryman," I say, accepting the tickets. "We are forever grateful."

"Before you go," the Ferryman says, his voice raspy but filled with curiosity, "what did you think of the Sylvariel?"

Aiden and I exchange glances, and sadness grips me. "He was a wise old druid who showed me the way."

The Ferryman's eyes widen with intrigue. "Tell me more," he implores, his frail hand resting on his cot as he lowers himself onto it.

So I recount the tale of our encounter with the Sylvariel, of the ancient Oath my mother made, the trials we faced, and the wisdom we gained. As I speak, the Ferryman listens attentively, occasionally nodding as he absorbs the details.

When I finish, he sits in thoughtful silence. "The Sylvariel has always been a mysterious figure, even to us who dwell in the Misty Village. You're lucky to have spent so much time with him."

I lower my gaze, memories rushing through my mind and tears threatening to spill. "The Sylvariel was my grandfather, and I aim to use his wisdom to protect the Groves and stop the King's destructive plans."

The Ferryman nods in understanding. "Your journey is not one I envy, but it is one of great significance. You carry a heavy burden, Faelyn. However, the Groves have a way of choosing their guardians wisely." He tries several times to lift from his cot but fails, then finally, with one final push, he staggers up and walks over to me with a determined look on his face. "If you ever need anything wood elf, I'm on your side."

I smile at the Ferryman's genuine offer, impressed by his resilience. I extend my hand, and he takes it with a firm grip. His rough, calloused hands tell the tale of a lifetime spent on the water, yet there's a warmth and kindness to them that reassures me. Maybe High Elves aren't all bad. I think of my time at the Salty Slug and chuckle.

As we leave the Ferryman's hut and head towards the docks, a mysterious stranger emerges from the shadows. The stranger's presence is shrouded in an almost magical veil, making it difficult to discern any details of their features. I sense a hidden aura of danger, and the way they move hints at a shadowy dexterity—a seasoned rogue or thief, perhaps.

"Excuse me," the stranger says, their voice low and gravelly, adding to the air of intrigue that surrounds them. "Do you know the significance of the amulet you carry?"

My hand instinctively moves to clutch the Amulet of Renewal hanging around my neck, guarding it like a precious secret. The amulet faintly glows in response to the stranger's question. "What do you mean?" I inquire, my voice tinged with suspicion. "Who are you?"

"The amulet is an ancient and powerful relic," the stranger continues. "It has the power to resurrect the dead."

The stranger's words hang in the air, leaving us with more questions than answers. "Who are you?" Aiden asks, his hand hovering over his dagger's hilt.

"That's not important," the stranger remains elusive, as if the darkness itself has given them form. They offer no name and, with a puff of smoke, they disappear into the mist as quickly as they appeared, leaving Aiden and me with more questions than answers.

Aiden takes a swipe at the now empty shadows and warns, "I'm not just a bard you know."

I smile at him, and look down at his ornamental dagger and feign holding him back for his own good. "He's gone Aiden."

"He?" Aiden exclaims.

"Yes. He." I say. "He was a shadowblade, from what I can tell." I walk to the alley where the man stood and inspect the area. He let off some sort of muted smoke bomb before he disappeared. And as I scour the rooftops, I can't make out where he might have gone.

"Shadowblade you say." Aiden scratches his chin. "He could want something to sell to get tickets to the tournament."

I nod in agreement, tightly clutching the Amulet. "Well, I've worked too damn hard for anyone to just take it." I declare.

We continue towards the docks; the mist growing thicker as we near the water's edge. The Elven ferry awaits, a magnificent vessel that's a work of art in itself. Its slender, graceful design seems to mimic the shapes of the ancient trees, and the bow of the boat is adorned with intricate carvings of leaves and vines, as if the forest itself had lent its beauty to the craft.

The ferry, although docked, appears to glide upon a magical fog, an enchantment that surrounds it, making the vessel seem almost ethereal. This fog has an other-worldly quality, shimmering with a faint, silvery sheen that captures the light of the moon, transforming the ferry into a radiant ghost ship, that weaves through the mists. I glean information from it, as if the ancient trees that form the hull speak to me in the ancient language I've become accustomed to hearing. They say that the mist is enchanted, and that it's a protection guarding who is allowed onto the capital island.

As we step aboard, the sense of mystery deepens. We know we're leaving the familiar world behind and heading into the heart of the unknown. With each step forward, I can't help but feel that the amulet has chosen this path for me, and our destiny is now entwined with the fate of Faelyndelle. But that's not all. I can't shake the feeling that we are being watched.

The mist thickens, and the air grows colder as we journey down the river. We talk for some time, anxiously waiting to see the tall spired buildings of the Capital, but the mist is so thick it obscures everything. Suddenly, the ferry rocks violently, and we hear a loud crash from below.

Aiden and I exchange a panicked look as we make our way towards the source of the commotion. The mist has grown so thick that we can barely see our hands in front of our faces. The hull moans, reminding me of it's warning. We fumble through the darkness. I call out but nobody answers. I reach back just to know Aiden is still by my side. When he finally grips my hand, I breathe a sigh of relief, and we move forward.

Before we reach the lower deck, we see shadows moving below deck. I brace myself, then realize that a force of armed men have boarded the ferry. They are dressed in sleek, unmarked leather armor, their faces obscured by the mist. They move with practiced efficiency, their daggers at the ready.

"Who are you?" Aiden demands, his voice shaky.

One man steps forward, a cruel grin on his face. "We're here for the girl," he snarls.

My heart sinks as I realize what's happening. The King's guard has come for me. I clutch the amulet tightly, my mind racing as I try to think of a way out of this situation. The mist is obscuring my natural magic. I'm powerless.

Aiden draws his golden dagger, his eyes blazing with fury and my heart sinks knowing it is only a trinket. "You'll have to go through me first," he declares, his stance ready for a fight.

I take a deep breath, focusing my energy on the amulet of renewal. I can feel its power coursing through me, empowering my every move. The hull calls to me, warning me that danger lurks and that I am being censored. Even with the Amulet, I feel defenceless.

The first wave of attackers lunges towards us, their daggers drawn. I sidestep and strike, my movements graceful and deadly. Although I can't call on the surrounding magic, my melee abilities take hold. Aiden fights with a fierce determination, his blade flashing in the air. One of the King's guard slashes Aiden, splitting his dagger in half.

The clunk of the gold hitting the deck, a calamity of our troubles.

The King's men are well-trained and well-equipped, easily overpowering us in this dense fog we're ill prepared for. They press us hard, their numbers overwhelming.

Suddenly, I feel a sharp pain in my arm. I look down to see a dagger protruding from my flesh. I stumble, my mind clouded by the pain. My arm that a wraith has scratched, been broken by Malvolia, and now pierced by a shadow-blade. Just my luck.

Aiden rushes to my side, but it's too late. The men close in, their weapons raised for the final blow.

And then, everything changes.

The amulet of renewal blazes with a brilliant light, enveloping me in its glow. I feel my strength returning, my wounds healing before my very eyes. With a surge of power, I push back the attackers, sending them flying across the deck. Some hit the sides of the ferry and topple over into the cold depths the river, and others writhe in pain from the light.

But the victory is short-lived. As I reach for the amulet, I feel a sharp tug as someone is pulling it away from me. I vigorously swipe several times, hitting nothing but air. Then I turn to see a shadowy figure, cloaked in shadows. The stranger holds the amulet aloft, a wicked smile on his lips. Although I see him smile, I can't seem to make out the details of his face. He races away from me, diving into the river with a splash.

And then, without warning, the ferry explodes.

I am thrown into the water and sink, my body battered and bruised. Sinking further, it becomes dark until I hit the bottom, a jagged rock slicing through my leathers. I have two options; die at the bottom of the river or swim to the light and fill my lungs with air. The choice is simple. With a surge of energy, I kick the jagged rocks, and within moments, I gasp for air as I breach the surface of the water. The icy current pulls me downstream, threatening to drag me under again. Aiden is beside me, gasping, his arms flailing as he tries to keep his head above water.

I grab hold of his arm, determined not to let him go again. "We have to get to shore," I yell, my ears ringing and voice hoarse from the explosion. "Come on, Aiden!" We kick and paddle, struggling against the strong current.

The shores of the capital are within sight, but they seem impossibly far away. I can hear the sound of rushing water in my ears, drowning out all other noise. It steals my focus, tempting me to give up, but I'm resolute and fight the current.

"We're almost there," Aiden gasps, his face contorted with pain as he gulps more water than he breathes air.

And then, just when it seems like we might not make it, we feel the solid ground beneath our feet. We stagger onto the shore, our clothes clinging to our bodies, our lungs burning from the effort of the swim. "We have to find the shadowblade," I say, my voice firm despite the exhaustion.

"He has the amulet. We can't let him get away." Aiden glugs, waterlogged. "I'm with you, Faelyn."

We clamber through the shallows, heading down the shoreline, our footsteps echoing on the rocky terrain. The capital looms in the distance, a beacon of unknown adventure in the midst of chaos. But we have a long journey ahead of us, and the fate of the kingdom hangs in the balance.

Printed in Great Britain
by Amazon

40088709R00198